# PARASITE

Jason Parrish

2019

Copyright © 2019 Jason Parrish
ISBN 978-0-9979544-1-8
East Star Publishing, 2019

# AKNOWLEDGEMENTS

I would like to give special thanks to some great people who helped bring this book to life. My niece, Kaitlee Riese, who never fails to call me out on plot holes or poor writing. Tiffney Shankles, Susan Oates, and Casey Walton, whose insights and attention to detail made this novel readable. Thank you all. Finally, to Delia, my wife and first reader. Without her encouragement and patient support, this second novel never would have happened. Thanks for believing.

# 1

**I CRIED** the night I realized it lived inside me. The parasite hid itself well. I heard tales of it, most in my village had, but I never took them for truth. No one did. Not my parents, nor my teachers, no one; even when the man came and pleaded with us to believe. I thought him mad, a raving lunatic bent on spreading fear and obsessed with a disease we couldn't comprehend. He called himself an Outrider. We called him a fool.

We lived as we had for centuries. Same as my grandparents and their parents before. We were born. We labored. We died. Then came the long sleep. Complete darkness. Cessation of all awareness, all existence. Our village taught this generation after generation. Now I know it is a lie. Now I know they are all infected. A living evil swims in spoiled blood as it courses through our veins. Blood, the source of life.

I haven't passed through the gates of my village in over a year, so I have no idea who sleeps and who remains. I pray my parents and little sister still breathe the air of this world. I haven't proved the best son or brother, but I love them, and they need to hear the truth.

I've lost much along the way; friends, innocence, and for a time, my sanity. As I lay in this strange bed, mindlessly stroking the gold pendant around my neck and listening to laughter from the hall, I know it was worth it. The struggle, the pain, days I wasn't sure of my destination, or if the cure was a lie. Then I remember the girl. The one who found me dying in the Wastelands, rescued me, and introduced me to The Physician—the One with the cure.

This is my testimony of that journey...my search for truth. I'm writing it now because the way home to Bethman is filled with danger. If I don't survive to see my family again, they need to know what I've discovered.

It all began the day a stranger brought both death and life to my village.

# Bethman

## 2

**THE OUTRIDER'S** horse kicked up clouds of dust as he rode past my family's field. The man's long leather jacket resembled the kind I had only seen in magazines preserved from before the decay. A time of machines, when our ancient ancestors warred to the brink of extinction. Elders taught stories of the old world and its slow march to death. Outlandish tales of flying machines, glass that came alive with moving images and sounds, and communication across earth. All so fantastic, no one would have ever believed they once existed if it wasn't for a crate of books kept at the school. A lifetime of the old world condensed into thirty pounds of paper.

I stopped tending the dirt and watched the man and his horse approach. Our eyes met, and he dipped his head. The rake slipped from my hand onto hard earth as he made his way past rows of wilted corn and along the road into Bethman.

When I reached him, nearly all Bethman's hundred and twenty-one residents crowded the streets. The rest would be along in short measure. Word travels fast in a small community like mine, and a visitor was a newsworthy event. I pushed my way through the whispering crowd and took Elder Frank by the arm. "What's happening?"

He shook his head without turning.

"Help you?" William Gourd, Chief Elder and de-facto keeper of peace, spoke first.

The visitor in leather didn't reply. Instead he lifted his hat, slapped it on his thigh, and sent a burst of dust billowing into the air. He scanned the crowd with no expression.

"Said, can I help you stranger?" Gourd took a cautious step forward and shot a quick glance at his friend, Elder Frank.

The stranger finally spoke. "No need for alarm friend." He held his hands out, reassuring us he meant no harm. "I've come with a message." His accent, rhythmic and formal, was like nothing I had ever heard before and did nothing to endear him to my neighbors.

A low murmur swept through Bethman. More villagers had heard word of a visitor and crowded into the town square. The Ulrich twins positioned themselves atop Old Soldier. The statue was ancient and worn; the soldier, dignified. The man's identity was long forgotten or erased, though the sword hanging from his belt suggested a veteran from a war long ago. A hero I suppose, at least to someone. I'm certain his adversaries thought different.

Cora, my little sister who came along eight years ago when I was eighteen, ran to my side and punched me in the arm. "What's going on?"

I picked her up and held her over my head. "A going away party for you. Mom and dad are trading you away for a nice horse."

She giggled as I sat her down. "Cole!"

"Do mom and dad know you're here?"

"They're by the statue." She pointed to Old Soldier in the center of the square. "I saw Alice and wanted to watch with her."

Alice, Elder Franks only daughter, slid her hand from his and scooted close to Cora. Inseparable since both could walk, Alice and Cora's friendship defied adult logic. Alice loved to talk, dance, and sing. My little sister preferred listening, watching, and reading. Alice delighted in meeting new people. Cora dreaded any function that required prolonged conversation.

"Aww, I thought you came over here to be with me." I smiled and kissed the top of Cora's head as Alice took her arm and whispered something in her ear. They both giggled and turned to the man in leather.

The stranger waited for the late comers to join and continued. "My name is Charles, and I am an Outrider."

Whispers became a frenzy of conversation and exclamations. Some inched away from the stranger. We had heard tales of people called Outriders. Stories told around dying campfires of mad men who traveled earth spreading fear and lies about disease and monsters. Sowing discord among friends and family. Sometimes in these stories, spirits of the forest possessed them, and madness spread to two or three people they encountered. It was rumored those unfortunate souls often left the safe confines of Bethman in search of treasure, answers, or a cure, depending on which version you heard. Most never came back, and those who did returned deranged and had to be put down. Other times Outriders raided villages and took children captive. Some said to sell as slaves, others claimed to grow their numbers. Over time common themes emerged with an Outrider visit: disease, death, madness and exodus. And a message. It always started with a message.

\*\*\*

"**M**ove along stranger." William's voice held strong despite his obvious concern. "Don't need you spreading your poison here."

A voice from the crowd called out. "Let him speak." A neighbor, though I'm not sure who. "Let him say what he came for."

Several agreed, but the Outrider didn't move.

Alice broke from Cora's grip, and walked to the man. "I want to hear."

"Come back!" Cora reached for her friend but missed.

"Alice no!" Frank stiffened but made no effort to stop his daughter. Whether out of cowardice or confusion we'll never know, but I imagine the question haunted Frank the rest of his short life.

I wasn't sure what to expect. Would the man grab her, loft her onto his horse and ride away? A possibility according to legend. Maybe he would kill her. I didn't notice a blade, but those were easily concealed. Also, snapping her slender neck would be simple enough. I pulled my six-inch blade and carefully slipped it into Elder Frank's palm. He slid it into his belt but rested his hand on its handle. His eyes never left the stranger or his little girl.

Alice stopped in front of Charles the Outrider and held out a delicate hand. "I'm Alice."

By now, not even a whisper stirred through the crowd. A hundred and twenty-one people held their breath in anticipation of what the stranger might do. I took Cora by the shoulder and drew her close.

"Don't you touch her! Don't you dare touch her!" Frank's cry shattered the silence. "You keep your filthy hands off my baby!"

Alice swirled around. A sliver of sunlight flickered in her eyes. Eyes full of wonder and the pure curiosity of a child too young to experience the heartache of lost first love. "It's okay daddy. I want to hear him talk. I like how he sounds."

Frank stepped forward, paused, and cautioned another step. "Get away from him darling. Come here to daddy." He motioned her to him, gaze locked on the Outrider.

Charles held up his hands and shifted away from Alice. Only a couple of feet, but enough to show he had no ill intent. "See, no harm intended. I only wish to speak my message and be on my way."

The gesture momentarily pacified Elder Frank, but his grip tightened on the handle of my blade. The gathering breathed a collective sigh of relief. Fierce violence wasn't unheard of in our isolated corner of the world, but most people didn't enjoy putting someone down.

The Chief Elder drew close to the man. "Speak it quickly and be gone with you."

"Very well." The Outrider paused, scanned the crowd again, and continued. "I come to tell you of a sickness that has invaded our world. An ancient parasite playing havoc with our eyes, our minds, the core of who we are."

"Lies!" The cry came from a group of grey-haired women. Several heads nodded in agreement and the low murmur resumed.

The Chief Elder held out a hand and the clamor died. "People, we agreed to let him speak. True, we've heard the myth before, but we must be faithful to our word. He has done us no wrong...yet." He turned to the Outrider. "Be quick about it, stranger."

7

The Outrider offered a slight nod and continued. "This parasite infects every one of you. It has since your birth." A few loud objections arose, but the Outrider continued. "It survives by deceit. It survives by blinding the host to its existence." He paused. "But I have come to tell you of a cure."

The man stared at me, but I had heard enough. Frank eased my blade from his belt, and I nodded. Better a stranger's blood spilled than risk letting this man infect my friends or family. Or worse, lose a child to this madman. If our legends contained just half-truth, either was a possibility. In the moment I could have stopped it, I didn't. I kept my silence.

"Even me? It's in me?" The voice, full of concern and confusion, came from Alice. Tears toppled over her cheekbone when she raised her head and looked the Outrider in the face.

That's when it happened. When my world changed forever. The Outrider placed his hand on Alice's head, a simple act of consolation for which blood spilled. Frank raised the knife and lunged, a look of wild anger in his eyes.

It all happened in less than five seconds, but as I watched Frank accidently plunge my knife into his daughter's chest, time stopped. Frame by frame images as the Outrider pushed Alice aside and stepped in front of her. Frank, face contorted in anger, knife raised, adjusted his angle as the Outrider held up callused hands. A woman's panicked scream. A man, most probably the Chief Elder, yelled Frank's name. Alice jumped from behind the Outrider with confused eyes. Her last word cut short by a rusted blade meant for the stomach of the Outrider. "Da-"

Frank's eyes grew impossibly large as Alice dropped at his feet, blood pulsing out around my knife, spurting in rhythm with her dying heart. Frank's momentum carried him to the ground with her. His eyes closed... opened...and the light went out of him. His head fell onto the dirt with a thud. Tiny puffs of dust beside his nose gave the only evidence he was still alive.

Within seconds we converged on the stranger. A dozen men and women pummeled him with fists and boots. Blood splattered my shirt when his nose broke under my fist. Those that couldn't get close enough cheered us on. I glimpsed Cora kneeling by her friend's body. The look of horror on my little sister's face is a memory I'll always carry.

Through the chaos, dust, and blind rage, the stranger slipped from the pile of punches and kicks and sprinted down an alley beside the meeting hall. He left his horse and right pinky behind. We searched the surrounding hills two days without success.

We put Frank down three days after he killed his daughter. Madness set in, and we had no choice. The Chief Elder blamed it on the sickness Outriders spread. I wondered if grief had taken such a firm grip that all hope of sanity was lost. My mind waged war on itself. If I hadn't given him my blade, Alice might still be alive. Instead, both father and daughter died, and the Outrider escaped town with little more than bruises and a lost finger.

The night after we put Frank down, I awoke panicked and drenched in sweat. My chest grew tight and the room swam. I sat on the edge of my bed and tried to catch my breath. After a moment it came, though rapid and shallow. The Outrider. I dreamed he looked at me when he spoke the words about a parasite. He looked as if he could see it swimming through my veins, and I wanted to kill him. I wanted to kill him because he was a liar. The disease was a lie. Invisible worlds. Unseen monsters. Lies.

Cora hadn't spoken since she saw Alice die and had only gotten out of bed to pee. Mom and dad said she'd be fine, "just give her time", but I worried the Outrider's poison had infected her fragile body. I couldn't shake the dream. More precisely, I couldn't shake the Outriders eyes as they peered into my thoughts. My breath steadied. I reached to the small wooden table beside my bed and grabbed the knife my grandfather had given me before he died. I rolled it over in my hand. Its six-inch blade and solid oak handle balanced perfectly. Until Alice, it had only spilled the blood of deer, pheasant, and the occasional wild hog. Weeks later, a friend would also die by its sharp edge as it sliced into her stomach.

Late that afternoon I saw her; the girl that would save my life. Standing on a hill above my parents' small farm, her short and slender frame hinted at a girl of no more than ten. Had Alice escaped the grave, woke from the long sleep? But it wasn't Alice, and it wasn't any of the other girls from Bethman. I knew them all.

The moment I saw the girl I knew my life would never be the same. Her presence stirred powerful emotions I couldn't comprehend or ignore. I didn't feel the parasite living in me then or the next day; however, the thought that the myth might be true did enter my mind.

Less than two weeks later, fighting madness, I left my home in search of truth. Cora still hadn't spoken, and I worried we were going to lose her. I needed to know if the sickness was real, and if so, bring home a cure. The story of my long pilgrimage begins when I met my first two companions.

Alton. Then Willy.

# Grandview

## 3

**A TRAVLER** like myself, I met Alton two days after I left Bethman. I topped a small hill and saw him propped on his cane beside the road, staring at the cloudless sky. My first instinct was to ignore him. He looked frail and harmless, but something seemed off. He reminded me of a neighbor from my childhood. Every morning, the man walked to the center of his potato field, sat in the dirt, and read poetry to his plants. One day he disappeared, and I never saw him again. I wasn't surprised, people like him disappeared from Bethman all the time.

I picked up my pace and lowered my eyes as I passed.

"Beautiful, isn't it?"

I turned my head, and he locked eyes with me before I knew what happened.

"Ever wonder why the sky is blue? Why not green or yellow?"

"Interesting." I looked away and kept walking.

"It's sometimes red though. Never green, but red. So, what is the truth?"

I paused at the word 'truth' but didn't turn around.

"I've seen it orange, grey, pink...but never brown. So, what is the truth? Is it really blue or is there more?"

I almost answered, but instead nodded and started walking.

"Truth is like that you know." He called after me. "Rarely is it as simple as it first looks."

I stopped and walked back to the man. I didn't worship a particular god: I wasn't religious at all, but I wasn't fool enough to dismiss the possibility of a greater power capable of arranging encounters such as this.

"My name's Cole." I dipped my head in greeting, and he returned the gesture.

"Alton. Where you headed?"

"I'm not sure."

"My kind of traveler. Want some company?"

I didn't, but my thirst for answers convinced me I met the man for a reason, and I said yes.

***

The next day we stumbled onto Grandview. I smelled the village before I saw it. We rounded a sharp bend, and the air turned rotten. I imagined a waste field full of rancid fruit. The smell was sweet, yet so revolting it took complete concentration not to vomit. I glanced at Alton, and he already had his kerchief covering his mouth and nose.

"What's that?"

My new friend held his tongue, but it didn't take long to see the answer. Dozens of bodies hung from trees like silent wind chimes. I stopped and reached for Alton. If decomposing corpses unsettled me, I worried my aged companion might slip into the long sleep at the sight. His cold, boney fingers clasped my wrist. Neither of us spoke. Night hid his eyes, but I imagined how they looked. Much like mine, wide and confused.

Alton broke the silence. "Not by the neck." He pointed to the closest figure.

He was right. Rope looped under the arms. Flies buzzed around rotting feet, barely visible in the dim moonlight.

"What is this? Who are they?"

Alton stepped closer to the spoiled flesh. I reached to pull him back, but he jerked free. "Let me look."

"Are you crazy old man? We should go. Now!" I tried to keep my voice at a whisper but failed miserably.

Alton didn't seem affected by my alarm. "You asked the questions son, and I intend to find out." He moved to the tree, shooed away a swarm of flies, and studied the body. Smells of death escaped as bone, fabric, and rotted muscle tore away and dropped to the ground when he jabbed a denim covered leg with his cane.

"Now, Alton. We need to leave now." Not as strong as before, but my intended urgency came through.

"They can't hurt us." He poked the hanging man one more time as if to prove his point, prompting a hoard of beetles to scurry from the safety of their dark home. "See, nothing but a handful of bugs." I detected a hint of wonder, or maybe even joy, in Alton's voice.

The withering ball of insects, now feasting on what remained of the hanged man's decomposing foot, was more than I could take. The man's lower leg looked alive...alive and dying. I started to run but doubled over and vomited. For a moment, I was certain my knees would unhinge, and I'd end up sprawled out in the mess now puddled at my feet, but they held.

Alton's voice called from behind, but I couldn't answer until my world stopped spinning.

What was I doing? Searching for a cure to a sickness I doubted existed? And why? Because words from a lunatic wearing a leather coat had infected my mind and maybe my sister's as well? Or maybe because visions of a little girl, who might or might not be the phantom of Elder Frank's dead daughter, woke me in a panic every night?

I had no business in these woods. No business with a new companion who played with dangling corpses. No, not anymore. Not while a warm bed and people who loved me waited at home. A home where rotting bodies didn't hang from trees like party props waiting to spill a prize of beetles and maggots.

I spun when a hand fell on my shoulder. Alton took a step back, but his eyes didn't widen in surprise. "Only me son. Only me."

"I think it's time I go home."

He considered me for a moment. "If that's what you feel you must do, you have your reasons."

"Reasons? Reasons? Look there, and there, and there!"

He glanced over his shoulder at the corpses. "Those? I told you boy; they can't hurt you."

"Maybe not, but what put them there? Assassins, Outriders, or maybe it was the Shadows?"

He waved me off. "The Shadows? You've spent too many nights around the storyteller's campfire. Folklore for keeping a mother's child from wandering off into the night sky."

"You say."

"I know, but you're correct. Someone left them there. My guess would be Outriders. Vile creatures." He drew a breath and gently grasped my arm. "We'll move off the road, away from these," he waved over his shoulder, "and find a spot to rest for the night. We'll take shifts for a watch. If you feel the same in the light of day, we'll part ways."

I agreed. Traveling alone at night terrified me more than sleeping near the hanging men, and we found a small clearing about a hundred yards from the road. I sensed eyes watching as I slipped into my bag but dismissed it as the horror swinging from the trees. A dozen or more pair of empty sockets stared at me from half exposed skulls. For a moment I considered trading watches with Alton, but he had set himself on a fallen log and seemed alert.

Consciousness faded as I forced images of home into my thoughts. Slowly, Assassins, Outriders, and Shadows, vanished, replaced by mother's fresh bread: a list of chores waiting in the field: my sister's small hand stroking my cheek, coaxing me awake to play. Stroking and gently patting my cheek...urging me to wake up. Wake up.

I screamed when my eyes snapped open, and I saw the monster inches from my face.

It was deformed, a freak staring blankly at my forehead. I fumbled for my blade but came up empty. I grabbed a handful of dirt and flung it at the creature's one visible eye. He...it reeled and landed hard on its backside.

Alton called out from behind, but the thing moved to stand and had my full attention. My blade lay somewhere near my feet, but I didn't dare take my eyes off the beast.

Alton pressed behind me. "What is it?" he whispered.

Before I answered, it cried out. Not the wailing of an injured animal, but soft sobs of a child scolded by his mother. Head slumped and hands covering its face, it did look like a child. Too big for diapers, yet not nearly old enough to know the feel of a girl's soft lips.

"It's just a child, Cole. You strike it? Cut it?"

"No. I..."

"Well, you went on like one of your Shadows had you by the hair, carrying you off to hades."

He said the last as he shoved past me toward the figure, now sitting cross-legged, face still buried in his hands.

The creature didn't flinch from Alton's touch. Instead, two arms, one noticeably shorter, reached up. Alton took the boy to his chest, and for one horrifying moment I envisioned both toppling to the dirt. Their embrace was brief, and Alton sat the child on its feet and leaned in for a closer look.

My heart raced, but a feeling of relief slowly emerged. I managed a small step forward, then another. What I saw couldn't be human.

But it was. He was.

\*\*\*

**A**lton pulled a wooden twig from his pocket and started a fire.

Amazed, I watched the flame grow. "How did you do that? Where's your flint and steel?"

Alton cackled until he almost fell sideways into the new fire. "No magic. It's called a match. You can find them in most large villages." He gained his composure and eyed our new acquaintance. "You know what these are?"

The boy shook his head no.

"What do you know?" Alton's eyes narrowed. "Most ruined kids aren't worth the clean air they breathe."

The boy leaned closer into the light of our campfire. "To the contrary, Elder Sir, I'm well versed in many subjects."

He told us his name was Willy, and he was thirteen. He looked eight, maybe nine, but certainly not like a teenager. The boy's deformities came into full view when he leaned into the soft glow of the campfire. Dirty blond hair sprung forth in patches from his scalp and extended forehead. One eye bulged from its socket like a giant boil begging release. His other eye was missing, the space a smooth, dirt encrusted, concave of skin. Never in my life had I encountered anything like Willy. Never had I imagined such things were possible.

"I do so apologize for the fright, good sir. I beg your forgiveness." Willy bowed as he spoke. A show of respect, though I almost missed it, too startled by his high-brow speech. "I see not many travelers, for most pass-through during daylight." He lifted his head, smiled, and revealed grossly misshapen gums supporting only a few healthy teeth. "My mom and dad forbid me to come outside when light fills the sky."

"Don't take it hard child. Shame is powerful, especially shame in a son," Alton said.

I shot him a stern look, but the boy either didn't hear or let it pass.

"My father says there is freedom in darkness," Willy said.

"Freedom." Alton smiled along with the boy.

I stuck out my hand and withdrew quickly, realizing if he did the same, it would be with his worm-like arm. "My name is Cole, and this is Alton."

Alton grunted hello as Willy bowed his head. "Pleased we are met, good sirs."

"Where is your village?"

Willy pointed south, roughly the direction of the hanging corpses. "A mile past the Dead Trees."

"Dead Trees?"

"Trees full of dead Outriders. The ones you stopped to inspect. They're cursed with evil as ancient as it is strong."

"Cursed?"

"Our Council speaks of a time when a terrible goddess ruled our forest. She watched from the trees, while birds carried news from across her domain."

Alton cocked an eye at the boy. "She lived in trees like an animal?"

"No, Elder Sir," his countenance grew dark. "Legend claims she grew from the trees, gave them life."

"The one's with hanging...?"

"Yes, good sir, those."

"Who's responsible for stringing them up?" Alton asked first, but if he hadn't, I certainly would have.

"Us. I mean my village. I'm not permitted to attend the ceremony, but I've snuck and observed through the trees." He studied us for a moment, started to speak and hesitated.

"Go ahead, we're harmless." I couldn't look into his face, but the way he spoke, the sincerity and intelligence in his voice, mesmerized me. Also, the hurt. Subtle, buried deep but recognizable. I wanted to know more about this boy.

His voice waivered. "It's a brutal ritual. What they do when they catch an Outrider, I mean." His eye shifted away. The sight of it rotating outside its socket turned my stomach, but I'd emptied it earlier so the feeling passed. "Mother and father say it's necessary, what keeps us safe, but I don't like seeing it. Or hearing it. Neither does Vedia."

"Vedia?" Alton shifted his attention from a small rock to the boy.

"My friend. My only real friend. She meets me here some nights to play."

"Is she? I mean, do her parents make her stay inside during the day?"

"Is she like me?" He pointed to his face.

"No...well yes."

Willy smiled his terrible smile and laughed. "No. Nothing like me. Except in age maybe. I'm not sure about that. She's..." For the first time since we had gathered around the campfire, the young boy seemed to search for the correct word. "She's wonderful."

***

He told the story of how they'd first met, he and the girl. An Outrider had stumbled onto his village, Grandview.

"He wasn't the first Outrider to make that mistake, and surely won't be the last, but this was a young one. Barely out of his teens is my guess. My neighbors did as custom dictates, and offered him shelter, food, drink." Willy wiggled his arm, the short one, as if to say, "you get the idea." I nodded and looked away.

He continued. "Councilman Tiller, he's the oldest in Grandview, always keeps Outriders in the inn, top floor, last room on the left."

"He puts them in an inn then butchers them?"

"Please good sir, it's part of the story."

I motioned for him to hurry. I was curious, but my stomach heaved whenever I looked at the boy.

"Once well fed and rested, Councilman Tiller summoned the suspected Outrider to the meeting hall. Most, if not all, normal town people crammed in, perhaps three-hundred and fifty. Children and those of us deemed unshowable are never invited."

Alton cast a twig onto the fire. "Invited to what? Judging from what's stinking up the air, I assume it's not a welcome party."

"No, not a party. I've heard it called a trial, though we call it a testing."

Alton nodded as though he'd heard the term, and Willy continued. "I didn't see them bring him into the hall, but I was waiting when they finished. I'm certain they asked the same three questions asked of all suspected Outriders."

"Questions?"

Willy rolled his eye my way but didn't answer.

"I followed the crowd along the north road, in the shadows and far enough behind as not to be seen or heard. They could have taken him south. There's another patch of Dead Trees a mile that way, but the north road is most commonly used. It's the patch you discovered.

"No one saw or heard me, thank the gods, but I felt someone watching. I felt it in the darkness. I almost lost sight of the group when I slid into a thicket covered ditch and waited. Waited for whatever was watching to go away. Begging the gods it wasn't Shadows."

"Shadows? You know of the Shadows?" I asked.

Alton cast me an exasperated look, but I didn't pay him mind. If he refused to believe in the Shadows that was his choice.

Willy closed his eye and mumbled words I couldn't understand.

"Go on, it's okay. Do you know of them?" I asked.

"I beg, sir. Please forget I spoke that word." His round eye opened and swiveled again in my direction. "Please."

I let it drop, anxious for clarity on the ritual.

"Thank you, good sir."

Alton sighed, "Get on with it. My bones are crying out."

Willy glanced his direction, then at me and finished his story. "I arrived by the Dead Trees as they hoisted him up. He tried to speak; they all do. However, our ancestors learned long ago, words are hard formed without a tongue."

"You cut out his tongue?" My tone mixed surprise and disgust.

"Not I. Please sir, not I. But yes, after testing proved he was an Outrider, removal of the tongue was immediate."

Alton whirled his boney finger, urging the boy to speed his tale along.

"Yes. Anyway, with his hands and feet bound, he squirmed like a sacrificial worm dying on a hook." Willy squeezed his eye shut as if he were trying to erase the image from his mind. "An awful sight. Especially knowing what came next."

"For the sake of Father Earth, tell us about the girl!" Alton's outburst caught me off guard, and from the way Willy jerked, I knew he was startled.

Angry and more than a little embarrassed, I told Alton to shut up and let the boy finish.

"I apologize, Elder Sir. We are to the girl."

Alton grunted but said no more.

"Once the Outrider had been secured, this one's feet about chest high off the ground, the sporting line formed."

"Sporting?"

Willy closed his eye. "The game. A ritual as old or older than my grandpapa. I hate it and have never participated. I wouldn't even if they allowed it; you have to believe me." His voice quivered.

"Go ahead. I'm listening. We're listening." I made sure Alton heard.

"People form a line, sometimes it stretches into the forest, other times only thirty or forty people long. Councilman Tiller always swings first. Then the next oldest starts the sporting. Mister Jolly crafts their clubs from a pattern handed down from his father, who received it from his father, and so on."

Alton spun his finger. "We get the idea."

"Yes, sir. Legend is the clubs are modeled after a game ancients once played for recreation. Mister Jolly even burns letters into the sides, just like the pictures. One by one, people take a swing and pass to the next in line. The person who delivers the fatal blow wins whatever possessions the Outrider rode into town with." He paused, perhaps wanting to gauge our reaction. I was too astounded to speak. Alton held his peace also.

"I saw her right before Councilman Tiller swung. She was hidden behind a tree, no more than twenty feet away and watching Tiller. I heard her crying."

Alton leaned forward. "What did she look like?"

"Sir, please forgive me, it was dark. I can't say much, other than she looked about nine or ten years old and slender."

"She wasn't part of your village?" I asked.

"No, not that I know of. She did not say where she is from. I assume she escaped an Outrider and is in search of her family."

Alton's blasted finger again. "Go ahead."

"Yes, my apologies. Neither of us moved. She watched the sporting; I watched her. I don't know why, but I loved her the moment I saw her. Not the way mothers and fathers love one another, but the way...maybe the way a brother loves a sister, but stronger." He rolled his eye to the stars.

"Sounds of the sporting drifted through my head without sticking, as if it were far away. A sickening thud followed by jeers and laughter. Sounds of evil. Without warning, she turned to me."

A tear spilled down his misshapen face and the urge to embrace him overwhelmed me, but I held my place until he managed to go on.

"I wanted to run to her. Protect her from the animals I call neighbors and family, but she lifted her hand to stop me and smiled. No one had ever smiled at me."

\*\*\*

Willy hadn't learned her name that night. She vanished before the Outrider's insides spilled to the ground. "I turned away for a moment, and she was gone."

"When did you see her again?"

"Not for three nights, but I didn't venture outside to play until then. I..." Willy seemed to stumble over how to proceed. "Though I loved her, I did, I tell you." His look begged for me to believe him. He continued when I smiled my approval. "I couldn't tell a soul. Not ever."

"Why, because you watched the sporting?" I asked.

Willy shook his head, his protruding eye floated motionless. "No sir. It's the girl, Vedia. I can't let anyone in Grandview know about her. You must not tell; I beg you."

Alton let a rusty laugh escape from deep in his chest. "They not like the idea of you having a little girlfriend? Worried you might spawn a mutant as unfortunate as yourself?"

"Shut-up Alton!"

---

14

Willy didn't seem to mind the cruelty, or if he did, he didn't let on. "It's the testing."

"The testing of Outriders?" I asked.

"Suspected Outriders, kind sir. One of three questions asked is if they have ever met the girl of the forest."

Alton's lips pressed together in a tight grin. "Now, there's a story I'm anxious to hear," he stood and arched his back, "and when I finish my business behind those shrubs, you'll tell it."

Alton was already walking away when Willy answered. "Most certainly, Elder Sir."

"Don't worry about him." I cast a glance over my shoulder as Alton disappeared. "Born without a trace of charm. This girl, tell me more. What does she say?"

Questions rolled through my mind. Was this the girl from my dreams? Logically she couldn't be, but the way he described her gave me pause. Willy felt a draw I understood.

"Please, shouldn't we wait on Elder Sir to return? I will tell all I know when he does."

Alton seemed as anxious to hear about the girl as I. "Tell me this. Has she ever asked you-"?

Most of what happened next is a blur. Other parts I remember well. Never in my life had I felt pain like I did when the Night Cat leapt from the dark and latched onto my shoulder. Had I not moved my head at the last moment, I'm sure it would have snapped my neck and drug me into the trees. Fire raced down my arm and changed my world into a white-hot blur of agony. I reached across my body and grabbed for the cat, not knowing what I might grasp. At least one finger found an eye, I felt wetness as it popped, but its grip held tight. If anything, I stirred its rage.

Shouts from across the campfire. A sickening crunch by my ear. Hot, putrid breath rolled up my neck, and I flew backwards, pulled across rocks and dirt. The last image that flashed through my mind wasn't of home, chores, or mom. Before darkness overtook me, my mind recorded Willy, blade raised high, one bulbous eye, open wide, screeching and leaping through the air toward the beast. Even now, after all that happened during my journey, I still dream of that sight, of that sound. I still dream of Willy.

# 4

**THE TINKLE** of chimes filled my head. It was dark, cold, and my entire right side throbbed with a dull ache. I breathed deep and waited for death.

"You're awake?" A soft, timid voice joined the chimes in their song. "Easy, be easy I beg. Your fever is strong."

Not death. The cat hadn't taken me.

"Drink this." A young woman held a cup of steaming liquid to my mouth. Ginger and garlic assaulted my eyes; her matted, shoulder length hair smelled of the ingredients. I guessed her age at close to mine—twenty-five or twenty-six—but with a hard life. "Drink."

Cold metal gripped my wrist as I reached for the cup.

"Chains sir. The Council insisted until you are tested."

The drink tasted as it smelled. Sharp. Earthy.

"Thank you..."

"Susannah, or Susan if it pleases you." She dipped her head in a way that made me think of my sister Cora playing princess of the kingdom.

The automatic smile that appeared when I thought of Cora vanished when I remembered she might be sick. "Can you tell me what happened?"

She hesitated, looked over her shoulder, back to me, and over her shoulder again. "I mustn't. I'm sorry."

"You can't tell me why I'm here? Why I'm chained to a bed?"

No answer other than a timid shaking of her head and fear in her eyes.

"Are you afraid?"

Without another word, she sat the cup down within reach and hurried to the door.

"Wait! I didn't mean to frighten you. Susan, please."

She stopped. "When it's safer, I'll return." She scurried out without looking back.

Soft light filtered through the only window and offered a depressing view of my room. Water trickled down sections of stone walls, adding to murky puddles scattered about the stone floor. My stiff bed and a small table completed the room's furniture. From one corner, a rustling sound sent shivers up my neck. I closed my eyes and drew several deep breaths. The sound quieted, and the soft light faded. Time slowed, and sleep begged my sick body to relent. I did.

Hours, maybe months passed. I remember visitors, though I knew only two, Susan and Alton. I can't say whether we spoke or not. Heat, nausea, and pain. This is what I remember during my time chained to the bed as a suspected Outrider.

\*\*\*

I woke to a stranger sitting beside my bed. His leathered face and piercing blue eyes remained calm when I regarded him.

"Where am I?"

The stranger pulled a match from his bright red jacket, flicked it with his thumb, and lit a pipe hanging from the corner of his lips. Scents of vanilla and stale tobacco mingled with the stench of my own waste.

"Who are you?"

The man leaned back in his chair, blew another cloud of smoke and smiled. "Looks like you will live. Susan says your fever is leaving."

I did not like this man. The hard face and wispy white hair could belong to any of a dozen farmers in my village, but his teeth betrayed the truth. When he smiled, I saw them all and knew he lived a life of splendor.

"You didn't answer my questions," I said.

"Grandview and Tiller. Such rudeness to the man who saved your life."

"Saved my life?" I thought of the boy. "Where's Willy?"

"Sorry thing is fine. Took hard discipline from his father as I understand, but he isn't dead."

Relief overwhelmed me. I had only known the boy for a few hours, but I liked him. Maybe pity endeared him to me, but his story felt familiar. And of course, he had saved my life.

"I'd like to leave now."

"Sorry Cole, I can't allow that just yet."

Pain ripped through my shoulder when I lunged at Tiller.

"Easy, easy. You'll open your wounds. Susan's stitching is marvelous, but thread can only hold so long."

"Then let me out of these chains and let me see my friends."

"Friends? You mean sir Alton and our little ruined one?"

I lunged again and felt the stitches give.

"I must say, you're not helping your situation. Lashing out like a caged beast, no respect for your gracious hosts. Though, I will consider your upbringing in, what is the name of your village? Bellman, Beltman?"

"Bethman."

"Yes, Bethman. Peasants living in isolation, miles off the trade roads. Good people I'm sure, but primitive. We are a civilized society in Grandview. Trade with other villages, law and order, education. We are rebuilding the world, Cole. Rebuilding and framing it right this time."

"Are you going to let me see my friends?"

"No, I'm afraid not yet."

I wanted to strike out but my shoulder, now sticky through the bandages, wouldn't allow it. "Why? What have I done to you or your precious little town?"

I knew before the words slipped through his lips.

"You haven't been tested, my boy."

\*\*\*

**L**ater that night, Susan returned with more foul liquid and persuaded me to drink. I asked about Alton, and she told me he was staying in a room on the first floor. He had passed his testing and was free to leave—encouraged to leave actually—but refused to go without me.

"He asked to see you," she lowered her eyes, "but the Council will not allow it until your testing."

"I'm not an Outrider. I didn't come with a crazy message. I've seen with my own eyes the evil they spread. I saw it in my own village."

She glanced up briefly, opened her mouth to speak, but looked away.

"You have to believe me. You have to help me." I lifted my arm, the one not burning with infection, and jiggled the chain around my wrist.

"Please, sir Cole, no more talk. Roll to your side so I can change your bandages."

"No! I don't deserve this. I have done no wrong!" I felt like a child throwing a tantrum, but words spewed forth faster than I could stop them. "This is crazy! You're all crazy!"

Susan sobbed, but I didn't care.

"I've laid here, chained to this flea infested bed, rolling in my own mess, eating slop and drinking the putrid drink you force down my throat. You want to test me? Test me now. Ask me your questions! String me up and splatter my intestines all over your wooden club! Just be done with it."

"Please, sir. Please." Her voice cracked between breaths. "Please let me attend to your wounds."

My anger dissipated. Susan wasn't to blame; her actions showed only kindness. Still, she was one of them. I rolled to my side without another word.

The salve she smeared on my cuts was supposed to soothe, but instead burned like fire. Determined not to cry out and still furious, I bit into my pillow with enough force to rip the cloth as Susan applied new bandages. After a moment, the pain eased, though I would lay on my side for several hours. Susan knelt by my bed, eyes red and puffy. "Willy is gone."

I didn't grasp her words. Dead? Missing? My pain faded into the background. "Gone? What do you mean gone?"

She peeked toward the door and started to stand. I grabbed her wrist and yanked her to my face. "What do you mean gone?"

"He fled."

She struggled to break free, but I gripped harder. "He fled? Why? Where did he go?" Pain returned with a fury, but I didn't care.

"You're hurting me!" She yanked her arm, but my fingers dug into her skin. "Please stop. Please."

I relaxed my grip, but only slightly. "Is he okay?"

Her eyes shifted away before settling on mine. "If Tiller..." She bit her lip.

"Please." I begged.

"The Council found out about the girl. I don't know how, but they did. A group went to his home to question him, but when they opened the cellar, he was gone. His parents are with the Council now, and they've sent a group out looking for him."

"What does that mean?"

Susan choked back a sob.

"Look at me and tell me what that means."

"It means if they find him, he'll be tested."

***

**R**ain pelted the roof and dripped onto my bed. I twisted my neck and caught what I could with my tongue. I wondered if Alton had lived the same nightmare. I thought of Susan and wondered why she stayed in a community that terrified her. I thought of home, little Alice who had died at the feet of an Outrider...by my blade. I thought about the disease and wondered if it existed. If it did, would Cora survive until I knew the truth?

And Willy. What would Tiller do if he found him? I clenched my eyes shut, but the bloody image hovered in my mind.

***

**C**ouncilman Tiller and four men came for me that night and carried me to a large wooden building near the center of town. I smelled the hall before we reached the door. Its sharp aroma reminded me of medicine mother poured on my many cuts and scrapes as a child. The men of Bethman drank the same thing when harvest time ended and five days of partying began. They called it Firewater.

Cheers sprang from the large gathering as they led me to a platform near the front and drug me up its three steps. Torches, the height of a man, lit the stage from its sides. More torches and candles were scattered throughout. Moonlight filtered through several dirty windows, high along each side wall. I also spotted the source of the smell. Barrels of the medicine smelling drink lined the entrance wall. One, with no top, sat on the edge of the platform.

Rope cut into my wrists as men and women passed trays of meat and cheese among themselves. Everyone wore clothing more suited for social engagements than farming. Dresses embroidered with flowers and birds, jackets and pants without a patch, stain, or tear.

I scanned the room for Alton and saw him standing near the entrance talking to a giant man wearing a small black hat. They saluted an empty glass into the air when they saw me. Alton's smile and fresh clothes told his story.

"Ladies and gentleman." Tiller stepped forward on the platform. "Ladies and gentleman. Please, it's time we get started."

Polite applause rippled through the crowd.

"As you all know, we are here for a testing, our second this week."

Again, polite applause and several heads swiveled to the entrance. The big man wearing a small hat clapped Alton on the back.

"Let's hope this one turns out as fortunate as the first. If not, we have entertainment prepared." Cheers rose through the hall, and those near the door pounded on wooden barrels. Tiller summoned three men and a woman onto stage. All wore the same style clothes as the crowd. The only distinguishing feature was the white sash each wore across their chests.

"Council, are we ready to proceed?"

They nodded in turn.

"Very well." Tiller raised his hands to the sky and bowed his head. Without exception, the audience did likewise. "Father Earth, Mother Sky, gods of harvest and hunt, we beg you, give us wisdom. Before us stands a stranger, untested and therefore unclean in your sight. Grant us vision into truth. Grant us hearing against lies. Grant us strength to carry out our duty if he is proven false." Tiller dropped his hands and looked over the gathering. "All who agree, say so."

As one, the people spoke. "I agree."

The hair on my arms stood erect.

Tiller leaned in and whispered. "Your friend assures me all will be well if you speak truth. For your sake, I hope so." He stepped back and turned to the crowd. "Let the testing begin."

Polite applause fluttered though the hall. Four rows deep, a tray of cups slipped from a servant's palm and crashed to the floor. Those nearest the commotion jumped. A moment later, nervous laughter drifted among the spectators.

"Stranger, where is your home?"

The simple question caught me by surprise. "Bethman. Three days journey."

Tiller nodded as did several of the Council. "Let the record show the stranger claims the village of Bethman as home.

"Stranger, what do you know of the Shadows?"

"Only stories."

"Please elaborate."

My mouth went dry. No one who believed in Shadows talked about them. "May I have water?" My tongue felt thick and slow.

Tiller signaled to a woman, and she hurried out of sight. Within seconds, she returned with an elegant glass vase. I took the water and drank slowly.

"Enough." Tiller snatched it from my hands.

"In my village, some believe in Shadows, others do not. Of those that believe, no one agrees on exactly what they are, or their motives. The only consensus is they are monsters of night...creatures of darkness."

A Council member spoke. "Describe these beliefs."

Tiller shot the man a hard look but motioned me to answer.

"Some believe they are Night Cats, mutated by corrupt air left from the ancients' weapons. Others believe they are spirits of those who are gone from this world and come back to seek vengeance on those who wronged them. A few wonder if they are of this world at all."

"What do you believe?" Tiller asked.

"I don't know."

He considered me for a moment. "One last question. Stranger, have you met the girl of the forest?"

The question Willy spoke of. I thought of the girl on the hill and the girl from my dreams. Either could have been her.

"No, I have not."

Tiller turned and joined the Council without speaking. The crowd, who had remained silent, whispered among themselves as the huddle formed to my right. Near the entrance, Alton gave a slight dip of his head. A gesture I assumed meant to show his approval.

Hot, foul breath from behind rolled by my ear. A man, thick and scarred, shuffled to my side. His long blade tapped my thigh and eased to my waist.

Hushed disagreement arose from the huddled group. I considered my options and found no possible way of escape. Coarse rope bound my hands and feet tight. As if he read my mind, the thick man brought his knife to my ribs.

The faint murmur below fell silent as the huddle broke and Tiller walked to me. "Stranger, the Council will now give its verdict. Councilman Edwards?"

"He speaks lies. He is an Outrider."

"Councilman Brannon?"

"Not an Outrider."

"Councilwoman Heart?"

"He speaks truth. He is not an Outrider."

"Councilman Lansing?"

"He is an Outrider."

Tiller folded his arms across his chest. The only sound in the vast hall was the thud of his foot slowly tapping wooden planks. Finally, with well-rehearsed showmanship, he spread his arms wide. "He speaks truth. He is not an Outrider."

A mix of applause and cat-calls rose from the hall. I learned later the applause came from those who bet correctly on my fate. Many lost a great deal.

A blade flashed by my face, and my hands were free. Within seconds, so were my feet. I fell to the stage exhausted. Tiller reached for my hand, but I smacked it away. I wanted out. Far from these people. I wanted to go home and farm the field or climb a tall pine and fling myself into the creek like I did when I was younger.

"Cole, no need for aggression. It's over. You're free to go if you like. Or you may stay and rest.

Unchained of course." He laughed. "We have baths with warm water, meat," he leaned close. "The company of a woman if you like."

Shouts from the entrance drew our attention. I leaned around Tiller's legs for a clear view. A man and a woman walked the aisle, each clasping an arm of the hooded figure between them. Both middle-age and dressed in distinguished attire, their stern faces lacked emotion. The small hooded figure didn't struggle.

Tiller waved his arms to quiet the crowd. "Mr. and Mrs. Chambliss. Is this who I think it is?"

The woman curtsied and spoke. "Yes, Councilman Tiller."

The man, Mr. Chambliss, jerked the hood away. "He came home seeking help."

Tiller's lips stretched into a thin smile. "Willy Chambliss. We have three questions for you."

# 5

**TWO LANKY** men hoisted Willy onto stage. I reached for him, but Tiller grabbed my arm and pulled me away.

"No contact until after the testing."

I protested and felt the thick man's blade press against my side. Willy rolled his eye toward me, and for the first time I saw a frightened child, not the monster I had first mistaken him for.

"He's not an Outrider! He's-" A sharp sting below my ribs cut my plea short.

"One more word and I tell him to sink it through your liver." Tiller's fingers bit into my arm. "My patience is nearly depleted."

I backed away, and the sting in my side eased.

Tiller turned to Willy. "Willy Chambliss, where is your home?"

"Grandview," he said without hesitation.

"Let the record show Willy Chambliss claims Grandview as home." Whispers trickled among the people, silenced by Tiller's next question. "Willy Chambliss, what do you know of the Shadows?"

Willy recoiled at the word. "Sir, must I speak of them?"

"The choice to speak is yours, but if you do not, you understand the consequences."

He closed his eye. "Yes sir."

"Speak truth."

"I only know stories."

Tiller fixed his gaze on Willy's parents. "From your mother and father? Have they filled your ruined mind with myth and folklore?"

Mrs. Chambliss cried out first. "He's lying! We've never!"

Mr. Chambliss wrapped one arm around her shoulders and pointed the other at his son. "Recant your statement! How dare you speak lies about us to the Council after all we've provided for you, even after you came out ruined from your mother's womb!"

Tiller silenced them with his hand. "Do you recant?"

"No sir, but it wasn't them. They never speak of Shadows."

"Then who?"

Willy shrugged and the thick man smacked the back of his head. "Answer."

"From a friend."

Patches of laughter sprang from the floor. A deep voice boomed. "Raise your hand if you believe the boy has a friend." No one breathed or raised their hand.

Tiller snapped his fingers and three men secured the comedian and hauled him away. Muted whispers ceased when Tiller raised his hand. "Does this friend have a name."

"Yes," Willy said.

Mr. Chambliss called out in a pleading voice. "Tell the man his name, child. For the sake of your ma and pa, tell his name."

"It's a girl, and her name is Vedia."

Tiller glanced to the Council and back to Willy. "We have no child here by that name." He turned to the audience. "Citizens, are any here parents of a girl child called Vedia?"

Tiller waited, but no one spoke. He spun to Willy.

"Do not speak falsely to the Council. I ask one last time. Who speaks of the shadows?"

"I speak truth. My friend Vedia told me. She tells me much."

"Who is Vedia? Does she exist only in your mind? Another defect of your spoiled body?"

Willy remained silent.

"Tell us or be found false!" Tiller's voice exploded.

Willy glanced at me. Light from torches flickered off his wet face. I shook my head. Don't say it, Willy. Tell him Vedia is from another village. Tell him she's from the stars. Tell him he's right, Vedia comes to you in your mind. Tell him anything but what you told me and Alton.

"Sir Tiller, Vedia is the girl of the forest."

***

I've replayed the next few minutes over in my mind every day since. Many nights, sleep eludes me. Nights when the images become too real, and the smell of burning flesh turns my stomach. But I had to try and save him.

The crowd gasped in near perfect unison when Willy gave his final answer. Several shouted for his tongue; others clapped and shouted for firewater.

What I did next, I did without thinking. If I had considered the full consequences, I might have hesitated. I know I would have. One barrel of firewater was within reach, presumably for the evening's festivities, and with one shove I toppled it to its side. I wasn't certain it would burn, but its smell made me think it might.

Firewater flowed across the platform and spilled over the front in a small waterfall. I pulled a torch from its socket and hurled it. The platform ignited in flame.

That might have been the end if Councilman Tillers' pants hadn't caught fire. Several men working together might have fought the blaze and won. An orderly exit might have allowed most to escape. None of those things happened.

Tiller screamed out, either in pain or surprise, maybe both. He beat at his legs, a look of wild fury in his eyes. The thick man rushed across the platform and pulled him away from the flames. Safely out of their reach, he threw Tiller to the floor, tore off his shirt, and beat the Councilman's legs with his palms.

I moved quick. Fire blocked a straight path to Willy, but I circled around the back half of the stage. When I reached him, he simply held out his arms, and I slung him over my shoulder.

Panic swelled as smoke filled the hall. Men and women shoved and fought toward the entrance as the first row of benches caught, then the second. Tiller sat up, his pants charred and smoking, and yelled for order. No one obeyed. The thick man grabbed his arm and lifted Tiller to his feet. The Councilman let out a cry and collapsed.

Panic blocked the center aisle, just out of reach of the flames near the stage. More men and women stumbled over benches and along the walls.

"Is there another door?" I choked through the smoke now curling across the platform.

"Not that I know of, good sir." Willy clutched my shirt tight.

I circled behind the flames and hopped from the stage. My body screamed at the jolt when I landed hard and went to a knee. A flash of heat washed across my face as a burning woman stumbled by and fell beside me. Flames danced across her shoulders and around her neck. Strips of bloody flesh lifted from skin as her fingernails clawed at the fully engulfed dress. She reached out and touched my leg and I kicked her away. Two quick spasms, and the hand fell limp

The flow down the main aisle had stopped, but the shouts and curses had not. I stepped around the charred woman and worked my way forward along the wall.

"Please, leave me, sir Cole."

Three months before, I would have left him. Not then. Not after the nightmares about Alice and my rusted blade that ended up in her chest.

A ball of flame erupted from across the aisle. Then another. More screams. Wails of agony. A figure, so engulfed by fire it was impossible to tell whether man or woman, hurled themselves into the mass of people. A new bonfire sprang to life in the center of the hall.

"Listen to me." Smoke burned my lungs when I took a breath. "We can't go out the door. Is there another way?"

A crash from the front roared in my ears. A support beam had fallen, blocking the entrance and crushing a dozen people beneath blazing timber. Bits of wood and metal rained fire.

"No." Willy's words came hard through the thick smoke. "No other doors."

I slid along the wall, unable to see more than a few feet.

"Please help! Somebody help!" A man knelt beside a writhing body; its lower half wedged beneath two large timbers. "It's my son."

I paused. Heat pressed against my face, and my lungs cried for clean air. I scanned the mayhem, but smoke hung thick allowing no more than a glimpse of chaotic figures gone mad...clawing, pushing, burning.

"Please." The man's voice now a sob.

From behind. "Help him, sir, but do it quick." Willy panted the words.

"No time! We have to go!" I shouted over the roar of flames and cries of agony.

"We have to help them!"

I dropped Willy and swung to the trapped boy and his father. The boy wasn't exactly a boy but barely a man. Soot covered his acne scarred skin. Flames roared at the end of each eight-foot section of timber, consuming their way inward along the wood.

I pointed to the closest one. "Help me lift."

Pain shot through my palms when I grabbed the smoking wood, but me and the boy's father managed to slide it across the second timber and away.

A thunderous crash roared from across the hall and red-hot embers flittered down around us. A corner of the building had endured its limit.

"Hurry! Now!" We were out of time.

I don't know if the man heard me over the roar of fire and screams of the dying, but he grabbed one end of the remaining timber, and with strength I didn't know remained, we heaved it to the side.

"Thank you. Thank you," the son choked through smoke.

"Let's go!" His father reached, grabbed his hand, and yanked him forward.

The son cried out. "My foot!"

His father yanked again, putting all his weight behind the pull.

"Stop!"

I reached for Willy, but he wasn't there.

"Willy! Where are..." I couldn't manage another word, overcome with smoke and exhaustion. I pitched forward.

"Here sir. Here." Willy caught my fall.

He scooted a bench against the wall and pulled me to it. "I have a way." He pointed up. "The window."

Standing on the bench an average size man could reach it. I picked a four-foot plank from the floor and hurled it into the glass. "I'll lift you through." I spotted a discarded cane and handed it to him. "Clear the jagged edges with this but do it quick."

Another rush of heat swept across my back, and I glanced over my shoulder. More wall had collapsed into a torrent of fiery embers. A third of the roof followed.

"Now!"

I whirled around when a hand grasped my wrist. The man, eyes wide and face pale under streaks of soot. "My son. Can't walk. Beam busted his ankle."

I pushed him away and reached for Willy.

Willy smacked my hand away, his face fierce and determined. The same look when he saved me from the Night Cat. "Him first." He pointed to the man's son.

I started to protest but he cut my words short. "Him first!"

The boy's father took one arm, and I took the other. We led him to the bench as Willy finished clearing the remaining glass. The boy reached up, grabbed the seal and hoisted himself into the window with a grunt. He toppled through when we pushed. From the stage came a soft thud followed by a loud cry of agony.

Willy went next. He was lighter, but with only one good arm, we almost lost our balance lifting him high enough. Once into the window, he fell with ease.

"Go man! Go!" The man hoisted himself up. I gave a shove from below, and he slid into darkness.

Screams continued from behind, but they were fewer. I closed my eyes and jumped. My hands caught the windowsill, and I pulled with all the strength my shoulder allowed.

Cool air hit my lips and rushed down my body. I hit the ground hard. For a moment, I laid there, looking at the night sky, not believing I was free. We were free. Smoke billowed from the hall up to the stars. How many had died? Excited voices mingled with cracks and pops of the inferno. Not the horrific cries I had heard inside and not quite calm...just alive.

Suddenly I was being drug away from the building. I tilted my head. Willy and the man each had an arm and pulled me to safety. Numbed by horror, I didn't feel them grab me.

They dropped me by a small tree, away from the hall and scattered survivors.

"Can you walk?" The man knelt beside me.

"I think so."

"Then go. Go now while you can. I'll not stop you or the ruined child, but we're even. My debt to you is paid."

Many of the flaming bodies were those of his friends, neighbors, probably family. "I'm sorry. I..."

"Just go." He stood without another word, stepped toward his son, looked over his shoulder, "And never come back."

# 6

**WE WALKED** until the sounds of death faded. The smell never did. No one pursued us, concerned with the injured and dying...concerned with grief I suppose. How many had I killed? Forty? Fifty? Did it matter?

"Why did you tell me to help the boy?" I asked Willy.

"What do you mean?"

"The way they treated you. The way they ridiculed you your whole life."

He stopped and took my arm. "He would have died."

Willy walked on without me, but I called after him. "They were going to kill you! We could have died!"

He turned and smiled. A grotesque sight I learned to love. "Perhaps, but we didn't." He walked to me. "Have you watched someone die, knowing you might have saved them?"

My mouth went dry. "No," I lied.

"I have. Once." He paused and drew a breath. "Never again."

Willy continued along the path.

"Willy!" I caught up and spun him to me. "I did see someone die. I was part of it."

His smile vanished, but his eye stayed steady. "The boy you saved, his name is Jody. He was born six years before me. His parents and mine do business. When I was young, they spent much time together. One night, while they dined above, I waited in the cellar with my baby sister."

"Sister? You never mentioned a sister."

He looked away. "No, I don't speak of her often."

"Is she...like you?"

"Yes, born with deformities similar to mine." He ran his good hand through sparse patches of hair. "I waited for scraps. Mom usually prepared more than enough; I like to think on purpose. I heard glassware rattle and movement in the kitchen and knew we would soon eat. When the door opened, it wasn't mom. Jody crept down the stairs with a pot of scraps. He meant evil. Even with a single lit candle, I read his face.

"Della, my sister, started to cry. We hadn't eaten in two days other than a cup of tomato soup. She spit most up though."

"Your sister was a baby?"

"Yes, kind sir. Less than a year from the womb." He pulled a breath and continued. "Jody told me to make her 'shut up'."

I interrupted "How old was he?"

"Twelve. I was six." He waited a heartbeat. "I picked her up and tried to calm her, but it didn't work."

Willy fell silent and studied the night sky. Worry of Night Cats, Shadows, or hanging Outriders gave way to the sadness in Willy's eye.

"He killed her, didn't he?" I knew the answer halfway through his story but didn't want to watch him struggle recounting the memory. "Jody killed your baby sister."

"Yes," Willy said without looking at me. "I dream of her."

I wanted to ask more, but the sorrow in his eye stopped me, and we walked in silence. The sounds and smells of chaos dissipated, replaced by an occasional rustling of leaves, and call of forest insects. Familiar sounds. Natural Sounds. Sounds of life.

Willy broke the quiet. "Where is Elder Sir?"

I didn't know. The last time I saw him was before the fire, having a laugh along the back wall. "Gone I guess."

"Where will we go?"

"I don't know. Let's walk a little while longer and find a safe place to rest tonight. Tomorrow we'll figure it out."

Hooves clapped packed earth from behind, and I dove into a shallow ditch. Willy didn't move.

"Willy." I shouted under my breath.

Too late. He stepped back and lifted his arm then squealed with delight. "Elder Sir! Miss Susan! You brought Miss Susan!"

***

I helped Alton from his horse while Susan dismounted hers without help. Heavy smoke hung from both, especially Susan.

"What? How?" I had resigned myself to never seeing Alton again. Though part of me disliked him, knowing he hadn't deserted me brought hope.

"First, let's get off the road, then we'll talk. I'm fairly certain the good mister Tiller has more pressing matters to attend to now, but no need to tempt the gods."

We led the horses through light brush and into the forest. Alton first, then Willy and Susan. I anchored our band of fugitives, praying Alton was right about Tiller not following. Images of Dead Trees full of tongueless corpses lingered. Images and smells.

Twenty minutes in, we found a small clearing. Underbrush, toppled trees, and twisted saplings hid our fire from the road.

Susan broke the quiet. "I had to leave. I couldn't stay."

We all looked up at once. She paused, reading our faces in turn, and stopped on Willy. "I'm sorry. For how they...how we...treated you."

Willy leaned to her, but she held out her hand. "It's true. I should have stood up for you."

Willy tried to speak, and she stopped him again. "Please simply accept my apology."

Willy dipped his head and smiled. "I accept."

Several minutes of uncomfortable silence passed before I spoke. "Susan, how did you end up in Grandview to begin with?"

She glanced up through dirt-caked strands of hair. "I was young when my mother and father died. I don't remember her. I remember traveling with my father."

"What did he do?" I asked.

"He was an Outrider. We lived in a beautiful village called Hopewell when I was young. We rode into Grandview when I was ten, and I never left." She searched her satchel, pulled out a metal pendant and slid her fingers across its surface as we talked. "Tiller made me watch the testing. I wiped my father's blood from stage after they drug him away. Thank the gods I didn't see the rest." She rose slowly to her feet and gazed into the forest. "I had to throw away his tongue. I'll always feel it in my hands. If I wash them a thousand times, I'll feel it." She pushed dangling strands of hair away from her forehead. "One of the Councilmen—I don't remember who—stayed behind and locked me in Tiller's inn when I finished. I didn't see anyone for five days, other than when a servant brought food and water."

"What's that?" Alton glared at the pendant.

It glimmered as Susan held it to the light. "My father gave it to me when I was young."

"May I see it?" I held out my hand.

She paused and passed it to me. "My father said it is gold."

I had only seen the metal once before, when I was a child. I took the pendant and felt its weight. Heavier than it looked. "What is this?" I showed her the symbol etched on its face.

"I don't remember."

Alton peered over my shoulder. "Trouble, that's what it is. Big trouble."

"Elder Sir!" Willy said.

"Don't chastise me! I'll not stand disrespect from a child. Certainly not one as ruined as yourself."

"Enough Alton!" I handed the pendant to Susan and turned to Alton. "Please," my cordial tone came with great effort, "if you know, I would like to hear."

"Of course, I know. It's a sign the Outriders use: them and their delusional communities."

"There are communities of Outriders?" I asked.

"No, no, no. Outriders are relatively few, but there are communities full of people poisoned by their sorcery. They clamor over the cursed symbol like maggots on a carcass."

"Why? What is its meaning?" Willy asked.

Alton leaned forward toward the fire but didn't speak.

"Please, it was my father's."

He shook his head. "No. The myth itself has power. I can't risk poisoning you with their words."

His set jaw told me he meant it.

"Tell us the name of the sign. Surely that is safe." Susan choked back tears.

Alton cocked his head to her. "Nothing's safe with Outriders."

"Please." Her voice almost a whisper.

Alton sighed and launched a string of spit into the fire. "It's a word from the ancients. A vile word that speaks of death." He looked at each of us. "Outriders and their poor victims always speak of death and blood. Part of the sickness if you ask me."

"What is the word?" Susan placed her hand on his.

"It's called a cross."

We let the conversation end when Susan kissed the pendant and slowly tucked it into her satchel. If words alone carried power to poison, surely a token etched with their sacred symbol was dangerous.

Willy broke the uncomfortable silence. "How old was I, Miss Susan? When you came, did you know me?"

She looked at Willy and smiled. "You were born a year after I arrived. I remember very well." Susan opened her mouth to speak but stopped.

"Please continue, Miss Susan." Willy leaned forward with his seat off the ground.

"I helped bring you from your mother's womb. Part of my duties at Grandview included caring for new mothers. I remember you. I was eleven, and you were my first baby. And the way you cried and squirmed," she drifted into a quiet laugh, "You reminded me of a little puppy. I thought you were the best baby in all the world."

"Miss Susan." Willy beamed. "I only wish my mother and father would have let me have friends. We would have been good ones. What was it like for them, my parents? Were they happy when I was born?"

Susan tried to hide the truth, but sadness in her eyes betrayed her smile. "We would have been friends...good ones, but that doesn't mean we can't be friends now."

Willy blushed, while I watched the exchange in silence.

"I hate to interrupt such a special moment, but we have more important matters to discuss," Alton said. "Eventually Tiller will come. I say we move on to a more urgent topic."

"There isn't much more to say. I helped with births, nursed the sick, never married, and had no children of my own. Servants were allowed neither husband nor offspring." Her voice softened. "That's how you found me. An orphaned slave."

That night around our fire and the next day were good days.

# 7

**EITHER WE** lost our pursuers, or they had given up. We returned to the road, and within minutes encountered a wiry man with a round stomach as he struggled to lift a large barrel onto the back of a crude, nearly rotten wagon. Several more barrels lay scattered across the road, busted and leaking stout liquid. Hard wine from the smell, though I'd never tasted the drink. Alton urged us not to stop, and Susan agreed.

"Isn't our business, Cole," Alton said.

"He's right. Besides, what if he's hauling his load to Grandview?" Susan eyed the man with unmistakable distrust.

"He hasn't seen us yet and won't if we're lucky. Last thing we need this close to Grandview is a half-drunk peddler squawking about four strangers heading west." Alton had enough time to finish his sentence when we heard Willy introduce himself.

"Hello, good sir. May I offer you a hand?" He wiggled his gimp arm.

What we heard, what we saw, wasn't what we expected. The man lifted his head to the sound and froze. The barrel in his arms dropped and busted with a dull thud. Waves of pink liquid washed over his shoes, and Willy's. Neither moved. After what seemed like minutes, though seconds probably would be more accurate, the man screamed. He didn't charge the boy, nor did he turn and run, but his scream didn't stop...even when Willy's screams began.

And that's how we met Tick Grainger.

*** 

We sat in a circle outside his dilapidated shed. Me, Alton, Susan, and Tick on wooden crates with foam padding, Willy crossed-legged on the ground. Tick squinted against a setting sun; his target barely visible in the reddish orange glow peeking over a pine thicket. He drew a breath and let his sling fly. A puff of dirt sprang up in front of the rat, and it scurried beneath a pile of newly deposited trash bags. From the smell, this place had thousands of disease-ridden critters, and Tick still had an hour of light and a box full of grape sized metal balls.

"Want to try one?" Tick pushed the leather sling in my direction. "It's a bugger, but when ya do whack one," he let out a long whistle but said no more.
I declined. He loaded another shot and sent a ball over the same rat's head. "Suit yourself."

Tick and his wife grew up and were married in a village called Sugar Hill. Alton, Susan, and Willy had heard of it, though none had ever visited. He was a laborer, hiring on at harvest to haul corn, potatoes, whatever needed hauling. During winter, he hired on at a sawmill to stack wood and fetch supplies.
"Whatever I could, for whoever would have me." Tick loaded another ball, flicked the sling over his head, and sent it three feet behind a plump rat. It never looked away from the meal in its paws.

"Anyway, trouble came looking for us, and the Council kindly asked me and Cindy to leave town. Wanted my land is what I think. Dirty bunch of vultures is what they are." He paused, looked my direction, and continued when I gave an affirming nod. "We left, and that was about ten summers ago, I guess." He didn't elaborate, and none of us pressed.

"You're wife, Cindy. Is she here?" Susan asked.

"Naw. Said she was going to Grandview to trade for coffee, and she ain't come back."

"We didn't pass a lady along the way. When are you expecting her? It'll be dark soon," I asked.

Tick's short laugh rolled through his nose. "Buddy, that was three winters ago. I don't reckon she'll be here anytime soon.

"Cindy said I wasn't worth putting up with the stench. Good riddance is what I said. All she did was complain. 'The floor's rotten Tick. You look pregnant Tick. They ain't no such thing as little green monsters in the woods, Tick.' I tried to tell her they weren't green, they were black, but she wouldn't have it. Said I had 'problems'. Then she was gone. Poof, off to restock the coffee, and I ain't seen her since." He had lived in the shed going on ten years, the last three alone with no plans of moving or chasing her down.

A rustling sound near a pile of scrap metal caught our attention. Tick lifted his sling, leaned forward on the crate chair and stopped. "You sure any of you don't want a turn?"

Willy wiggled his arm, and Tick handed the sling over. "You need me to show you how?"

"No sir, I watched your technique."

Willy adjusted the ball, slipped his finger through the strap, and whirled the sling over his head. The ball flew, and twenty yards away a rat toppled from a pile of busted barrels and out of sight.

Tick flicked a green beetle off his arm and smiled. "One gone, five thousand to go. Nice shot, Willy. You sure you ain't never slung one?"

Willy handed the sling to Tick.

"Nah, you go ahead and keep it. I got two more."

Tick reached into the box and took a handful of balls. "Here, stuff these in your pocket. If y'all traveling, looks like you're the protection."

The smile on Willy's deformed face made him look almost normal. "Thank you, sir."

"Quit it with that sir stuff. My papa was a sir. I'm Tick. No more, no less." He smacked the boy's good arm. "Reckon you'll be wanting a place to rest. You're welcome to stay here...as long as y'all can pile up on the floor together. You can use those seat cushions for pillows if you want."

I liked the idea of a roof over my head, and Tick seemed harmless. "Thank you Tick, and if it's okay with my friends, we'll accept your offer."

"Yes, kind sir, if I may only ask one question," Willy said.

"What's on your mind? Ask Tick, he'll tell you."

"Yes, well...It's your speech. The accent is unfamiliar."

Tick threw back his head in laughter. "Ain't that something? I was thinking the same thing about you. I mean, all you Grandview folk talk funny, but you seem extra fancy." His laughter died, but his smile didn't. "You haven't traveled much have you? In this big world everybody talks a little different. My momma and daddy talked this way, so I guess I learned from them. I reckon if I had any kids, they'd talk like me." He winked at Willy. "Unless y'all made friends, and they started talking like you." This brought another round of laughter from

Tick, and we chatted outside till the sun hid itself completely below the horizon.

Tick stood first. "We better be getting on inside. Now's about the time jeeters start peeking out the woods."

"Jeeters?" Susan asked.

"The black critters that run around the woods at night." Tick looked at Susan like she should have learned the word as a child.

Willy took my hand and pulled me close. "Shadows. He's talking about the Shadows."

Tick cocked his head in our direction. "Yeah, heard em' called that too."

"I'd like to hear what you know of them if you don't mind. Them and a girl we're looking for." I said.

***

**We** crowded into Tick's shed, seat cushions in hand.

"I don't know nothing about no girl. Ain't seen a young'un out this far in, oh I don't know, three, maybe four years. But jeeters, they come around. Come 'round enough for me to believe in them."

Alton sounded a not so discreet humph. "Fairytales." Even for Alton, the tone was harsh.

"Oh, it's true. Get in your head, them things do. Start whispering in your mind."

"You've seen one up close?" I asked.

"Nah, I catch glimpses of them through the trees and along the road. I smell them too. Got a funny smell, them things."

Alton leaned close and whispered. "He's crazy, Cole." Then to Tick, "Thought you said they talked to you. What do they do, shout across the field?" He laughed the laugh of an old man.

Tick's eyes narrowed. "Jeeters ain't nothing to laugh about. They don't have to be close to talk to you. You just hear them in your thinking." He spat a brown stream of tobacco into the steel pot beside his chair. "Make you think you're crazy."

Willy wiggled his arm. "Sir Tick, if I may ask a question?"

"Roll with it, Little Man." He pulled a wad of leafy chew from a leather pouch and offered it to Willy. The boy wrinkled his nose and shook his head.

"Your loss," Tick said and passed the clump to Alton.

"Yes, good sir, as I was asking, when you hear them, what do they say?"

"What does who say?"

"The Shadows...jeeters as you know them."

"Ain't nothing you want to hear, Little Man."

"Please, sir Tick. I'm older than I look. Nearly a man." Willy straightened his back and stuck out his chest.

Alton gave an exaggerated sigh and rubbed his face. Tick glanced at me, and when I nodded for him to go on, he did.

"You can believe what you want, mister, but I ain't lying about them. Tick might be a lot of things, but he ain't no liar." He swiveled to Willy. "Little Man, I'll tell you this. They don't like it when you know it's them talking. No sir. Want you to think what they say comes from your own head. Make you think you're going crazy if you ain't careful."

We all sat in silence. The hair on my arms tingled to life. I wasn't ready to ask what he and Shadows talked about. Tick was odd, no argument there, but despite his paranoid tendencies, I liked him.

Alton sprung to his feet. "Okay, I've heard enough rubbish for one night. Mister Tick, I thank you for the offer of a roof, but if no one objects, I'll take my cushion and sleep under open sky. Done it most of my life anyway."

No one stopped him, and though we talked for another thirty minutes, the subject of Shadows died for the evening.

***

Gentle poking of my ribs blended with a dream of home. "Sir Cole. Wake up. Sir Cole."

Willy's voice. Not a dream.

"Sir Cole."

"What?"

"They're coming."

"Who's coming?"

"Tiller and his men. They're coming for us."

I rolled over and closed my eyes. "Go to sleep, Willy."

He jabbed my hip with his fist. "No. The horses, I hear them. They followed our tracks."

I flipped to my side and faced him. "How could you know that?"

Before he answered, Alton burst into the shed. "Time to go! Group of people coming through the woods. Six, maybe eight. All on horseback and carrying torches. Move people! Move!"

The force with which Alton spoke jolted me from the fog of drowsiness. I sprung to my feet, took a step, and tripped over Susan. She yelled out and cursed a god I had never heard of. From the far corner, Tick passed gas, mumbled, and rolled under his blanket.

Alton grabbed a large glass canister from beside the door and hurled it into the wall. Shards of glass

52

bounced off Tick's rough plank floor, but the explosion got everyone's attention.

"I said move!" Alton grabbed Willy, flung him toward the door, and the boy stumbled through with a cry. He ripped the blanket from Susan's grasp, slapped her hard across the face, and yanked her to her feet. "Stupid woman, I said we have to go!"

My first instinct was not to flee, but to slam my fist into the side of Alton's head. Susan had nursed me back from the brink of eternal sleep. I restrained my rage as a thin trickle of blood slid from her nose, underscoring the bright red imprint on her otherwise fair cheek. I hated Alton and vowed we'd part ways once safe. I wish now I had followed through. For her sake.

From the yard, Willy cried out, but I didn't catch what he said through the commotion inside the shed.

By now Tick was up, stripped to his undergarments, and scratching an angry rash on his thigh. "Take it them's the fellas you burned out?"

No one answered. Alton had already disappeared out the door and was yelling for Willy to ready our horses. I grabbed Susan and started after him.

"Hold up a second," Tick said.

I stopped and released Susan's arm. She sprinted into the darkness.

"Thanks for your kindness Tick, but no time for goodbyes."

"Give this to Willy, will you?" He tossed a sling across the room and glanced out the cracked window. "I'll stall them as long as I can."

I dipped my head and bolted into the night.

Alton, Willy, and Susan waited for me in the edge of the forest. From the tree line, torches bobbed like giant fireflies dancing to the sound of hooves beating a melody on hard earth. Shouts rang from the midst of waltzing lights, and the torches darted forward.

Alton reached down, grabbed my wrist, and with more strength than a man his age should possess, helped me onto his horse.

"Hold tight."

We raced for the cover offered by thick underbrush opposite the path we'd taken in—the path Tiller's men used to track us. Barely visible by the crescent moon, Willy clutched Susan's waist, his head buried in her back. Wisps of Alton's fine hair brushed across my face like threads of silk. We rode hard into the night and cries of hurt, both man and beast, rose from behind.

***

We rode deeper, slowed by thorns and fallen trees. The clearing around Tick's shed had grown quiet. Ahead, Susan and Willy's mount slowed to a stop. We eased to their side.

"Willy wants to stop." Susan sounded close to tears.

"No." Alton spurred our horse forward. "We keep going."

"Wait! Elder Sir, please wait."

Alton pulled to a stop and swung to the boy.

Willy didn't wait for him to argue. "He helped us. I'm not leaving him."

"We stay, we die," Alton snapped.

Willy slid from the horse and looked defiantly at him. "I'm not leaving him."

I wanted to press forward. I saw no reason to risk our lives for a man we'd known less than a day. One look at Willy told me his decision was made. He was going back.

"Wait!" I hopped to the ground and ran to him. "Hold on. Let's talk about this."

He stopped but didn't turn. Susan and Alton both dismounted. Neither attempted to hide their frustration.

"We can't risk it." I said as I walked to Willy.

"We can't leave him."

"He'll be fine." I tried to convince myself as much as him. "What do you want to do? Alton's not going back, and I doubt Susan will either."

"What about you, sir Cole? Will you return with me?"

"And do what? If some of Tiller's men are still around, we can't take them, not two of us. How about this? I'll speak with Alton and try to convince him to make camp here for the night. Come morning, if it's clear, you and I can hike to Tick's and check on him."

Willy considered this, his eye moving from me, west towards Tick's land, and back to me. "And if the Elder Sir decides to leave tonight?"

"We let him go."

"It's settled, but we keep watch. I'll take first," Willy said.

"Sure." I turned, intending to convince Alton and Susan and remembered the sling. "Oh, Tick told me to give this to you." I tossed it to him.

I smelled smoke as the sling left my hand and landed at Willy's feet. He faced west, toward the pinprick of light now filtering through the forest and cried out. "Sir Tick!" He grabbed the sling and sprinted into thick brush and darkness.

"Willy, no! Alton, help me!" I shouted over my shoulder, already dashing into the thicket.

I ran, blinded by night and thick forest. Ahead, close but pulling away, twigs snapped, and leaves crunched under Willy's feet. The smell of smoke intensified with every step, though dense growth and distance hid the source. Thorns cut into my skin and sweat stung my eyes, but I ran.

I ran until I burst through the undergrowth a half mile later. Tiller and his men were gone. Willy and Tick were nowhere in sight. The inferno that was once Tick's humble shed drew my complete attention. Flames, higher than the small abode should have allowed, lapped at distant stars.

"Willy!" I screamed into the blaze. I panicked, certain he had plunged into the fire, driven by a heart bigger than the body which held it. "Willy!"

"Over here, sir Cole!"

I peered in the direction of his voice, but after staring into bright fire, the night sky slipped into pure darkness.

"To your right." Tick's voice.

Faint images of the two sharpened as I jogged to them. I scooped Willy into my arms, kissed his cheek, and held him tight. "I thought I lost you." He squirmed to break free, but I pulled him close.

"Sir Cole. Sir Cole!" He was laughing now. "You're embarrassing me."

"Let him love on you, Little Man. People that care are hard to come by in this world." Tick's skinny arms were folded across his considerable belly. "Well, I reckon that went about as well as expected."

Willy broke free from my embrace and took Tick's hand. Ashes filled the air around them.

"Are you all right?" I asked Tick. A stupid question considering the view in front of us. I noticed a cut on his swollen lip and felt worse.

"I'll be fine. Hurt them worse than they got me."
He wiped a bit of blood from his chin and laughed. "They
ran right into the nets." He pointed to where Tiller and
his men had fallen. "Got them spread out on the ground
here and there around the house. They don't spring up or
nothing fancy, but they'll tangle a horse's hooves pretty
good." He paused. "Or Shadows."

"You're not hurt Sir Tick?" Willy asked.

"Nah, got a busted lip. Probably have a headache in
the morning, but I'm okay. Hate losing my stockpile
though. Nine barrels of drink and four bags of dried
tobacco. I was hoping my cellar wouldn't catch, but..."

I scanned the darkness as best I could but saw no
one. "Where did they go?"

Tick rubbed his jaw and chuckled. "Sent them
hobbling north. Told them you and the boy heard them
coming and stole my last loaf of bread on the way out the
door. The ones that could, worked me over pretty good,
lit my house on fire, then took out after you. I guess the
rest went home."

Alton and Susan emerged from the forest, horses in
tow. I waved them over and turned to Tick. "Thank you
for your kindness. I'm sorry about this."

He waved off my apology. "Don't worry about it.
Ain't been the same around here since Cindy went after
that coffee."

I laughed, but it came out forced.

"What will you do now sir Tick?" Willy once again
grabbed his hand.

"Don't know, Little Man. Can't hire on anywhere in
Grandview, and I think my days of selling Tiller firewater
for his testings are over." He knelt and looked Willy in
the eye. "Maybe I'll head west, see if I can find a village
to hire on as a laborer. Might even get lucky and find one

that enjoys an occasional swig and start making my stuff again."

I knew Willy's next words before they left his lips.

"Come with us."

With that invitation, Tick Grainger completed our circle of outcasts.

# 8

WE TRAVLED until dawn, hoping to put as much distance between ourselves and Grandview as possible. Susan and Alton led. Tick and I alternated sharing a horse with Willy, while the other walked. No one spoke, afraid the forest might answer.

Night lifted as we crested a barren ridge. I estimated we had traveled less than ten miles since Tick's shed. Less than I hoped, but more than I expected. "Anybody know where we are?" I asked, not expecting an answer.

"If my memory hasn't fouled, you're looking at New Babylon." Alton said and pointed to the sprawling village below.

"You've been there, Elder Sir?" Willy asked.

"I have, many times."

"Do you think it's safe?" Susan bit her lower lip.

Never in my life had I imagined a village so large. Buildings of all sizes and colors stretched across the valley. But something was wrong. With the rising sun at our backs, my view was clear. The streets were empty. No laborers shuffling off for a day's work. No farmers hauling fruits, vegetables, and meat to a morning market. No signs of life.

"It looks deserted," I said.

Alton laughed his old man laugh and stared out over the vast village. "No son, not deserted—still in bed." We all must have had the same look of confusion, judging by his dramatic sigh. He paused, turned to us and the newly risen sun, and winked at Willy. "New Babylon is a city of night. Your kind of place, right my boy?"

Tick hitched his pants and opened his mouth but didn't speak.

"Do you believe it's safe?" Willy asked.

Alton rubbed his chin. "Depends."

"Depends on what?" Susan asked.

"Depends on what you consider safe. Few Outriders, beasts are in cages, Shadows made of stone. Lots of thieves, assassins run free, women wear little."

"I think we should go around," Susan said.

Tick cocked his thumb toward Susan. "I'm with her. Place has a bad feel. Bad I tell you. We should go around."

"Sir Cole, may I ask a question?" Willy revolved his eye to me.

"Sure."

"Where are we going?"

I started to answer and realized I didn't know. I left Bethman for Cora, in search of truth. Truth about a disease of the mind or blood, truth about a cure if the disease was real, and truth about the girl from my dreams. Where was I going? I didn't know, and with embarrassment, I told them so.

Tick laughed first. Our newest companion smacked my arm and doubled over. "You mean to tell me I latched onto a bunch the likes of you, and you don't know where you're headed?"

"No." What else could I say? "I have no idea."

# New Babylon

## 9

WE SPENT the day sleeping on a hill overlooking New Babylon. When we awoke, the western sky burned deep red and orange, and the streets of the city below flowed with people and animals. Susan wanted to go back, or at least move from the hilltop, but Alton assured us we would be safe, even with a fire. Folks from there didn't bother travelers, they welcomed them in fact. We were still split on whether to go into the city. Susan and Tick decidedly against, Alton decidedly for, Willy leaning toward Susan and Tick, me leaning toward Alton.

"Susan. Tick." Alton chewed a bit of squirrel, one of eight Willy shot with his sling. "We need supplies, and New Babylon has them in abundance."

"Supplies for what? Supplies for where, Elder Sir?" Willy asked.

Alton pointed at me. "Ask him."

"I don't know, Willy."

Susan stood from her place beside Tick, sat beside me, and took my hand. "Maybe I can help. When you were with fever you spoke of madness. Many things I couldn't understand. You spoke of corn and a sister. You spoke of disease and a man named Charles. But mostly you spoke to a girl."

Alton lifted his eyes from the greasy meat in his hand. "You mean 'spoke of'?"

"Pardon me?"

"You said 'spoke to a girl'. You mean 'spoke of a girl'." Alton's interest in her choice of words puzzled me.

"No," Susan said. "He spoke to her in mumbled conversation." She turned to me. "The first few times it happened I believed you were speaking to me, but you were not."

Tick interrupted. "I don't mean to spoil sweet memories, but how does this get us any closer to figuring anything out?" He grabbed another roasted squirrel, his third, took a bite, and continued. "I mean, I'm all for you finding out what's eating at you, but I've got my own situation." He tore away another piece of meat and pointed to Willy. "And from what you told me, Little Man and Susan are in the same condition. No home. No work. No going back. Seems we all got some thinking to do before we stroll into a city that might or might not be safe." He tossed the remains of his meal into the fire. "I don't mean to be rude, but I think I need to hear a little more about what I've gotten myself into."

The group looked at me. All but Alton. He heard my story the night we met and didn't seem interested in sitting through a retelling. But they deserved to know. I wanted them to know.

"You're right. You deserve to know the whole story."

I told them of my village and the day an Outrider named Charles arrived. I told them of the message he told. The disease. His claim to know of a cure. I told them how I went from disbelief, to skepticism, to confusion. I told them of my dreams and how I first believed the girl was Elder Frank's daughter Alice. I told them about Cora and cried.

Alton stood over New Babylon. "If you want answers son, maybe I can help. I didn't want to mention it before because I'm old and where you want to go is a rough journey. May take months on horseback, many more on foot. Either way, I don't know if my aching body is up to it."

"And you are just now telling me?"

"It's like you said. Things moved pretty fast once we met the kid." He flicked his hand to Willy.

"Elder Sir. Please tell us about this place and how you know of it."

"Tell us," Susan said.

Alton raised a bushy eyebrow and sat.

"Alright, but then I'm going into the city with or without you." He looked at all of us. "I need real food and decent entertainment."

Around a campfire, on a hill overlooking the city of New Babylon, Alton told us of a place where I might find truth—the village of Lawsonville.

# 10

"**I TRAVEL**. It's what I do, how I survive. I had a family once, long ago. Now I spend my days roaming. I guess you might say I'm built for it." Alton rubbed his knee and winced.

"Tell us about your family," Willy said.

Alton's lips spread into a tight, thin line. "Maybe someday."

Willy dipped his head.

"I came across Lawsonville about twenty-five years ago. Nice place. Friendly people. Safe." He glanced at Susan. "Boring."

"They know of Outriders and the disease?" I asked.

He glared at me through upturned eyes. "Their society is built around them."

"And the girl? They speak of the girl?"

"Who? Your girl of the forest?" Alton asked.

"Vedia." Willy jumped into the discussion.

Alton glared at him. "Yes, Vedia, though I doubt your mysterious friend and the lass of Cole's dreams are one and the same." He looked at me, "but no, I didn't hear about a girl during my time there.

"Anyway, not much more to tell about Lawsonville. Nice. Comfortable. Safe."

For the first time in weeks, I had direction. A destination that might yield answers...a path by which to mark my steps. My circle of friends gave me hope, and I asked them to go with me.

Willy spoke without hesitation. "Sir Cole, you saved my life, but even if you hadn't, I would follow you."

"Little Man," Tick laughed, "if he hadn't saved your life, you wouldn't be going nowhere."

Willy flushed, but I caught a hint of his horrible smile. "Yes, sir Tick. My logic seems a mite askew pertaining to my previous statement."

Tick's face fell into an expressionless mask of confusion. I fought laughter as he tilted his head and squinted. When he finally burst into snorting cackles, we all joined in.

"Mite askew?" Tick managed through breaths. "You are one of a kind Little Man." More laughter. He took Willy in an embrace and swung him like a child's doll.

Several minutes later, we settled down. I held my aching side, while Susan and Tick wiped tear stained cheeks, dusty from days on the run. Willy, face still flush, glowed. I suppose we all needed the release.

Tick wiped his eyes. "I'm with Little Man. Ain't got nothing better to do and nowhere better to go."

I turned to Susan. "And you?"

She pushed tangled hair away from her face, grinned, and threw up her hands. "I certainly don't have anywhere else to go."

Alton's expression worried me.

"What about you Alton?" I asked. "You're the only one who knows the way."

We waited in silence as he seemed to consider. Sounds from New Babylon drifted up the slope and melded with the crackling fire. Shouts, laughter, music.

Torch light from the streets and open markets cast a soft glow across the horizon.

Alton pulled a rattled breath. "I'll go on one condition. We tarry in New Babylon for a spell." Susan started to speak, but he held out his hand. "We need food, and unless you can produce a wagon full of corn or have a barrel or two of Firewater stashed away, we have nothing to barter with. We'll need to labor for them."

"How long?" I asked.

"Don't know. A week, maybe as many as three. But if we don't stock up, we'll die in the Wastelands."

"Wastelands?" I asked.

Alton slowly nodded. "Lands spoiled by wars before the decay. Patches of land where food don't grow. You can't drink the water."

"Can't we work our way there from village to village?" I asked.

"You're not listening to me, son. They don't call them Wastelands because they like the name. There are no villages. Nothing west but hard travelers and nomads past New Babylon until you see Lawsonville's gate, and that's a month's ride."

"Can we go around?" Willy asked.

"We could take a trade route north then cut across and swing around. Or, we can take a southern route to the coast, follow it for a few weeks and come in that way. Only problem is we might freeze to death going north, and we'll be robbed of our supplies and left for dead anywhere near the southern coast. Land of wickedness is what I say."

Neither option appealed to me, and coupled with the extra weeks of travel, the wastelands seemed our only viable choice. "Can we survive?"

"It will be hard, but yes, we'll make it."

It was settled. The next night we would venture into New Babylon and gather provisions for our journey. In a week, maybe three, we would head into the Wastelands with Alton as our guide.

I'm not sure when things went wrong, but they did. Every journey has unexpected trials. Some, mere annoyances—bad weather, inaccurate directions, a broken wagon wheel. If only our troubles had been so mundane. We did walk into New Babylon the next day, but when we left for the Wastelands two months later, one friend was dead, Willy was blind, and it was my fault.

# 11

I DREAMED of the girl. We looked out over a city. She didn't speak but took my hand and led me down a path to the edge of New Babylon. People scurried along dusty roads, in and out of buildings. Most wore clothing made from material I didn't know, smooth and flowing as they walked. Others wore nothing. A group of young women approached but passed as if we didn't exist. They giggled as a man, bare chested and carrying a young lady over his shoulder, jogged by. From a distance, applause and cheers erupted. A moment later, a boy, no older than Willy, and also deformed, rushed past. He clutched a wooden flute to his chest. His cries for help drifted behind as he fled a laughing mob carrying blades and clubs. The boy stumbled, and they caught him. I turned away from the brutal sight, but I couldn't escape the sounds.

The little girl squeezed my hand. "The world is dying."

"Sir Cole, we need to speak." Willy's voice mingled with the sounds of my dream. "Sir Cole." He rattled me out of sleep.

"What?" I grumbled.

"Please, I need to talk to you."

I forced my eyes open and rolled to face him. He looked at the others still asleep, spread across patches of grass and under ripped strips of cloth. He motioned over his shoulder and whispered, "Alone."

I had never seen him so excited. Nervous energy seeped through his movements, held in check by sheer determination. I took his shoulder and walked to the tree line fifty steps from the campsite.

"She came." He bounced on the balls of his feet. "She was here."

"The girl? Not a dream? You talked with her?"

He peeked at our sleeping friends. "Yes. We spoke." He hesitated and rolled his eye to the ground. "She thinks New Babylon is a bad idea. She doesn't want us to go."

"She told you that?"

"Yes."

I didn't know what to say. I felt a strong connection to this girl...a terrifying connection. I wanted to believe she was a simple runaway, cast aside by her family and in search of another, but I knew it wasn't true. She had beckoned me, drawn me out of Bethman in search of truth. She invaded my dreams. "The world is dying," she had said. Of disease? I didn't know.

"Willy, we have to go into New Babylon. We need water, another horse, a wagon if we can find one."

He stared at me.

"What did she say? Did she specifically tell you not to go into the city?"

"She told me it was dying."

\*\*\*

We rode into New Babylon when the sun fell. Alton knew a man who owed him a favor and owned several homes he rented to travelers—sometimes for precious metal or stone, other times for labor or special favors. Alton refused to elaborate, except to say he had not spoken to the man for two years. He may or may not still live, but if he did, he'd find him. "New Babylon gets into your blood. Hard to leave once you've tasted its fruit." He winked and led us to a small clearing near the gate but away from the main road. We gathered around the largest of four benches lined along the walking path. Manicured shrubs, thick and the height of full-grown corn, hid the enclave from every side except one. Stones carved into the likeness of men, women, and creatures I didn't recognize, were scattered haphazardly throughout and gazed at the stars. Torches lit the walkway and entrance and cast a dim glow in the hauntingly beautiful garden.

"Wait here together. If anyone approaches, speak kindly, but don't engage in conversation. Keep careful watch until they move along," Alton said.

"What is this place Elder Sir?" Willy asked.

"They call it a tranquility garden. There's one at each gate and others scattered closer in. Don't get much use by natives, but travelers who aren't accustomed to New Babylon's," he paused until a slight grin crept across his face, "unique lifestyle let's call it, often require a place of rest and solitude. Don't worry, you'll be safe here if you stay together.

"I'll be back as soon as possible. Maybe an hour, maybe five. If my old friend Herman is living, I know where to find him." Alton trod the path to the main road.

We watched in silence until he rounded the corner. Tick dropped to the wooden bench with a thud. "Ain't so bad is it, Little Man? Going to have us a roof, a bed, probably bread."

Willy sat beside him, hands clasped in his lap, his eye rolling side to side, but he didn't reply. Even through deformities, worry is a universal look.

I knelt by his side. "I know you didn't want to come but thank you. You saved my life, and I saved yours. We're square, but I couldn't do this without you. Besides, what if Vedia is wrong? She's a little girl, and little girls have wild imaginations." I smiled, hoping to cover my doubt.

He looked up, still not amused. "But she told me. She warned us."

Tick inched sideways and made room for Susan as she sat beside him. "Willy, if you want to leave, I'm with you. This place bothers me." She shifted her eyes to me. "It's an evil place."

"Evil? We haven't been here an hour, and you've judged an entire city? I've seen evil...we brought you out of evil," I said.

Tick spoke up. "Easy on her Cole. She's scared, and I got to say, I ain't too thrilled about spending a week crammed into a place swarming with people like bees in a hive." He turned to Susan and Willy, "But we need rations. We need rest, and if Alton says we'll be okay, I believe him."

Susan huffed and turned away.

"Susan," I said, and she let me rest my hand on her knee. "Alton says Lawsonville is full of wisdom. Full of records from the old world and this one. If we stay together," I flipped a glance to Tick and Willy, "we'll all find truth."

She peered around at me. "My father died chasing the truth."

She eased from the bench and walked toward one of the stone women. I moved to follow, but Tick took my arm. "Let her be for a bit. She needs time to sort out the past few days."

I suppose she did, but my dream of the girl, and her words, "the world is dying," wouldn't fade. Neither would the image of a crazed mob chasing a boy who reminded me all too much of Willy. "Tick, together is the only way we can do it. Susan can't survive on her own. None of us can. If she leaves, she'll die. If you and Willy leave with her, I'll go on alone, or with Alton, and probably die."

Willy puffed out his chest. "Sir Cole, I'll not leave you!"

Touched by his sincerity, I ran my fingers across his head and over patches of hair, coarse and dead to the touch. "Thank you, but I told you, we're square. If you can't linger here, I understand."

He pulled away from my touch. "I'll stay because you are my friend, not because of an unpaid debt."

Tick leaned forward, "If you ask me, it's simple Willy. You and Susan go back to the hill. Wait it out; while me, Cole, and Alton gather what we need. We load everybody up, then one quick trip through town and out the other side."

Susan wandered to another stone carving, this one a life size figure with the body of a man and head of a dog. She ran a hand along its snout and quickly drew back.

Tick stood, "I'll talk to her."

I turned to Willy as Tick went to Susan. "What do you think? You're more than capable of taking care of her for a few days. I can talk to Alton, maybe we'll work out a way to labor here and sleep at the camp."

Willy feigned a smile. "Who will take care of you and Tick?"

We laughed and sat in silence watching Susan and Tick walk from carving to carving. They moved slowly, talking as they went. We waited until they circled around to the bench.

Susan spoke first. "I want to help, but only if we agree to stay together."

Before long, Alton returned. "Herman can't give us a room, but he has work. Enough to earn our way through the Wastelands." Alton sat on the bench alone as we circled around. "Susan, you and Willy are helping Herman's son with his freak shows. Cole, you and Tick can haul lumber. Herman has a dozen loads in Blanch. None of you have a problem, do you?"

Susan shook her head. "I thought we were sticking together." She looked at me. "You said we would stick together."

Tick bobbed his head in agreement. "Yeah, and where's Blanch?"

Alton smacked his cane on the ground. "It's the only way! Yes, we won't be together all the time, but you'll not be alone either. This is the work available on short notice, so I suggest you take it and thank me." He took a breath and looked at Tick. "And Blanch is just a short ride north. Next village up."

"Elder Sir, I'm pleased you found labor, but I am concerned about the position you have secured for me."

"Always concerned, aren't you?" Alton said. "Don't worry, my ruined little friend. I'm sure you will be running errands or sweeping floors. No performances for you." He pointed to Susan. "And you my dear, will help collect admission fees." He slapped his knee and rose. "See, all taken care of."

\*\*\*

Everyone but Alton started work that night. We pressed about his contribution to our cause, but he claimed he was "coordinating our efforts and negotiating with various merchants." It might have been true. He knew more people than Herman in New Babylon.

Big Rodge, Herman's overgrown son, picked Susan and Willy up from the tranquility garden in a covered wagon, while we waited on our two-hour ride into Blanch. Tick and I would spend the night loading timber, sleep until late afternoon, and be back in New Babylon by dusk to unload. The routine would begin anew after sundown. I hated splitting our group. I think we all did, but we convinced ourselves the reward outweighed the risk.

I hugged Susan and wished her well. Her soft green eyes hid the fear I know she felt. Willy shook my hand and with a dip of his head, wished me a safe journey. I ruffled a large patch of hair and thanked him before he jumped into Tick's arms. They embraced like father and son.

"Take care of Sir Cole," I heard Willy whisper to Tick before he and Susan walked hand in hand to the waiting wagon.

# 12

**TICK DIDN'T** want to leave the garden, but our ride wouldn't arrive for another hour. The smells and sounds of the city aroused my curiosity. Meats, incense, and perfumes mingled in the air along with sweat and urine. Merchants and patrons haggled over prices. Women and men loved in plain view, while children played with burning sticks nearby. A beggar held up his pants as he rattled a can of coins to those that cared to hear. I wandered toward a row of tables away from the throng of people.

"See a treasure you like?" A diminutive man with soiled teeth and leathered skin peered at me from behind bushy eyebrows. "It's all authentic."

"Authentic?"

"From the old world." The man cocked his head. "Name's Arnie. Best trader in New Babylon."

I returned his greeting. "Cole. Pleased to meet you."

Arnie slipped a cigar between his lips. "Where you from? Blanch? The eastern shores?" He dug a strand of meat from his teeth, sniffed it, and popped it into his mouth. "Not the southern coast...no, you're much too pale."

I didn't know there were eastern shores. "Bethman. East, but not to the coast."

"Bethman? Never heard of it. Tell me, what brings you to the greatest city on earth?"

"Work." It wasn't a complete lie. "Hauling lumber from Blanch."

He grunted, reached for an item on the table, and shoved it to me. "Blanch is a rough place. You'll want this."

I flipped the small container over in my hands. "Pepper Spray. What is it?"

"See?" He pointed to a small hole near one end. "Point it at a face and push the red button. Like hot spikes through the peepers."

"Thank you, but no." I sat the pepper spray down and eyed an odd cube. Small squares of various colors covered each side.

"Ah, the mind cube." Arnie's cigar bounced as he talked. "Mysterious object indeed."

"Mind cube?" I twisted one side, and to my surprise it moved. "How does it work?"

"Some say the ancients used it to test their young. See how long it took to match each side." He tossed his hands into the air. "I don't know if it's true, but it could be." He took the cube and laid it on the table. "You look like a man more concerned with matters of spirit than of mind. I obtained a fine piece that might interest you." He retrieved a cloth bag and laid in front of me. "A quick peek. You won't be disappointed."

He pulled out a small black ball and handed it to me. I ran my hand over its smooth surface, tracing my finger along the number eight on its top.

"Turn it over," he said.

I did and almost dropped it. A ghostly blue triangle appeared in the small window carved into its belly. Through murky liquid I read the words 'outlook good'.

Arnie gave a high pitch laugh. "Does it not like you?"

"It says 'outlook good'. What is it?"

"The ancients used it for divination. Do you know the word?"

"Never heard it."

"Whenever an important decision had to be made, they consulted the gods. This is one way they talked to them. I'll show you."

He reached into his pocket, pulled out a handful of seeds, laid most on the table, and swallowed the rest. "Okay, hand it over."

"What are those?" I pointed to the pile.

"Rosewood seeds. Come from a tree in the Wastelands and hard found. They clear the mind for communication with the gods and goddesses. Now, give it to me."

I did, and he shook it. "Is my new friend Cole worthy of possessing a link to the gods?"

He rolled it over and read the answer aloud. "It is certain."

"Do you think I'm a fool?"

He feigned surprise. "Of course not." He pulled his cigar and tossed it aside. "But the seeds, they're an experience you don't want to miss."

"Why?"

"No good way to explain." White flakes of skin drifted to the table as he scratched his chin. "They open your mind to senses you never knew existed. Colors you've never seen, sounds you've never heard." Arnie fished in his pocket for another cigar. "They open your mind to a world you could never imagine. Many have found the meaning of life in them." He leaned closer. "Care for a sample?"

On impulse, I grabbed several seeds and popped them into my mouth.

"Chew them if you want. They're bitter, but you'll get the full effect."

I chewed and swallowed hard. Arnie smiled when I grimaced. "Careful, Rosewood hits fast. If it's your first time, you might want to get to where you're going. The streets of New Babylon turn nasty most nights. Dangerous place if you're not careful."

They did work fast. From the main street, shouts of ecstasy arose. Blood rushed to my head as I glanced back. Multitudes of sounds separated from one another, and I heard each individually. Outlines blurred, but colors became vivid. Time lost its rigid nature.

From in front, a familiar voice said my name. I heard but couldn't place its origin.

"Cole!" Cool water splashed the side of my face. "Over here."

Arnie was waving his hands and smiling. "Told you." He handed me the ball. "Try it. You never know what you might see with the seeds opening your mind."

I shook the ball and forgot to ask a question. Within its dark waters, the triangle spun. Swirling white bubbles concealed its words as the piece rotated. I can't say how long I stood there, mesmerized by its impossible motion. Finally, it slowed, and I waited on wisdom. White bubbles gave way to its blue triangle. Horrified, I stared at the image. Alice's clear blue eyes held mine for a moment, then sunk into murky waters.

"Tell me what it says, my friend." Arnie leaned across the table.

"I..." I couldn't speak and for a moment couldn't release the ball.

Arnie's cackle rang in my ears as tears streamed down his face. "Must be a bad one. Happens, but don't worry. It'll pass. Always does."

I lunged for his throat, missed, and threw the ball at his head. He caught it and laughed harder. "Don't be angry, my friend. That was a lesson."

I reached out again with the same result. "Lesson?"

Arnie raised his finger. "Be careful of what and who you trust in New Babylon. Not everyone is as helpful as your friend Arnie. Place is full of crooks and thieves." He replaced the ball into its bag. "I'll admit, my dealings are frequently one-sided, but I like you. Here, take these." He gathered a handful of Rosewood seeds and dumped them in my hand. "No barter expected for this first batch. Have fun while you're here and come see me when you need more."

I stuffed the seeds into my pocket and walked away. Each step brought greater awareness of my surroundings. Complex patterns of light and shade emerged from blazing torches. Each moving image left a visual trail of itself lingering behind. Sounds became colorful and smells took on texture. Overwhelmed with sudden euphoria, I turned back to Arnie, but he was gone.

***

I may never know how I found my way back to the tranquility garden and Tick. I remember people, lots of them, watching me as I walked. A large man who stank of firewater and mold took my hand and tried pulling me into an alley, but I squirmed away and melted into the flowing mass of bodies. The sounds, the aromas, the sensation of touch and timelessness, all captivated me, and I knew Arnie hadn't given me enough Rosewood to last a week.

# 13

**TWO DAYS** later, Tick and I dropped our load of timber at Big Rodge's mill, a vast wood structure situated near New Babylon's northern gate. Tired, hungry, and in a foul mood, I hadn't spoken to Tick most of our trip home from Blanch. The Rosewood seeds remained in my pocket untouched. Twice, I had taken them out. Once to throw them away and once to swallow. I did neither.

I knew there was a problem when Susan met us halfway down the hill in a dead run. She doubled over, and out of breath, leaned against my horse and tried to speak. She managed gasping, incomprehensible sentences.

"What's wrong?" I scanned the camp for Alton or Willy but saw neither and dismounted. "Susan!" I grabbed her shoulders. "Breathe."

"Willy." Deep breath. "He's gone."

"Gone? What do you mean gone?" Tick jumped off his horse.

"Gone. They took him."

"Who took him?" My mind raced, and before Susan could answer, I continued. "Where's Alton?"

She caught her breath. "Alton's in the city trying to find answers. He left early this morning when I told him."

"Told him what?" Tick again. "What do you mean gone?"

"Tell us everything you know," I said.

She did.

"Big Rodge owns most of the entertainment in town. Theater, places to gamble, houses where women..." she paused, "are the entertainment." I nodded, though I had never heard of such a place. "We worked at the theater, Marvels and Wonders. I counted those who passed into the main door. Another woman took fees, and a nice young man kept order in line."

"Where was Willy?" I asked.

"I didn't see him until later; when the crowds left, and we met to come here. Big Rodge made him work on the dock unloading wagons of supplies. He said he liked it. Yesterday, we slept until sundown. He told me it was his best sleep in months. Willy killed a rabbit for supper, and then later, we headed back to town for work."

"Where was Alton?" Tick asked.

Susan shook her head. "I don't know. Willy and I assumed he was laboring in town, but I didn't see him until today."

Tick looked toward New Babylon.

"Willy and I parted ways at the theater, and that was the last time I saw him. I waited and waited, but he never showed, so I went to look for him. Most of the crowd was either gone or passed out in the dirt, but I found Big Rodge, and he told me." Through sobs she said, "He told me a group of men took him away in a covered wagon."

Tick moved beside her, took her into his arms and cried with her. "We'll find Little Man. Don't you worry. We'll find him and bring him back." He turned away, but not before I saw tears. "Won't we Cole? We'll bring him back."

I tried my best to smile, told him we would, and walked to the edge of the slope overlooking New Babylon. I didn't cry, not yet, but I hurt. The city was quiet, settling down for the day. A few horses trotted along otherwise empty streets. Scattered shouts of drunken revelry spewed from various quarters of the city, but those would soon end. Much later, as the sun settled and torches came to life, so again would the streets. Was Willy locked in another cellar or chained to a stone wall? Or was he along a dusty road, headed for forced labor in one of the forsaken villages scattered around this part of earth? I tried to imagine him planning his escape, killing his abductors, and running to freedom. He was courageous. He was smart. But he was a little boy, and all I could think about was him bound and afraid, begging not to be harmed. I heard his voice. "Please good sirs, be kind to me."

I chewed a handful of Rosewood seeds and let the world slip away.

# 14

**TICK WANTED** to go into New Babylon and search every building, alley, and shrub. I thought we'd be best served waiting on Alton's return. He knew the area and a few people. Susan flipped between the two choices depending on whose voice rose higher.

Before the shouts became violent, Alton crested the rise, and without dismounting, waved us over. "Big Rodge is waiting. He and his dad are meeting us at the theater."

Tick sprinted for his horse as fast as his round belly and spindle legs allowed. I took Susan's hand. "You should stay."

Her eyes narrowed, and her grip tightened around my fingers. "I'm not a child. I can handle myself in the city."

"I know you can, but if he escapes, he'll come here first."

She hesitated, then released my hand. "Find him."

"You coming Cole? Big Rodge won't wait all day." Alton's finger spun like a windmill.

I mounted, and less than an hour later we walked through the doors of Marvels and Wonders. Big Rodge met us in the greeting hall, a large open room inside the entry. Alton led, followed by Tick, then me. Paintings, some framed, others splashed directly onto plank walls, covered the room. Depictions of ghastly creatures stared down from high. One drew my eye. I wandered to it as Alton and Big Rodge huddled in a corner. It wasn't a creature at all. Not like the others. Amongst images of five-legged deer and wingless birds, a boy, younger than Willy, stared back. His petite, pale body was covered in angry red boils and sagged under the weight of his enormous head. No smile. No flicker of life in either eye. A simple wooden flute hung limp from his hand. He looked like the boy from my dream—the one beaten to death by the laughing mob.

Big Rodge's boots smacked the floor like cracking timber as he walked to me. "His name was Franklin, but we called him Melody. Trees came alive when he played that flute. Played it day and night." His hands were clasped at his waist. "People loved him, especially travelers from lands around the southern sea."

"Why the southern sea?"

He studied the picture. I saw sadness hidden behind Rodge's stern eyes and wondered what had happened to Melody.

"Because they rarely see any ruined ones there." Alton crept to my right and gazed at the painting. "They're around, but not like the eastern sea or parts of the flatlands."

Big Rodge grunted his approval. "Saved him from a group of Outriders." He pointed to Melody. "Took him in, let him work the shows, made him part of our family."

Tick talked with Rodge's dad across the room, marveling over several more stone statues.

Big Rodge continued. "Died last year. Spoiled ones never last long...children or animals."

"Alton says war from before the great decay causes it. Is that what you think?" I asked.

"I do. It's what our scholars say. Weapons from the ancient world spoiled the land and water. Chemicals and sickness made by man. Their devices created mountains of fire and left soil useless for farming. Scholars believe that is why most of the spoiled come from areas around the wastelands." He shrugged. "But what do I know? We give ruined creatures purpose. No one wants to roast a chicken born without wings or a pig with two heads. Here they have use. They entertain and keep people and goods flowing through our city. Kids though, ruined kids like Melody who are smart enough to interact with society, are hard to find."

"Not if you know where to look." Alton peeked around me and shot the big man a wink. "What he means is in many villages that border the Wastelands, if a child comes out ruined, its parents 'put it down' as you might say." He stifled a laugh.

His flippant attitude sickened me. "That's funny?" My taste for Alton grew more sour by the day. "It's funny to kill a baby because they come out like him?" I gestured to the painting of Melody.

"Easy, son." Alton glanced at Big Rodge. "You'll have to forgive him, he's not a traveler. Our little friend, Willy, was the first ruined one he'd ever seen."

"And stop calling him ruined!" My jaws ached from clenching so tight.

Big Rodge clasped my arm with a grip that left a bruise. "No fighting in Marvels and Wonders unless it's part of the show." He relaxed his grip. "What Alton means is most ruined ones," he paused, waiting for me to correct him I suppose. When I didn't, he continued, "are nothing more than lifeless bags of blood and bones. They can't talk. Most can't walk, never can. They eat and make waste. Besides, only a few make it more than ten years, even less see their twentieth spring."

"Tell him about Blanch and the cemetery beside Teller Creek." Alton waved to Big Rodge.

"Blanch? Where Tick and I hauled timber from?" I asked.

Rodge chuckled. "That's the only Blanch near New Babylon. Years ago, the town dedicated an entire plot of land for the burial of ruined children. Proper marking for graves, manicured landscape, very peaceful place. Must have a thousand mounds now. Every year they offer one to...Alton, which god is it?"

"Heqet, and she's a goddess."

"That's right, Heqet. Every year they give the first ruined one to her. We send wagons of meat and firewater for the festival. Glorious time. They claim if Heqet is pleased with the sacrifice, less rejects are born that year. More healthy children equal more hands working the lumber fields. More hands in the fields equals more trade."

"And that makes it okay to put down babies?"

"What I'm saying, is parents of ruined ones have their reasons, and when the deed must be done, it is done with compassion and a heavy heart."

Big Rodge sauntered toward Tick and Herman. His heavy steps echoed through the hall, while Alton and I followed. I didn't know if I liked the man. His pristine clothes and clean hands were not marks of a man who labored. But, the loss of Melody, whatever their relationship had been, seemed to affect him deeply.

Tick swirled to us as we neared. "Jeeters. They got statues of jeeters." His mixed look of fear and fascination made me laugh.

"He means Shadows, Rodge." Alton stepped to a carving and ran his hand across its head. "A reason I don't call New Babylon home. I love the entertainment," he looked to Big Rodge, "but its fascination with this creature is more than I can stomach. Anyway, shouldn't we get on with what we came for?"

Alton was right. Swept away by the grandeur and novelty of the greeting hall, I had, for a moment, forgotten the urgency of our visit. By Tick's slumped shoulders, I knew he had also.

"Certainly." Big Rodge turned to a set of double doors. "If you'll follow me, I'll take you to the warehouse."

***

Beyond the greeting hall doors, a room as large as my family's corn field opened to us. We stepped down from a small ledge which jutted out from every wall except one and onto a dirt floor. I heard a chorus of muffled sounds, animals maybe but I wasn't certain. Chairs of various color and material dotted the ledge and floor in no discernable pattern. A large door centered the far wall. Other than our party and the chairs, the room was empty.

"This is the main show floor." Big Rodge swept his hands through the air. "An hour or so before sundown, we roll the entertainment through that door," he pointed to the far wall, "and ready the drink carts."

"Entertainment?" I asked. The sounds, animal I was sure now, grew clearer.

"The wonders and marvels. Oddities. Ruined creation."

"Don't think I'm doubting you, mister," Tick said, "but people pay you to see that stuff?"

Big Rodge, Herman, and Alton chuckled in unison, and Rodge answered. "Oh, they pay for that and..." he clapped Alton on the shoulder, "other forms of enjoyment. We try and accommodate every weary traveler and curious mind."

We reached the far wall and Big Rodge stopped and slid the massive door open. "Our warehouse."

Putrid air washed across my face. The area was as large as the main room. Except this one wasn't empty. A myriad of rolling cages, both wood and metal, lined the wall. Cattle with extra legs, hairless dogs with eyes set at odd angles, a Night Cat, smaller than a toddler, yet bearing the protruding fangs of an adult. There had to be two-hundred specimens, all deformed and many of which I had never encountered.

"Over here is where your young friend was taken." Big Rodge led us to another sliding door which opened to the outside. "He was unloading feed when it happened."

We walked into sunlight, but the stench lingered. "My assistant saw men come from the west," Big Rodge pointed along the side of the building and down a narrow service road. "She tried to stop them, but what's one woman against four hard men?"

"Any idea on who they are?" I asked. "Alton says you think they're Outriders."

"I do. We've had trouble with them before. I sent a team of men north toward Blanch and another south to Newton. Ten men in all. The Blanch group will circle west toward the Wastelands and the others will circle east. If your friend is still alive, they'll track him."

"If." The word stuck in my mind. If he's still alive. If I had listened to him and stayed out of New Babylon. If I had taken my dream of the girl and this place seriously.

Tick shook his head. "Tick don't like it. Tick don't like it one bit. Why would someone want a kid...you know...like Willy?"

Herman spoke for the first time since leaving the greeting hall. "I can answer."

"Father, now isn't the time." Big Rodge cast a quick glance at his dad.

Herman waved his son off. "It's no secret. I'm surprised these two didn't see any while working in Blanch."

"See any what?" Tick and I had spent several daylight hours there and more on the road leading to the village, but there wasn't much to see. Farmland mostly. Rows of tomatoes, beans, grapes, and yes, corn. We never visited the town center since the timber patches we worked skirted the eastern farms.

"Forced labor is big business in most towns and cities along the Wastelands. Blanch, to the north, Newton and Slygo with its citrus orchards to the south. They all rely on it for their crops."

Big Rodge took the conversation. "Too many children born ruined and filling the cemetery. Not enough hands cutting lumber and plowing fields."

Herman cracked his knuckles. "Without forced labor, they'd wither and die like so many cities since the decay." He paused, turned, and started into the warehouse. "So would we."

We followed him into the stench, all but Tick, who called out from behind. "Hold on fellas." I stopped inside the door and welcomed a chance to step back into suitable air. "I may not be a master of business like you two," Tick wiggled a finger at Herman and his son, "or a traveler like Alton, but I don't get it. How'd they get so bad off, they need to make slaves of kids?"

Rodge sighed and flashed a weak smile. "Let me ask you a question, mister Tick. When you look around New Babylon what do you see?"

Tick scratched his head. "Don't know. Lots of buildings. Lots of people at night I guess." He looked at Big Rodge like a student who didn't quite grasp the question but wanted to give it a try anyway.

"Yes, at times, New Babylon is the largest city within a week's ride. Thousands flow through on their way to the southern sea, out of the Wastelands, or in your case, into the Wastelands. They linger several days or weeks, some never leave. Maybe a better question is what didn't you see?" He paused for only a moment. "Farmland. There are no farms in New Babylon. Our native population is relatively small to our size, meaning most people you see are visitors. Our neighbors to the north and south supply us with everything from fruits for our wines, to lumber and stone for our buildings. We in turn offer free services or hard metals. Our demand is high, hence their need for extra labor."

Tick grunted a nod. His arrangement with the tavern in Grandview had been similar, though on a much smaller scale. "So, you think these Outriders took Willy and what, sold him to one of your neighbors? Still doesn't make sense. Willy is...well you know what I mean. He ain't the strongest fellow with that little arm of his."

Big Rodge did more than chuckle this time. "No, I suppose not, but the boy is a worker. Trust me, I'm certain my men will find him laboring on one of the larger farms in a nearby border town. They know where to look."

"And if they do find him? What? Will the..." I searched for the word, "buyer release him without a fight?"

"Depends on who it is. Some owe us favors, others will want payment. Either can be arranged. I feel partly responsible for this mix-up." He clapped Alton on the back and turned to the warehouse. "For now, it's best we wait until my men send word. Of course, father and I don't expect you to labor with this worry on your hearts. We'll give you a day's wage apiece. As I said before, I feel partly responsible.

"While we wait, might I suggest you explore our great city. Many fabulous sights to behold and pleasures to experience." He glanced over his shoulder to me. "I understand you search for information about a disease."

Caught by surprise, I managed a weak yes. "I've heard a village named Lawsonville might have answers."

"Lawsonville? We have everything you'll ever need here. Finest collection of books from the old world, most capable doctors and scientists, gifted philosophers and intellectuals. I'll have a friend—Felica is her name—show you around the university. Splendid center of knowledge in this part of the world. Or, if you need physical stimulation rather than mental," he took Alton around the shoulder, "my friend is well aware of our excellence in that trade."

***

**O**nce outside, Tick pulled me to him. "Let's go look for him."

"Where? We don't know this part of earth." I searched for Alton and found him admiring another stone statue across the street. "Besides, if Big Rodge says his men will find him, I believe him. I don't like him, but I believe he has the means to save Willy."

"I don't trust him."

"You don't trust anyone." I thought he would laugh, but he didn't. "Okay, we give them a few days, if there are no updates, we go. The story makes sense, and if it's true, Willy isn't in any danger. What if we get caught?"

Tick offered his usual expressionless stare.

"They'll kill us and him. That's what they'll do. Big Rodge has the power and knowledge to save him. We would only get in the way."

Revelation eased into Tick's eyes, followed by a look of helplessness. I hurt for him. He found a counterpart in Willy. Two outcasts, judged by society, different in age, personality, appearance, every comparison except one. Heart.

"What do you say? Let the man use his resources?" I asked.

"I guess you're right. Only a few days though. If we ain't heard nothing, I'm going."

Alton strolled up beside us but remained silent.

"Fair enough. Now, we need rest." I said.

"Sure," Tick started to mount his horse, "but I still don't trust the fat man and his fancy clothes"

# 15

TICK AND I waited in front of New Babylon's Center of Education, Arts, and Spirituality. Rodge's friend, Felicia Sumter, agreed to show me around. Tick wasn't interested in exploring the stately rectangular stone building, but he was curious about her and how she knew Rodge.

"Got to be somebody that knows something. I'm telling you Cole, that Big Rodge character is trouble. It's his eyes...his eyes. I couldn't place it before, but that's it."

"His eyes?" Tick's persistent paranoia was taking a toll on my patience.

"They're shifty."

"Shifty?"

"Yeah, like he's trying to see if you believe what he's saying."

I looked away, hoping to see Felicia descending the stairs. I considered Tick a friend, but one best enjoyed in moderation. Even his peculiar speech, a novelty at first, now frustrated my ears. "You can go if you'd like. I'll wait for her."

"Nah, it's okay. I'll stick around. Maybe I should check this place out with you. You know, ask questions?"

"We can cover more ground separate. You ask around the city. Tonight, we'll meet at camp and fill Susan and Alton in on what we uncovered."

His face softened into a smile. "You're right. Don't know why I didn't think of that. It's…"

"What is it?" I asked with more than a hint of frustration.

"Well, I'm not exactly what you'd call a city fellow. All these people make me nervous, and when I get nervous, I tend to ramble."

I glanced up and down the nearly deserted street. It would be another two hours until the city came alive at dusk. "You'll be fine. Just don't accuse Rodge and his father of anything."

A pleasant voice saved me from the conversation. "Mister Cole, I presume?"

A slender woman of about my age strolled the narrow stone steps and held out her hand. "I'm Felicia Sumter."

I froze, arms by my side, gazing at her. My mind stalled, attempting to process her beauty. Dark brown hair to her shoulders, eyes the color of a cloudless sky, and skin smooth like a child.

"Hey there, I'm Tick, and this is Cole." Tick shoved his hand past me.

"Nice to meet you, Tick. Will you be joining us?"

"Tick has other business to attend to." I stuck out a clammy hand. "Cole Creek. Nice to meet you."

I waited for her to snatch her hand away once she felt its damp coolness, but she didn't. Her coy smile told me she knew I was nervous, but instead of cringing and pulling away, she let the touch linger.

"Nice to meet you, Cole Creek." She slowly broke contact. "You can call me Felicia."

\*\*\*

We toured the temple rooms first, six in all. Each housed an altar to one of their gods. I didn't recognize the names of most; each village or city bows before their own deity. Even a village as small as Bethman displayed a simple stone altar to the god of harvest, Rezzi, though I wasn't a firm believer, and the elders no longer celebrated traditional rituals. Only a few older villagers gathered twice a year and offered the sacrifice of an ox and two crows.

"This is Renenet, goddess of harvest." Felicia led me to the door of a brightly lit room. Torches lined the walls, their smoke rising and disappearing through uneven rectangles directly above each one. Seated on a throne along the far wall, was the likeness of a woman with the head of a serpent. Flames reflected off her eyes and gave the illusion of movement.

"Our god of harvest is Rezzi," I mentioned casually. "We have an alt-"

Her open hand smashed into my cheek before I finished the sentence. The crack sounded like dried timber popping in fire.

"I'm sorry." Cool eyes betrayed her words. "But you mustn't speak blasphemy in her temple." She gently caressed my face, still hot and stinging from her slap. "There is no goddess of harvest other than Renenet." She fell to her knees and pulled me to mine. "Good and gracious Renenet, please forgive this traveler. He comes from a heathen land and knows not of your name or goodness." Her lips continued to move but without words.

We knelt, her gaze toward the floor, mine wandering the shrine, still shocked by Felicia's outburst. Primitive drawings depicted laborers harvesting wheat and corn, merchants hauling their harvest to market...everyday village life. In each scene, a likeness of the goddess hovered above the fields. Torch light danced along the images and, like Renenet's eyes, created an illusion of movement among the crops. I longed for a few Rosewood seeds to elevate the experience.

"Come now, we must go." Felicia stood. "The goddess has forgiven you."

She disappeared into the hallway. "I'll show you the rest of our complex."

I managed a nod but felt frozen in place. The drawings, how did they move? They didn't of course, but the illusion was beyond my comprehension.

She laid a hand on my shoulder and knelt beside me. "Amazing, isn't it? You'll see many wonders in New Babylon, but the temple rooms are my favorite."

Her hand slid from my shoulder and gently clasped my own.

"I can understand why. They moved, the drawings, like they were alive, like they...?" I couldn't finish.

Her lips, full and tempting, curled into a smile. "A mysterious wonder." She leaned in and kissed my cheek, still warm and tender from her strike. "Perhaps I'll show you more one day." Her words brushed across my ear like a feather.

We walked in quiet comfort the length of the hall hand in hand. To our right, double doors opened into a vast corridor lined with shelves of books. Thousands of volumes in one location. I never imagined such a thing possible. I never imagined so many books existed. We stopped, and she pointed to a balcony across the room.

"Those are the Books of Knowledge."

Uniform in their dark red color, the rows consumed the rear wall of the balcony. "Books of Knowledge?"

"Yes, over eight-hundred volumes total. The only known complete collection on earth."

"What are they?"

She laughed. "What aren't they? Stories of earth before the decay, tales of great civilizations, drawings and images of machines when they still moved and talked."

"May I see them?"

"Perhaps, but not today. I have someone I would like you to meet." She clasped my hand again, and I followed her into the hallway to a rather ordinary door. "Alton informed us you seek answers concerning the disease Outriders speak of."

"You know of it?"

Her laughter echoed down the hall. "You do come from an isolated part of earth. Of course, I know of it. Their myths are well known."

"You're convinced they are myths. Why?"

We came to the ordinary door and stopped. "I believe you'll find your answer behind this door."

*** 

Wick Proctor, a wiry man lacking hair or smile, brushed past me without a glance. "Don't touch anything while you're here." He settled behind a small table, scattered with glass tubes and books. "Make it quick."

"Mister Proctor, be polite. This is Cole Creek, guest of Herman and Rodge." She pivoted to me. "Cole, I would like to introduce you to Wick Proctor. Director of Medicine in New Babylon."

Wick didn't look up from his work. "What can I help you with?"

Felicia walked to him, speaking as she went. "A word, Mister Proctor."

They huddled beside the table in animated conversation. Finally, Wick spoke. "Forgive me. I don't receive many visitors, but Felicia has informed me you seek answers about the disease of Outriders. I am happy to assist any way I can."

Felicia never told me what she said to Wick, but I'm certain it involved Big Rodge and his father.

"Thank you for your time." I glanced at Felicia. "Many say this disease is a myth. Is this your belief also?"

"Depends. If you mean the disease Outriders speak of, yes, it is a myth. If you speak of the disease Outriders carry and spread, then no, that is not a myth." He motioned me to the table. "I have studied both for many years. Some say it is a waste of time, considering the many ailments we suffer in New Babylon, but I rather enjoy research." He handed me a stack of papers. "Read through these, and we'll talk. When you feel comfortable with the material, tell Felicia."

He hurried us into the hall and closed the door.

# 16

I WOKE from a nap the same way as I had laid down, with Susan sitting cross-legged beside me, flipping through Proctor's research. She paused and ran her finger across a page.

"What do you think?" I asked.

We were alone on the hill. Tick was in the city asking questions, and Alton had decided to tag along. The day before, Tick had scuffled with two of Herman's timber hands. He had confronted them at a bar as they laughed and joked about the ruined one-eyed kid. Tick left with the worst of the brawl, but he didn't care. I believe he would have killed those men if it would have brought Willy back.

Susan handed over the stack of paper. "I think he spent a lot of time on those questions."

"Does it make sense?"

"Most, but not all." She hesitated, and I knew she wanted to say more.

"Go on. What is it?"

"He mentions the girl. The one Willy claims is real."

He had mentioned her. There she was, scribbled on paper along with a list of other symptoms of madness, including both visual and audible hallucinations. Carried by Outriders and passed to unsuspecting persons, Proctor claimed the sickness wasn't natural. In detail, his work laid out his theory of how Outriders used plants and minerals in creating their wicked poison. He speculated a dried powder rather than liquid. Testimony and interrogations of dozens of affected people, mostly travelers, carried common themes. First hallucinations, followed by sleeplessness or nightmares, often both. Eventually paranoia took hold and, convinced malice swam in their blood, they became obsessed with finding a cure to a disease that doesn't exist.

The words hit me hard. I first dreamed of the girl after an Outrider invaded Bethman. Sleep resisted me, and when it came, was restless. Stories of madness and infection consumed my thoughts and drove me from my home in search of answers.

"Do you think I'm paranoid?" I asked Susan. "Have I shown signs?"

She puffed a strand of hair off her lips twice. It was the first time I really noticed them...her lips. Beautiful. Delicate. Scarred. "No. Not that I have seen. Do you feel paranoid?" She asked.

I didn't know. I wanted the truth. I wanted answers about the girl, about the disease of Outriders, about spoiled blood and madness. But paranoid? "No. I want truth."

"And you think it's in there?" She pointed to the stack of papers. "You believe this is what you're looking for?"

"Perhaps. Proctor promised to meet with me again."

"May I ask you a question?" Her body faced me as we sat.

"Sure."

"What about Willy?"

His name struck my chest. He was out there, maybe laboring in chains, maybe dead, and all I had thought about was a phantom girl and hypothetical sickness. But Susan had no right to judge me. More than a dozen men were searching. Men who knew the territory and people. Men trained to fight. I would only slow them, and I told her so.

"What about him?" I asked. "You think I forgot my friend? Do you think I'm selfish enough to put this..." I shook the papers in her face, "above Willy?"

Susan's calm voice froze my anger. "I don't. What I'm asking is, do you believe Willy is mad. Do you think he is sick?"

I couldn't respond. He claimed friendship with the girl. He claimed he knew her name. He claimed she called to him, drew him to her. He claimed he loved her.

"You see," Susan continued, "either our friend, our Willy, is going mad with the disease of Outriders, or," she grabbed Proctor's notes, "this is a lie."

Before I processed what she said, shouts from the path caught us by surprise. Dust rolled behind Susan's horse in a hazy wave. It was Alton, and when he stopped beside us, he didn't dismount.

"Tick's hurt. Bad this time."

Neither Susan nor I moved.

"Did you hear me? Tick's hurt. We took him to Dr. Proctor, but it doesn't look good." Alton was breathing hard. "Running his uneducated mouth again."

# 17

**ALTON FILLED** us in as we waited for Tick to regain consciousness. Herman's men, the two he tangled with before, saw our friend outside Marvels and Wonders stopping people on the street to ask about Willy. According to Alton's account, Tick was the aggressor. Herman's men asked him to move along, and Tick refused. They exchanged words, and Tick swung. The shorter of the two pulled a wooden club from his belt and caught Tick flush across the jaw. Tick hit the ground, but the men didn't stop until Big Rodge himself burst outside and wrestled them off.

"I told him to shut-up and let it be," Alton said, "but he wouldn't let it go. Now look at him. Eyes swollen shut, head split like a melon, only the gods know what his insides look like."

"What does Wick say?" Susan asked through fresh tears.

"It's hard to tell for certain," Proctor appeared by the door of Tick's small room, "but the next couple of days should tell us a lot. We stopped his bleeding, and he is breathing, but I can't say for how long."

He walked to Tick's bed, checked the bloody bandage around his head, and frowned. "It's reopened. I need to see to this, so if you don't mind." He flicked his hand toward the door. "Felicia can help with your needs."

"When can we see him again?" Susan asked, not sobbing now, but in a voice low and cracking.

"Later today, but I doubt he'll be awake. Even if he is, I want him to rest. Find Felicia, tell her to show you the library. I'll meet you there when I'm finished, and we can have our chat, Mr. Creek." He shooed us away.

We didn't have to search for Felicia. She was standing in the hall when we walked out.

"The library? You saw a glimpse earlier." She touched my arm as she spoke. "How about I give you and your friends a tour?"

***

**P**roctor joined us an hour later. I had spent most of the time browsing the Books of Knowledge. Sorted and labeled, some alphabetically, others by year, I picked one marked 2003. Its pages enchanted me as I looked centuries into the past. I was fascinated by its images of buildings whose tops reached into the clouds and machinery that flew like birds. Clothing, food, streets: all different, beautiful, and absurd.

Horrified, but entranced by a story of the mechanical birds flying into buildings and killing thousands, I didn't hear Proctor ease beside me.

"Fascinating, aren't they? A glimpse of the world left behind." He pulled a book, moved over three rows, and took another. "Knowledge is what gives us power. It gives us hope."

"Hope for what?" I asked.

He looked both surprised and amused. "Hope for us. Hope for the world." He led me to a small table overlooking the floor below. Alton and Susan listened as Felicia pawed over another stone figure—a crow or raven—with wings large enough to canopy over a wagon.

"How's Tick?" I asked Proctor. Again, mesmerized by my search, thoughts of him had drifted to the far reaches of my mind. Never gone, but certainly overshadowed by my drive for the truth.

The doctor slid his glasses to their rightful place on his nose. "I think he'll make it if he lives through the night. I re-sutured the gash on his head and gave him medicine for pain."

He laid his books on the table. "I take it you read my research?"

I laid my 2003 book beside his. "I did."

"And?" He leaned forward and folded his arms.

"I think I understand. You believe Outriders carry a disease or poison, but the disease they tell others about is a myth."

His smile and tone were condescending. "A simple explanation, but yes, I suppose you understand." He settled in his chair and stared at me for a moment. When I didn't respond, he continued. "I want you to see something." He opened a book, flipped the pages until he found what he was looking for, and shoved it across the table. "Read this while I check on our friends."

His footsteps descended the stairs as I read a familiar word—drugs. The older women in Bethman used the term interchangeably with medicine, but the drugs described in the book didn't resemble any healing potion spoken of back home. I knew of mushrooms, but most I couldn't pronounce; Heroin, Ecstasy, and Marijuana. A couple were merely random letters with no obvious meaning: LSD and PCP.

I read the descriptions of each. Beads of sweat dripped on the old paper as I studied various symptoms. Hallucinations of color and sound, disturbed sleep, alternating feelings of paranoia and euphoria, bursts of energy, periods of lethargy. Had the Outrider who came to my village, what was his name...Carl? Cameron? Charles? Yes, Charles. Had he infected me with one of his drugs? And if so, how many in Bethman suffered from their effects?

The dull thud of Proctor's boots smacking stairs sounded throughout the library.

"Well," he said, taking his seat, "read anything thought provoking?"

"How? How do they do it?" I closed my eyes and concentrated on the day Alice died. Did the Outrider blow in my face or touch my skin? Had he poisoned the water or air before he rode into town?

"I have a few theories but let me ask you. Did what you read sound familiar? Hallucinations perhaps?" He cocked his head and flashed a half smile. "Paranoia? Alton mentioned your trouble sleeping."

I didn't speak, and he opened his second book.

"As for the disease Outriders speak of," he flipped through several pages, "let me explain how illness works."

He spent an hour teaching me medicine of the old world. Unimaginable theories. Tiny creatures, too small for human sight, lived in water: food: dirt: the air we breathe. A whole universe, varied in type, function, and purpose, existed before and after the great decay. Invisible monsters with names like virus and bacteria flourished in our world and thrived in our bodies.

"This is the cause of sickness, these creatures and many more like them. Natural organisms found throughout earth. The cause of everything from fever to mental illness. The body and head, Cole, body and head. And natural organisms are treated with real medicine" He leaned back and smiled. "I believe Outriders use many different potions to spread their sickness. Virus, Bacteria, Parasites. A brilliant plan really."

He made sense, and I hated it. I hated him.

"The world before knew this." He slammed his finger onto the page. "And though we have not maintained the technology, we have kept the knowledge."

"And knowledge gives us hope." I heard myself murmur.

"Yes Cole. It gives us hope."

\*\*\*

Felicia showed us to our rooms. Three well-furnished spaces lined along another wing of the building. According to her, dignitaries from neighboring cities, towns, and villages, occasionally chose to stay at the Center during visits. They enjoyed its relative peace as opposed to an inn or traveler's house. She claimed an official delegation from Newton once spent a week without leaving the library. Another, from the southern coast, spent three days drinking firewater, enjoying the company of women, and harassing Proctor.

I fell onto my bed, the softest I had ever known, and tried to think. By himself, somewhere in the building, Tick was either resting or dying. Outside the gates of New Babylon, Willy was scared or maybe dead. My friends and my family might have been poisoned at the hands of an Outrider. Poisoned like me. At least they weren't going soft under six feet of Bethman's hard soil with Alice and her daddy.

I jolted up at a light rapping on my door. I hoped it was Susan, but when I opened it, Felicia's beautiful face greeted me.

"Care for company?" She slid past me as she spoke.

I wanted to say no. My mouth formed the word, but no sound escaped.

"I'll take that as a yes." She moved to the hand carved desk and admired a painting above. "Do you know what this is?"

Four children, all in a type of uniform and each wearing a cap, sat side by side on a bench. Most wore smiles and one held a club with the name Louisville carved in black. I shuddered and looked away. The club looked exactly as I had imagined.

Felicia stifled a laugh. "I forgot. Alton told me about your time in Grandview. I can remove it if you'd like."

"No, it's fine." It wasn't fine but asking her to take it away felt childish. "It took me by surprise."

"We aren't that cruel here in New Babylon. We certainly don't encourage Outriders and their lies, but few in this city would go to such extremes as the fine citizens of Grandview. We believe people should live their lives as they wish. Partake of all the pleasures given us by the gods." Her hand touched mine for a heartbeat. "What do you think?"

"I don't know. I don't know what-" She leaned in to kiss me, and I flinched. "Please don't."

"Why?" A playful smile rested on her lips.

Why indeed? I wanted her, but something inside urged me to resist. I had never experienced the struggle and said the first thing that came to me. "What if I am sick? What if the Outrider did poison me, and I pass it along to you?"

She laughed at this. "Oh, my dear Cole. You are sick, I'm sure of it. But it's not contagious. The poison of Outriders is strong but not deadly. It will wear off with proper treatment." She took my hands and drew me close. Her warm body melted my resolve. "Start healing with me."

And I did.

# 18

**FOUR DAYS** passed. Tick hovered on the edge of consciousness: alert at times, asleep or blabbering incoherently the rest. I know because Susan stayed by his side day and night. I only saw Tick two out of those four days. One was the day after Felicia came to my room. I went to see him, but he was asleep. The second time, two days later, but I didn't linger. He talked like a man drunk on firewater, and Susan didn't look at me. I spent the afternoon in the library, visiting stories of the old world with Rosewood seeds as my guide.

Alton stayed away, partaking of the plentiful bounty New Babylon offered lonely travelers. He returned to the Center once to check on Tick, and I asked about Willy. No new word from Big Rodge's men. They had searched Blanch and were now combing smaller villages along the Wasteland border. Slowly, I resigned myself to his fate and hated myself for not caring.

I spent those four days enjoying the effects of Rosewood seeds. Concern for Willy and Tick gave way to pleasure. I passed time alone in the library, asleep in my room, or with Felicia. I didn't love her but found her touch irresistible. We talked about the Books of Knowledge, and what I'd studied. We walked hand in hand through the gardens outside the Center, discussing what life before the decay must have been like. Twice a day, dawn and dusk, she led me into the temple rooms where she worshiped Renenet. I indulged her and kneeled before the statue. In truth, the room fascinated me. My village passed down stories of the old world like any other I suppose, and the one I found most outrageous was of moving pictures: images on glass that came to life. Not many believed, including me, but the Books of Knowledge proved the stories true. They called the moving images television. I imagined the moving pictures in Renenet's temple looked much the same, only rough and crude in comparison.

On the fifth day, Felicia left for an overnight errand in Blanch. Susan slept by Tick's bed, but I hadn't heard from Alton. I wandered the halls, trying to recall the reasons I had begun my journey. I believed I was sick. The Outrider from home had somehow infected me with his poison and sent my mind mad. I still heard screams from Grandview and smelled burning flesh. I had thought them savage, but I was the savage one. The good people of Grandview only wanted to protect themselves. I hadn't understood the madness Outriders' poison caused. Neither did Willy. Poor ruined child, if we could find him alive, I determined we would isolate him here at the Center. Let time work its cure. I would show him the Books of Knowledge and explain drugs, viruses and bacteria. Convince him the girl was no more than a hallucination brought about by the sorcery of Outrider poison.

I had never entered Renenet's temple alone, but I was lost. The prospect of crushing Willy's hope weighed on me. The girl, Vedia, had been his only friend, but he had us now—Tick, Susan, and me. "If he still lives," I muttered to the empty hall.

The goddess's room was exactly as before. The great statue commanded the far wall, its eyes trained on the entrance. Torches cast flickering light in the space and gave life to peasants and slaves working the fields. I knelt, my hands pressed against cool stone, and bowed my head.

No words came. I wasn't a follower of Renenet or any other god or goddess. Her presence didn't fill me with awe or dread, nor did it fill me with hope. I glanced up, wishing for a sign of life in the goddess carved of stone, but saw nothing other than her eyes, which glimmered. An illusion of the torches' fire.

Despair washed over me as the walls performed the same trick. The farmer, pushing his cart. A group of women carrying water from a flowing stream. A man, dressed in robes and carrying a staff, lifted his face to the statue and spoke silent words. Each went through their motions, reached a point, and began the routine anew.

No magic. No higher being asserting power over nature. All carefully crafted illusions set in motion by the flickering light of torches.

Disgusted with the temple, disgusted with life, I pressed my face to the floor. From my right, odd motion caught my attention. A peasant woman had stopped, water jug in hand, while the others moved along. She swiveled her head toward me. Fear and curiosity held me in place as more images ceased their labor and pivoted my direction. From all sides, moving pictures turned to the entrance and stilled.

I tried to stand and couldn't. My muscles rebelled against my mind's command.

The images dropped. Every image. Every man, woman, and child fell to their knees as one. I tried to scream, but no breath came. I tried to gain my feet, but my knees no longer worked. I tried to close my eyes to the insanity, but they wouldn't obey.

My breath caught when a hand fell onto my shoulder. Afraid to look, but terrified not to, I turned my head.

"Hello, Cole." The little girl from my dreams. The girl of the forest, Vedia.

Unable to speak and unsure if my mind was now gone, I scanned the room. Every figure still bowed. I saw them clearly, though flames no longer leapt from their holders. Wind gently swayed carvings of tall grass along one wall; a stream made of stone flowed along the edge of a field. But the men and women didn't lift their faces from the ground.

The girl spoke again. "It's time we met." Her smile, not the torches, lit the room.

My vision faded, and I lurched forward. One final word flashed through my mind before I passed out. A terrifying word, foreign to my vocabulary.

Holy.

***

I awoke in my room alone, disoriented and thirsty. I stumbled to the desk and drew a cup of water from a clay pot Felicia had left. My parched throat rejoiced at the cool refreshment.

Holy. The word screamed into my head. I didn't know it, never heard it, but I knew what it meant. Not because I read it in the Books of Knowledge or learned it as a child in Bethman, but because I felt it. I felt her.

And the images! I steadied myself against the table as the memory came to life in my mind. Dozens of rough carved figures, chiseled into the walls and painted with a simple oil or dye, had turned to the girl and fell to their knees. Trees, corn, and grass swayed in a wind that didn't exist. The steady rhythm of their movement hypnotized me.

A knock at my door sounded, and I dropped the cup. It fell and shattered on cold stone. Felicia hurried in at the sound.

"Cole!" She saw me and stopped. "Are you okay?"

"I'm fine," I lied. "A little clumsy this morning I guess."

"Morning? It's nearing dusk. Are you sure you're alright?"

"I'm fine."

"Good, because I have wonderful news! Tick's awake and asking for you." She ran to me and took me into her arms. "He's going to be fine. Wick says in another day or two he can leave." She pulled away slightly. "Or stay. You're all welcome until you find a place of your own."

I eased from her embrace and moved to the bed. I wanted to tell her of the girl and what happened in Renenet's temple, but my instinct said no.

"I haven't decided what to do," I said.

She made her way across the room and joined me. "Cole, look at me." Her soft, beautiful hands cupped my chin and tilted my head to her. "You're getting better. The poison is losing its effect. Tick is better, and we may have a lead on Willy-"

I stopped her. "They found Willy?"

"No. Not yet, but I received word one of Rodge's groups is checking a ranch west of Blanch. They think he's there." She slid her hand from my chin up my cheek. "They are almost certain."

I kissed her. Out of joy or relief or confusion or simple lust, I don't know, but I kissed her, and all other thoughts fled.

\*\*\*

Full dark came by the time I found Arnie and the seeds I desperately needed. I promised myself I would see Tick after Felicia left. I promised a lot during my time in New Babylon.

Arnie sat a book aside as I approached. "My friend Cole! Change your mind about the divination ball?" A half-smile crept up his face. He knew why I had returned.

"I'm out of Rosewood," I said.

He reached under the table and produced a small bag. "I'm not. My product is good?"

"It's good." Of course, I had nothing to compare it to. "How much do you have?"

"As much as you can afford."

I fished three coins from my pocket and tossed them on the table. Arnie snatched the bag. "Come back when you're serious."

I panicked. I hadn't considered the cost. "How much? How much for all you have?"

He sniffled. "Anything other than gold would be a waste of our time."

Gold. I had only seen it twice. Once, as a child when my father received a piece for land, and again when Susan showed us her pendant. "Gold? How am I supposed to find gold?"

"You're in New Babylon. There is gold to be found."

"Please, just a handful for now."

"I'm afraid not. Bring me gold and these are yours. Until then..." he stuffed the bag under the table.

My first thought was to return to the Center for my blade, kill him, and take his seeds. My second was Susan's pendant. The choice to betray a friend was easier than I expected.

# 19

I TOOK Susan's pendant from her satchel while she slept by Tick's bedside and finished my business with Arnie before dawn. The trader paid very well for the pendant. I found Felicia, and we walked to Tick's room. I hoped he wouldn't hear me open his door because I wanted to be there when he woke. He looked better...miraculously better, but I hadn't seen him in three days. Ravaged by guilt, I fought the urge to flee as Susan stirred from her chair. She kissed Tick's forehead and left without a word or a glance to me. She could never know I traded away her father's gift. Felicia took my arm and smiled as Susan passed us.

"Well, would you look at that." Tick stirred and took a cup of water from the stand beside his bed. "You made a friend." He took a sip and belched without shame. "You ain't replacing old Tick, are you?"

I wasn't ready to explain my complicated situation yet. "They think Big Rodge found Willy."

"Yeah, I know. Susan told me. Word gets around fast here." He took another sip and sat his cup aside. "Of course, what do I know? Might be like that in all big cities." He slid off the edge and eased to his feet. "Ain't heard anything about Alton. Susan said she ain't seen him since I busted up those boys that put me in here."

"He's around. Enjoying New Babylon's night entertainment from what I hear," I said.

"Figures. Old man like him gets all the fun, I get laid up in a bed with nothing but hurt bones and dreams of jeeters."

"Jeeters?" Felicia asked. I had almost forgotten she was beside me.

"Shadows," I clarified.

"Jeeters, Shadows, all the same to me." Tick eased another soft belch.

"Susan stayed by your bed the whole time." I said.

"She did, did she?" Tick's lips spread into a smile and revealed more lost teeth. "She's a fine woman. Fine woman indeed."

"Felicia!" Proctor burst into the room. "Something's happened." He paused and caught his breath. "Something's happened to Renenet's temple. Come!" He turned and sprinted down the hall. "Come now!"

Felicia went ahead as I helped Tick gain his feet. "Go on. I got this." He waved me away. "I'll catch up."

Felicia and Proctor stood outside Renenet's door: Proctor motionless, eyes wide. Felicia held her hand to her mouth. Muffled cries escaped through her fingers.

"What? What is it?" I hurried up behind them.

Neither answered, but they didn't have to. Prostrate across the floor, head separated from its body, lay the goddess Renenet. Her lifeless eyes fixed on the place I had knelt...the place the girl had stood.

I braced myself against the doorframe as light from the torches worked their magic. Farmers harvested. Children danced. Women carried water.

But something was missing...the robe wearing priest with his staff held to the sky. Instead, a mounted horse trotted by the stream where he once stood, a horse not there before. The man in the saddle wore a long leather coat, his gaze fixed ahead. On his sleeve was sown the familiar symbol from Susan's pendant.

***

When Alton returned to the Center, I expected him to look worn and haggard, but his eyes gleamed. Susan, Tick, Alton, and I gathered in Tick's room, while Felicia and Proctor worried over the mess in Renenet's shrine.

"Why is the doctor so upset?" Alton eased into a chair across from Tick's bed.

"A statue tipped over and lost its head. Guess it was an important one." Tick said.

Susan poured Tick a cup of water. "Drink this. I know you feel better, but you need to keep water in you."

I watched her care for Tick...the gentle way she spoke. Her soft touch as she checked a healing cut. Her concern over his slightest discomfort. Just like she cared for me in Grandview. "Do you need help?" I couldn't think of anything else to say, but guilt demanded I try. "Are you hungry? I can go grab you and Tick bread." I glanced at Alton. "You too."

Alton waved me off, and Susan turned to Tick. "Are you hungry?"

"I could eat." Tick said.

"That would be fine." Susan's tone was cold, but it was a start.

I left and searched for Felicia. She always brought the food, and it occurred to me I had no idea where it came from. It didn't take long to find her and Proctor. I followed loud pounding from the direction of the temple rooms and found them outside Renenet's entrance. A sheet of wood covered the doorway with a sign forbidding entry. They both glared at me as I approached.

"What do you know of this?" Proctor's thin cheeks burned bright pink.

His question caught me off guard. "I...I don't know. I was with you when it happened."

Felicia took my hand but looked up at the doctor. "Wick, calm down." She stroked my fingers with her thumb and a tingle of excitement crept up my arm. "We'll commission a new carving. Bigger, more elaborate. Renenet will forgive us."

Proctor replied with a grunt, but his jaw relaxed.

"Wick," Felicia rubbed his arm with her free hand, "she'll forgive us."

Her power over men obviously extended beyond me because when she touched him, a smile spread across his face. "You're right. She will." He blushed again. "I don't know why I care so much. You're the one with faith in such philosophies, not me. I can only assume your presence at the Center is beginning to affect my thinking."

Still stroking my hand with her thumb, she winked at Proctor. "I have a way."

Never in my life had I wanted a woman as much as her, yet I felt an equally powerful need to escape. A story from the Books of Knowledge came to mind. A man addicted to a drug. I can't remember the name, there were so many, but he spent every waking hour obsessing about it. Where might he find it? How might he obtain it? The drug consumed his mind and body. Yet, he hated it. It destroyed his family and alienated his friends. He knew it was killing him, or would kill him, but he couldn't stop. Felicia was my drug.

\*\*\*

**B**ig Rodge came with news his men had spotted Willy at a ranch west of Blanch, on the border of the Wastelands. Tick wanted to go after him. I told him he wasn't healed, that he needed rest, but the stubborn fool didn't listen. He asked me to go, and I almost did, but Felicia begged me to stay with her. Torn between love and lust, I chose lust. Lust and the escape Rosewood offered.

Tick left for Blanch alone with only his horse and Big Rodge's lie. He slipped out of the center while Susan slept, afraid she would try and come with him—afraid she would stop him. He didn't find Willy in Blanch. Instead, later that night, I found our friend in a cage across the street waiting to perform.

*** 

Felicia drifted into silent sleep. Restless and disgusted with myself, I downed more seeds and ventured into the streets of New Babylon. I stumbled my way to Marvels and Wonders. An elderly man, fat and reeking of urine, pushed past, but I barely felt him. Nor did I care when a strong hand groped me from behind. Touch, smell, time...all altered by Rosewood. Each sense strangely beautiful and extraordinarily deceptive. I doubled over and vomited, another occasional Rosewood effect. Two hairy women laughed and handed me a scarf. I wiped my mouth and chewed three more seeds. The laughing women disappeared into a sea of color and sound without a word.

A sign hung over the door. William the Lion Slayer. A perfect drawing of my friend Willy, sling in hand, a look of despair on his face. A better man would have been angry, even repulsed. I was neither. I felt only empty curiosity.

I rode a wave of people through the doors, fumbled around in my pockets for admission, and made my way through the mass of people. There, alone in a metal cage the length and width of twelve horses, stood Willy. People swarmed for the best view. Children squealed in delight and pointed to various oddities scattered amongst the crowd. Workers carried trays of food and drink to those enjoying the entertainment. Frozen by confusion, anger, and fear, I stared in horrified silence; my mind a rolling fog of emotions.

A burly man emerged from the warehouse door. White hair flowed over his bare shoulders. Gasps and several shrieks erupted as the crowd parted. When they moved, I saw the cause of alarm. A Night Cat struggled against ropes that bound its legs and jaws. Though young and half the size of an adult beast, its sharp fangs and claws glistened in the torch light.

Another man, this one the height of a toddler and wearing orange pants and a green jacket, opened the cage's wide door and stepped away, while his partner deposited the cat inside. The crowd cheered when the door slammed closed, and the short man in flamboyant clothes reached between the bars and sliced the Night Cat's restraints.

The animal gained his feet and glared at Willy. The two circled each other; Willy with his sling, and the cat with its fangs. The throng of spectators grew silent. A young woman rammed into my shoulder as she sprinted forward for a better view. I hardly noticed.

A familiar hand slid around my waist from behind and caressed my stomach.

"Don't worry, Rodge sedated the cat. He's not fool enough to lose his newest star so soon." Felicia's perfume drifted by my cheek. "He's sick you know." She pressed against me, allowing the full pleasure of her warm breath across my ear and the heat of her body against my back. "Too sick for rehabilitation."

Without warning, the cat sprang. Its head tilted at a slight angle; front claws extended. I registered a flash from Willy, and the Night Cat dropped. First a gasp, then roars of approval swept through the audience. Willy slunk to the edge of the cage and plopped down. He was trembling. For a moment, my heart broke for him.

Felicia whispered, and she was my world again. "Come back to the Center with me. We'll talk."

Someone called my name, and though I heard through a muffled haze of Rosewood and Felicia, the voice sounded familiar. "Who...?"

Felica brought her fingers to my lips, eased several more seeds onto my tongue, and sealed the offering with a kiss. Her touch intoxicated me.

I heard my name again. From the cage. Willy?

"Cole?" Felica's voice hijacked my attention. "It is one thing to claim dreams and visions of the girl, but Willy insists she speaks to him...that he's touched her. Once the sickness has progressed to those types of hallucinations..." she paused, "there is no cure."

I thought of Renenet's temple. It seemed real enough. The girl had spoken to me. She knew my name. Of course, if it was a hallucination, she would. But her smile...it lit the room. And the images, they strayed from a continuous loop of routine chores and fell to their knees. And the sudden appearance of an Outrider in place of Renenet's priest with his staff held to the sky. And the word, foreign to my tongue, yet familiar in a way I couldn't comprehend. Holy.

Felica and I waited in silence as the crowd lost interest in Willy's cage and focused on other exhibits. The burly man roped Willy and hauled him away. His tiny assistant followed with the carcass of the Night Cat dragging behind.

Felicia squeezed my hand. "Let it be. Willy has purpose now."

"Does Alton know?"

"No, I don't see how he could. Tonight was Willy's first performance, I put his poster up myself this morning. Besides, from what I hear, Alton has kept himself busy with other pleasures."

"Why would Big Rodge lie? Why put him on display so I can see?" My words sounded muddled, as if I were speaking into a pillow. The familiar fog of Rosewood worked its magic.

"You know why he lied. Your other friends wouldn't have agreed with Willy's new role. You however," she reached into her bag, "understand how sick he is." Susan's gold pendant dangled from her hand.

"How?" I slurred, but she understood.

She winked. "Rodge knows all the regular traders, and Arnie's one of his favorites. He'll keep your secret if you keep his."

I swiped at the pendant, but she was quick, and it disappeared into her bag.

I tried to respond but couldn't. The right words never formed a cohesive sentence for my mouth to utter.

"Shh. Don't talk." She took my hand. "I'll walk you home." Her tongue played on her lips as she whispered, and my resolve melted. I followed her to the Center, and we didn't speak anymore of Willy. We didn't speak at all.

I needed her. I craved her. I hated her.

# 20

**I WOKE** alone, nauseous, with one word on my mind.

Holy.

I slipped out of bed, dressed, and crept the deserted hall toward the library. I had meant to ask Felicia about the word—surely, she or Proctor knew of it—but once again her touch had cleansed my mind of all but her.

Footsteps, too heavy for Felicia or Proctor, echoed through the corridor. I ducked into a small enclave that served as a showcase for various artwork and relics and waited. The dull thud as each foot connected with the stone floor sounded like boots. Rodge's men searching for Proctor or Felicia perhaps. Or a drunkard in search of rest or food. The sound faded, and I peeked into an empty hall. I felt foolish. No one would care if I spent time with the Books of Knowledge.

I reached the library without incident and eased in. Moonlight bled through upper windows, casting a dull glow on the stairs and one wall of shelves. The balcony, home to the Books of Knowledge, sat in darkness. Navigating the stairs, I stopped midway to allow my eyes to adjust. Slowly, the shelves and table above came into focus.

I stopped near the top and listened. The silence eased my anxiety. I passed the table and noticed an odd book. Out of place and different from the others, a note rested on its ancient cover.

*COLE- A Book of Truth*

My knees buckled, and I slumped forward into the table. Behind me, volumes of information waited to be absorbed. Books of Knowledge, treasures I had never imagined existed three weeks ago, that contained all the world ever knew. Yet the book under the note pulled at me. It terrified me. I gathered my courage and slid the note away. The first word of its title took my breath. Holy.

I stared at the book in stunned awe. Lines and creases crossed its cover like tiny cracks in parched earth. My fingers trembled as I ran them over the words Holy Bible. Part of me expected fire to leap from the leather or music to flow from my fingers.

I read the note again, sat it aside, and grabbed it once more. Was this a hallucination? I laid my hand on the book for assurance. Not a hallucination. Then what? A greater breakdown of my mind? Had someone played a cruel but effective game with my sanity? Maybe. Or maybe the girl was real, and that possibility terrified me.

I opened the book and read. "In the beginning..."

# 21

**RODGE SENT** Felica on a three-day errand to Newton the next afternoon. She didn't share the details, and I didn't press. I tried reading The Book but fell asleep halfway through a story about a flood. I woke up lonely and chewed a few Rosewood seeds. I didn't know how much I had come to rely on Felicia's touch. Determined not to waste the night, I fumbled beside the bed for my bag of seeds and ventured into the streets.

I drifted among the throng of revelers, enchanted by the sights, smells, and sounds. I didn't intentionally seek out Marvels and Wonders but found myself outside the entrance. A group of gangly teenagers huddled around a poster by the door. I walked to them and pushed my way to the front.

"Watch it!" One of the boys shoved my shoulder, but I didn't turn. I couldn't take my eyes off the poster announcing Willy's second fight.

Another shove but a different voice. "What's your problem?"

I managed a single word, "Willy," before an arm wrapped around my throat from behind.

"My friend asked what your problem is?"

One of the two girls in the group laughed. "He looks stoned."

"Is that it?" The other girl asked. "What have you got? Mushrooms? Rosewood?"

I looked up at the word, and the arm around my throat tightened.

The girl smiled. "Rosewood." She flicked her head at the boy who shoved me.

He reached into my jacket, found the bag of seeds, and tossed them to the girl. She caught it and stuffed it into the cloth pouch around her waist.

A pale man with long dark hair and no shirt, stopped. For a moment, I thought he might help. Instead, he smiled and walked into Marvels and Wonders without looking back. No one else paid us any attention.

I struggled to free myself, and the boy who had his arm around my throat slung me to the ground. The group of thieves sprinted off in different directions before I gained my feet. No one but me cared.

A mass of sweaty flesh pressed me forward and through the doors of Marvels and Wonders. I escaped the human current in the lobby and began fighting my way back to the entrance. I knew my Rosewood was gone, but I had to at least try and recover it.

A large hand fell on my shoulder before I reached the door. "Cole," Big Rodge spun me around, "come to cheer your boy on tonight?"

"They took my seeds."

"Who?" He tried to hide a smile.

"The kids stole my Rosewood."

Rodge shook his head. "It's a shame what New Babylon has become." He let go of my shoulder and motioned for me to follow him. "Willy's fight is about to begin."

"You don't understand! They took all I had!" I cried.

He stopped and looked over his shoulder at me. "Your seeds are gone my friend. Trade for more."

"With what?"

A smile crept across Rodge's lips. "There's always a way in a city like New Babylon."

"I take it you have a suggestion."

His smile faded. "I'm taking wagers on Willy's fight tonight. Maybe you and I can find a solution."

"If I had anything to wager, I could just get the seeds."

"I'm willing to discuss different terms," Big Rodge said. "How much Rosewood do you need to make it through the week?"

I looked away and didn't answer.

"Maybe you want enough to last a month," Rodge said and chuckled. "I know the pull of Rosewood. It's a hunger that is difficult to tame."

"I don't need a lecture! I need something to barter with!"

"Here's my offer. If Willy wins, I'll give you enough gold for a month's worth of seeds." Rodge said.

"And if he loses?" I asked.

"If he loses, you'll pay with two months of labor in my lumber mill."

"Two? For only a month of seeds?"

"I'm giving you better odds than anyone else. Take it or leave it." Rodge said.

"How do I know you'll keep your word?"

"You dare insult me after the kindness I have shown to you and your friends? I've fed you. I've sheltered you. I've provided work and hospitality."

I held up my hand. "It's a deal. Enough gold for a month supply or two months in the lumber mill."

"Good." He turned and started walking again. "You can sit with me. I've got the best seat in the house."

"Thank you, but no. I can't let Willy see me. Not again. I'll watch from the crowd." The thought of Willy calling out my name again made my stomach turn.

"Very well. I hope the boy is as much of a fighter as I suspect."

"He dropped your last Night Cat without much effort, didn't he?" I asked.

Rodge smiled, turned to walk away, then stopped. "I certainly hope you don't make it a habit of basing your wagers on past performances...especially against the house." He chuckled and continued toward the arena.

"What does that mean?" I yelled after him.

He disappeared through the doors without answering.

*** 

I blended into the mass of people without incident. The smell of urine and firewater saturated the air. Across the massive room, someone blew a horn and the audience quieted.

The young woman beside me leaned close. "They're taking wagers on this one."

I nodded and tried not to make eye contact with Willy.

The woman pulled a wad of dried tobacco from her pocket and stuffed it into a small pipe. "I put ten silver coins on the cat."

Again, I nodded and added a weak smile.

"My cousin is friends with one of the workers who cleans the cages." The woman struck a match, held the flame to the pipe, and drew in a breath. "He said Rodge drugged the cat for the first fight." She released a stream of smoke into the air. "Not this one though."

I grabbed her arm and jerked her to me. "What did you say?"

"Let go of me!"

I released her arm and turned away from Willy and the cage. "Okay. I'm sorry. Calm down." I raised my palms and took a step back. "Did you say the Night Cat isn't drugged?"

"Yeah. Why do you care? You didn't wager on the ruined kid, did you?" She took another puff on her pipe and studied my eyes. "If you did, you're an idiot." A blast of stale tobacco smoke hit my face before she walked away.

Cheers erupted from the spectators, and I turned to the cage. Willy and the Cat were already circling. Even from a distance, I saw fear in Willy's eye as he gripped his sling. Someone threw a piece of meat into the cage and the crowd burst into laughter. Rodge motioned to several of his workers who, to the delight of the audience, forcefully removed a large balding man from the arena.

Before Rodge's men closed the door behind the meat thrower, the Night Cat sprang. I turned in time to see Willy dive to his left and avoid its extended claws. The cat slammed the metal bars hard and stumbled back but gained its composure fast.

Willy struggled to his feet and whirled the sling over his head. I didn't see the ball fly, but I heard it hit the arena wall on the far side of the room. The audience released a collective sigh of disappointment.

The giant cat lowered his shoulders and took a slow step toward my friend. Willy reached into the bag around his waist and fumbled out another metal ball. As he positioned his sling to load it, the cat sprang again. I screamed for him to dive, but he dropped to the floor and rolled. The cat overshot him but hooked a claw in the strap to Willy's bag. The forward motion sent Willy into a roll, and though he held on to his sling, it was empty. The bag flew across the cage and a torrent of metal balls rained through the bars.

Willy found his feet as the night cat turned and crouched. Without ammunition, I was certain Willy would die. I would lose a friend and two months of freedom to Big Rodge's lumber mill.

Willy held the empty sling close to his face, and the cat inched forward another step. The cat's tail twitched; I knew the show was almost over. Willy's good hand flew towards his mouth as if shielding himself from the inevitable onslaught of fangs and razor like claw. An instant later, Willy flicked his wrist, and a ball flashed in the torchlight.

Willy's ball flew before the beast's back paws left the floor. His aim was true, and the cat's life ended before it hit the ground. Gasps, followed by cheers, filled the arena. Only later did I learn that Tick had taught Willy to stash an extra shot between his cheek and gum. "Just in case, Little Man," he had said.

I waited until workers carried Willy and the dead cat away, then found Big Rodge. He paid my winnings without protest.

"That boy of yours is going to make me a lot of money." Rodge counted gold coins into my hand as he spoke. "Had one hid in his mouth. Sneaky runt, isn't he?"

I didn't reply, but I don't think Rodge cared.

He finished counting and sent me away with a slap on the back. "Don't worry, I'll give him a day or two rest. Can't burn the crowd out. Got to give them something to anticipate." He winked. "Business, my good friend. Business."

I found my way to the lobby and into the street. I had business to take care of myself...business with my friend Arnie.

*** 

Arnie saw me coming and called out. "My friend Cole Creek. The traveler in search of truth." He waved me to him. "Come. Come. I have something I want to show you."

His booth was deserted when I walked up. "I need more seeds."

"More seeds already? You are enjoying them!" Arnie's eyes sparkled with delight.

"Do you have any or not?"

The trader held up his hands. "Of course, but first, look." A necklace dropped and dangled from his fingers. "Beautiful, isn't it? I understand it was unearthed near the outskirts of your home village. You're from Bethman, correct?"

I nodded and followed the dangling charm with my eyes as it swung from the chain in a slow arc. "What is it?"

"It's a silver necklace with a white trimmed dove charm. Ancient, yet divinely exquisite. Wouldn't you agree?"

"Can I take a closer look?" I reached for the charm, but Arnie snatched it away.

"Sorry, it is already sold. I'm just temporarily holding it for him." He rolled the necklace in a white cloth and slid it into his pocket. "I thought you might enjoy seeing an ancient relic from home. I'm always fascinated by treasures from before The Decay." He patted his pocket. "Who wore the charm? What is its story? Is it one of sorrow, or one of joy? Fascinating to ponder, isn't it?"

"Sure." I opened my palm and showed Arnie my winnings. "How much Rosewood will this get me?"

"Ah yes, back to the present." He leaned over the table and peered at the small pile of coins. "You're sure you wouldn't rather have food and supplies? I only ask because I like you. You are," he stroked his chin, "unlike most of my customers."

I shook my head. "Rodge has been taking care of us."

"Be careful my friend. Nothing is free. There is always a price to pay."

"Are you going to give me the seeds, or do I need to find them somewhere else?"

He shrugged and produced a small cloth pouch. "Two-hundred seeds. Enough to last a month or more." His hard eyes relaxed, and his mouth rose into an easy smile. "If you show restraint that is. Although, from what I hear, restraint isn't a quality at which you excel."

"Are you going to sell them to me or not?"

"Relax my friend." He tossed the pouch of seeds onto the table. "We have a deal."

I dropped my winnings into his outstretched hand. "Thank you."

"It's always a pleasure."

I crammed the seeds into my pocket and turned to walk away. His voice called out from behind before I took my third step.

"Cole! There is one more thing." He motioned me to him. "You're a good customer, so I'm going to help you and your friends."

"How?" I asked, genuinely intrigued by the thought.

"Earlier, a young man, a stranger in New Babylon, came by my table asking questions about you."

"Me? Who knows I'm here?"

He held up his hands. "Let me finish. He knew your name and said you might be traveling with a ruined child. He's from a village you visited, Grandview."

My knees started to buckle but held. "Tiller."

Arnie shook his head. "Sounds familiar but that wasn't the young man's name. This boy's name was Jody, but before he left, two of his friends joined us around my table."

"What did they say? Please."

"Right now, they are the only three in the city. There is another group searching in Blanch, and one more searching in Newton. They are working their way to New Babylon."

"Did they say anything else? Where are they staying? How many men total?"

"One friend was going to the center, but I wouldn't worry about Felica turning you in."

"What about Proctor?" I asked.

Arnie laughed and shook his head. "Haven't you learned anything in your time with him? Proctor will do what Felica tells him to do."

"Do you know their plans?"

"The friend is searching the streets, but I sent him to the other side of the city." He dipped his head. "A thank-you for your business. However, Jody is your immediate concern."

"Why?"

"He left to search Marvels and Wonders."

\*\*\*

I worked my way through the bustling streets, toward Marvels and Wonders. Part of me wanted to run. Avoiding Tiller's men would be easier alone. My friends didn't need me. Rodge was taking care of Willy. Tick would look after Susan. And Alton knew more about the world than all of us combined.

I ducked into the deserted alley beside Marvels and Wonders, chewed a handful of seeds and planned my next move. Tiller's men were coming from the north and south. Arnie didn't mention a group riding from the east, but that was the direction of Grandview, which made it a risky choice. My best option seemed to be west, through The Wastelands and to Lawsonville.

The seeds began to work their sorcery, and I leaned against the side of the building. If I expected to make it through The Wastelands, I'd need plenty of supplies. The thought of leaving my friends behind crept into my mind. They would be fine. They didn't need me.

I took a deep breath and tried to focus. Supplies. Food and water. How could I get them? My best hope was Big Rodge. He controlled enough resources to equip a thousand men for the journey. I banged my fist against the wall, and then it came. Willy made Rodge money. Tiller's men wanted Willy. I could partner with Rodge to protect Willy and kill Tiller's men in exchange for food and water. I might even convince him to give me a wagon. The plan solved two problems; supplies for my trip and protection from the men of Grandview.

Invigorated, I stumbled out of the alley to the front of Marvels and Wonders. Groups of men and women loitered around the entrance laughing and yelling. I grabbed an abandoned cup of water from the group and splashed my face. The crowd seemed to engulf me, and my breaths became quick and labored. My mind struggled to form coherent thoughts. Too many seeds. Not enough seeds.

I stumbled back into the alley and found my way to the warehouse entrance of Marvels and Wonders. Away from the throng of stinking people, I could rest until the Rosewood leveled off. When a worker opened the door to load a wagon or escape the warehouse smell, I would ask to see Rodge and offer my services against Tiller.

To my surprise, when I plopped down against the door, it swung open, spilling me into the warehouse. The stench of animal waste hit me hard, and I covered my nose to keep from gagging.

Loud voices from down the hall startled me, and I ducked behind a large wooden box. I didn't understand all the words, but the tone was clear. Someone was pleading for their life. Two, possibly three, other voices mixed with the first.

I peered around the corner and saw soft light flickering from a room at the end of the corridor. Curiosity drew me from behind the box and toward the light. I crept along the edge of the wall until I had a clear view inside the room. No one could see me from where I stood, but my hands still shook uncontrollably.

Big Rodge and two of his men (the big one and little one from Willy's fight) stood around a young man tied to a chair. From my vantage, the man's identity was clear. It was Jody. The man who had killed Willy's sister as a boy. Tears streamed down his cheeks and fell onto the bloody stump that was once his hand. Hidden deep in the shadows, I watched in silence.

"How many are there?" Rodge shouted.

Jody didn't answer—or couldn't answer.

"How many?" A meaty fist slammed down on what remained of Jody's hand.

The big man put a blade to Jody's throat when he screamed.

"Not yet. Give him time to catch his breath." Rodge rested his hand on Jody's shoulder.

A flash of movement from the dark corner of the room drew my eye. A small creature, chained around the neck, sprinted toward the men. The chain pulled taut and jerked the creature backwards into a patch of light.

"Please, I'll go with him. If he leaves my friends alone, I'll go with him." I knew Willy's voice better than my own.

Rodge didn't acknowledge Willy, and instead motioned to his hired man. "Take off a finger."

Before Jody screamed again, the blade flashed, and a finger fell to the floor. From the darkness, three large rats scurried to the base of the chair and scuffled over the snack.

Rodge knelt in front of Jody, and the rats hustled out of sight. "I feed them my dead attractions. Think of them as my pets." He stroked Jody's hair with a calmness that terrified me. "Of course, people might pay to see them eat someone alive. Human depravity is good for business. Maybe if you talk, I'll leave you a few fingers. It's going to be difficult fighting them off with two useless stumps."

"Please Jody, tell him." Willy cried out from the darkness.

Rodge stood, turned to Willy, and backhanded him to the floor. "Another word, and I'll cut off your squirmy little arm." He motioned again, and another of Jody's fingers fell to the floor.

Jody cried out but managed to speak. "Please! They killed half of my village in a fire. We just want justice. Please!"

Rodge towered over the chair and grabbed Jody by the hair. "How many and where?"

"About twenty in all. Three of us came to New Babylon. The rest rode to Blanch and Newton. They're working their way here."

Rodge let go of Jody and stepped back. "Is there a reward for their heads?"

Jody didn't respond.

"I asked if there is a reward for their heads?" Rodge took the blade, wiped its bloody handle on his shirt, and sliced off Jody's middle finger. "When I ask a question, I expect an answer."

Jody's breath came in quick, labored gasps. "No. Tiller doesn't make deals."

"That's unfortunate because without compensation, I can't allow you or your friends to steal my prize exhibit."

Rodge brought the six-inch blade down hard on Jody's wrist twice in quick succession, and his remaining hand fell to the floor with a sickening thud. The young man from Grandview slumped back in the chair.

"He'll be dead before the next show. Make sure the rope is tight and toss him in the corner." Rodge wiped the blade on his shirt. "Once the rats have had their fill, toss the body to one of the Night Cats. In the meantime, gather every man we have and find Jody's friends. Spread the word in Newton and Blanch. This time tomorrow, I want twenty more bodies laid out in time for feeding."

I staggered back and hurried down the hall. Sounds of shuffling and laugher followed me, but I made it to the backdoor. Outside, the cool night air hit my damp skin. I tried to run, but my legs buckled, so I laid in the dirt and closed my eyes. I couldn't leave Willy with that monster. I couldn't leave any of my friends.

\*\*\*

I spent hours thinking of and rejecting ideas. We needed to leave New Babylon and hope neither Rodge nor Tiller caught us. How would we make it across the Wastelands with no supplies? What was the best way to elude two groups of dangerous men? Could I ever forgive myself for stealing Susan's pendant? Drowning in a sea of uncertainty, I gave up and accepted the escape my seeds offered.

The next morning, I opened the book called Holy Bible, read a dozen pages, but unable to concentrate, slammed it shut. I counted out six seeds and dry swallowed without chewing. Within seconds, a stream of ludicrous ideas screamed through my head. I laid on my bed and let them come. Finally, numb to time and emotion, I surrendered to darkness and drifted into dreamless sleep.

# 22

**TWO THINGS** happened the next morning. First, I formulated a plan that would keep my secrets, provide us supplies, and maybe save Willy. Then Tick stumbled into town.

He busted into my room and woke me from a dream about Felicia. "He ain't out there, Cole."

Surprised and groggy, I slid a shirt over my head. I had wanted to ease into the conversation about Willy, but the words spilled out. "I know. He's here."

"He's what? How?" Tick's haggard face came to life.

"Sit down, and I'll tell you. But first, you need to tell me what happened to you."

"He's okay, ain't he?"

"He's fine. We have work to do, but he's going to be fine."

"Where is he? What do you mean work?"

The hard look in Tick's eyes bothered me, and I chose my next words carefully. "He's with Rodge, and I promise he's not harmed. We'll talk about it," I forced a smile, "but first I need to know what happened in Blanch."

He stared at me hard for a moment before continuing. "Okay, I got there and asked around. It ain't a big place, about the size of Grandview, maybe smaller, so I figured it'd be easy. I talked to a dozen people, and no one had seen any of Big Rodge's men." He stopped and cocked his head to me. "Funny ain't it? Well, I got to thinking maybe they was trying to be sneaky, and headed west, toward the Wastelands. That's where he told us they found him, right? West of Blanch."

I nodded but didn't speak. I worried that if Tick knew Tiller and his men had tracked us to New Babylon, he would forget an important detail. The mind plays funny tricks with our memories when worry shoves its way to the forefront of our thoughts.

"I rode along a ridge to get a better look. Maybe see those ranches Big Rodge was talking about, but they weren't there." He paused and leaned toward me. "You get what I'm saying, Cole? There wasn't nothing but dirt as far as I could see. No buildings. No trees. No grass."

"The Wastelands."

"Yep, the Wastelands. Deadest place I ever seen. I rode a couple of miles each way along the overlook, but the view didn't change. Dirt, dirt, dirt, and rocks. I wondered if maybe I got what Big Rodge said confused. Maybe he meant east of Blanch. I started back, and that's when it happened.

"These two fellows jumped out from behind a rock and started yelling. Horse reared up and tossed me off like I was a rabbit on a bull, but I landed lucky. Before I got to my feet, another man popped out from behind a tree. All of them carried blades, big ones. I figured that was it for Tick. A bunch of assassins was going to cut me to pieces, steal my clothes, and take my horse. After all the scrapes we been through, that's how it was going to end for me." He paused and smacked his lips. "You got any water?"

I poured him a cup and handed it over. "What happened?"

He drank it in one swig and answered with a belch. "Jeeters. That's what happened." He squinted hard. "Yeah, I said it. Jeeters. I didn't see them, but I heard them, and I saw something."

"I believe you."

"They were just about on me...the assassins or whoever they were,"

I interrupted him. "They were Tiller's men."

"They were who? Tiller's men?" His face bore the look of thorough confusion.

"I'll get to that."

He stared a moment longer, then continued. "Well, they were just about on me when the tops of trees started rustling. You know, like they do when a big storm's about to blow in. Only, there wasn't any wind. None. They didn't notice it, or if they did, they didn't stop. Just kept coming.

"All the sudden, it seemed like the tops of those trees was about to come right apart. Leaves were falling, branches cracking, and then the men did stop...stopped and looked up. And that's when it happened. It got so bright I thought the sun had fell into my lap. Then it was gone—the light, the sounds, everything except for those men. But now, get this Cole, here's the part I don't understand. They was all blind, but I could see." He poured himself another cup and took a sip. "I caught up with my horse halfway down the ridge and rode hard till we saw the gates of New Babylon. Figured you and me could ride back and check the east side together."

"What makes you think what you saw were Shadows? Jeeters, I mean."

Tick's eyes narrowed under his brow. "Ain't nothing on earth can do stuff like that except jeeters."

"What if you're wrong?"

I laid out my story, starting with the truth. I told him about the girl in Renenet's temple, and how I found the book called Holy. I told him about Tiller's men tracking us and Jody's first and last meeting with Big Rodge.

I ended my story with the lies. I told Tick I had begged for Willy's freedom and offered myself as his replacement. I told him Big Rodge promised to kill Susan if I threatened his business.

He cried when I told him of Willy and how I found him. I assured him Rodge didn't want his star performer harmed, but Tick's hurt morphed to anger. He loved the boy and convincing him not to storm into Marvels and Wonders took over an hour. My stack of lies would have crumbled had I not stopped him.

Tick calmed when I laid out my plan. We would rescue Willy, and the four of us, Willy, Tick, Susan, and myself would flee south with enough food and water to last a week. We decided to keep our plan from Alton. I didn't trust his history with Big Rodge, and neither did Tick. Alton could wallow in the lies and evil of New Babylon until he died.

*** 

**O**ur best hope rested in Rodge's anger toward Tiller and his posse. If he had sent his men after Tiller, we had a chance. Let the two keep each other occupied until we could slip out of the city.

That afternoon, I sent word to Felicia that I wanted her to go with me to see Big Rodge. I had a business proposition and could use her support. I hoped having her along would convince him of my sincerity and quell any suspicions. While we met, Tick and Susan would locate Willy and wait. I told them about the room at the end of the hall and warned them about the rats. Once I secured Rodge's trust and supplies, they would free him and meet me on the hill.

Felicia and I arrived at Marvels and Wonders late afternoon, hours before the shows began. Big Rodge met us in the lobby.

"Cole," he extended his plump hand, "I'm happy to hear you've accepted the unfortunate situation of your young acquaintance. Sad, how the world treats those who are different, but he'll be safe here. I'll make certain he's well cared for."

His look of concern and swinging jowl stirred my rage, but I played the part. "Yes, it's sad, but thank you."

"And for the young man to have been sickened by an Outrider's poison..." He closed his eyes and sighed. "well, it's horrible."

I tried to hide my anger.

"But," he said, "he's in a good place now. A place where he can thrive and have use in the world. You understand, don't you?"

I summoned my strength, took a breath, and lied. "I do, and that's why I'm here. I have a business proposition for you."

His eyes brightened. "Felicia told me, though she didn't elaborate. I'm listening."

"Several weeks ago, I came across a village with two of these ruined children; twins about Willy's age." I stopped to gauge his reaction.

"Go on."

"The parents offered them to me for a price. They couldn't afford to feed them any longer but couldn't stomach putting them down."

"And why didn't you take them? A businessman would sense the opportunity."

I kept my answer simple. Lies tend to unravel the more intricate they become. "I didn't have enough to barter."

"You let that stop you? Anything worth buying is worth taking." He slapped my shoulder. "A lesson I learned long ago. Just look." He waved his arm around the lobby. "Now, where is the village?"

"That's the heart of my offer. I will return for the ruined ones and negotiate a price to relieve their parents of the burden. Once secured, I will bring them to you."

"Why don't I send my men for them and bypass dealing with you? I don't see a need to negotiate."

I prayed I was right about Rodge's men searching for Tiller and called his bluff. "Your men wouldn't find the village. It's a two-day ride from any road. You'd waste weeks of supplies and might never stumble onto it."

"Okay, okay." He smacked me on the shoulder. "I'll play along. What are your conditions?"

"First, the barter comes from your pocket, not mine, and if I can negotiate a lower price, I keep the difference."

He smiled. "Of course. What else?"

"Second, you grant me at least six weeks' supplies for the journey."

"Six weeks? Absurd! Two weeks. I have shown you and your friends nothing but kindness and you insult me?"

"Everyone in New Babylon has been remarkably kind, but there will be three of us coming back. Six weeks' worth of supplies, and I turn the children over to you. I keep any extra food and water in addition to anything extra I negotiate from the parents."

"Is that all?"

"No, there's one more condition. You'll give me your word you will care for Willy."

His gaze didn't falter as he rubbed his chin. "Alright, you have a deal. You trade like you've lived here all your life Cole. When do you leave?"

"Tonight, if possible. Tick went to Blanch in search of Willy, and I want to be gone when he gets back. He is fond of the boy but doesn't understand what the poison has done to him. I'd prefer our friend Susan and your doctor explain it to him. He and I didn't part on pleasant terms, and I think it best if I'm already gone when they talk."

"Smart man. I can take care of the problem if you wish."

"Not necessary, but thanks."

He never mentioned Tiller our entire conversation. I knew in his mind, Tick was already dead somewhere between New Babylon and Blanch. If the men from Grandview hadn't killed him, Rodge would order his men to hunt him down. I was also certain that Rodge would never give me a wagon full of supplies and send me off alone. If he believed my story about the two ruined kids, and I think he did, one of his men would follow me. Once I led them to the children, he would kill me and bring them to Marvels and Wonders. I hoped Big Rodge's greed blinded him to my lies, and it did.

"As you wish." His voice carried little tone. "Follow me, and we'll get you loaded."

He led me through the main arena to the double doors and into the warehouse. A couple of workers milled about; setting chairs, hanging signs, and other pre-show chores. Somewhere, hidden in the thick brush along the road, Tick and Susan waited on me to pass with Rodge's supplies and signal all was well. I scanned the visible portion of the warehouse for Willy but saw only animals, pitiful in appearance and vigor. A mob of hairless chickens shuffled by my leg. One stopped and pecked my foot, and I kicked. Its head flopped to the side and hung limp. It took three steps and lurched forward without a sound. Its friends and family continued without a squawk.

"Wait here." Big Rodge disappeared behind yet another door and didn't say a word about his chicken.

I wandered the main portion of the warehouse and searched for any sign of my friend but found nothing. I hoped he was still in the room at the end of the hall but didn't want to make Big Rodge suspicious by sneaking around. Within minutes, Big Rodge returned with both the burly man from earlier and his miniature assistant. The sight of them concerned me. I had assumed they left with Rodge's other men to find Tiller's group.

"Sven and Venn will see to your supplies. I can loan you a small wagon, but if it returns damaged, you pay." He glanced at the big man. "One way or another."

"Thank you."

Sven, the big one, and Venn, the miniature, loaded crates and bags for an hour. I tried to help, but the little one knocked my hand away from a box of potatoes and pointed to a stone bench. I sat in silence, waiting for an opportunity to loosen the backdoor latch for Tick and Susan.

I could run. Take what Rodge gave me for barter and the supplies and flee, but where would I go? He knew where I was born. Even if he didn't find me in Bethman, he'd kill my family. Shouts from the wagon broke out. An argument between Sven and Venn had come to blows. I shifted to the door and loosed the latch, while the two scuffled in the dirt. By the time I sat back down, they were up and working again.

Sven and Venn finished loading the wagon with only a few cross words. I offered a bow of thanks and rolled toward the gate. I prayed Tick and Susan saw me wave my hat above my head. We had supplies, and the lock was loose. All we needed was Willy.

*** 

I made it to our old hilltop campsite without incident. The rise offered a stunning view of New Babylon coming to life. Music, at times harsh, at other times soft and melodic, filled the air. Currents of tiny figures flowed this way and that along dirty streets. I wondered if Alton was among them and knew instantly he was. For a man who claimed no home, New Babylon suited him well. I took comfort knowing soon, I would be rid of him forever.

Night passed as I waited on my friends. I watched the moon arch across the sky and wondered if any villages existed there. I checked our supplies, read The Holy Book, and checked the supplies again. Time crawled along, and I convinced myself Rodge had discovered Tick and Susan. I reconsidered riding for Bethman. If I made it without Tiller's men capturing me, perhaps I'd be safe among friends and family.

The idea faded, replaced by fear that my madness had grown to insanity, and if I did return home, I would be put down like Elder Frank. I shivered as his name brought an image of Alice and the puddle of blood soaking into the ground beside her lifeless body. If I was mad, if the Outrider had infected me with his poison, I deserved to be put down.

I rested on hard dirt, and my hand landed on The Holy Book. It was real. I opened it and pulled out the note. Also real. But the girl, the images in Renenet's temple, the Books of Knowledge, the parasite I had begun to feel writhing in my body: they made no sense, and the battle raging in my mind exhausted me. If I returned home, I would never find truth, and if I didn't discover truth, the war within my body and mind would kill me.

Night entered its last hour, the time when moon and stars dim as the sun prepares to begin its travel across the sky. The time of night when utter darkness and silence take their first step in retreat. The revelry from New Babylon slowed to sporadic shouts and drunken laughter as people sought shelter from the coming light.

At the limits of sanity, certain Tick and Susan had been discovered, I summoned the courage to go after them. I didn't have a plan other than keep away from Big Rodge and his two mismatched hirelings. I debated taking our loaded wagon, but decided if I was discovered, a quick getaway would be in my best interest. I unhooked it, stuffed The Holy Book into a side satchel around the horse's neck, and rode for Marvels and Wonders.

# 23

**SOFT LIGHT** filtered through dusty air as the sun crested the horizon. I worked my way along backstreets and alleys to the rear of Marvels and Wonders, though at this early hour the streets were mostly deserted. I listened through the warehouse doors for any sign of Big Rodge's laborers, but all was quiet, so I pulled my blade and pushed. The doors swung easy, and I was inside.

I hid behind a stack of crates and waited. I saw no one, but from a far corner of the vast structure, muffled bangs and shouts rang out. They started, continued for a few moments, stopped, and started again.

Cages, boxes, and stacked lumber littered the floor and provided good cover as I worked my way to the sound. The stench of animal waste hung thick in the hot, unmoving air. Rodents scurried along the walls and disappeared under piles of wood and feed. The place which had fascinated me upon my first visit now repulsed me.

I rounded another stack of crates and stopped cold at the sight of Tick, Susan, and Willy pacing in a cage. My chest tightened, and the heavy air became impossible to inhale. I panicked. I wanted to rush the cage, fling open the door and free them, but my body wouldn't move.

Tick struck the bars hard and shouted. "Trap! Trap!"

Confused, not understanding his warning was meant for me, my legs finally engaged. I took three steps before Tick's eyes caught mine. "Cole, run!"

His words registered, and I rushed forward intent on saving my friends but not knowing how.

A blinding pain arched across my neck and sent me sprawling to the floor.

"I told you he would come for them." Felicia's beautifully seductive voice came from my right. "You owe me a horse."

I struggled from my knees to my feet. Big Rodge tossed a cracked board aside as the burly man and his sidekick appeared from behind a stack of feed bags.

The little one grabbed my blade and flashed it in front of my stomach. "Let me do it."

"Easy, Venn. Toss it over." Sven caught it by the handle.

Big Rodge folded his arms and studied me. "I trusted you had changed. I trusted you understood the madness of your friends." He flicked his head toward Felicia. "Obviously, she knows you better than I."

Venn gave a shrill laugh. Sven, my blade by his side, didn't move.

Willy's voice broke my heart. "Please, master Rodge. I'll stay and work for you. I'll perform every night if you like."

"Shut your malformed mouth!" Rodge didn't move his eyes from me as he spoke. "What I do with them is no concern of yours."

"But please, good master-"

Rodge snapped his finger, and Sven opened the cage and backhanded Willy, knocking him to the ground. A blade cut through my shirt when I stepped toward them.

"Move again and I'll spill your insides and feed them to our pets." Venn wiggled his blade at my midsection.

"Yes, Felicia," Rodge said, "you'll have your horse. And you'll have Mr. Cole to do with as you please. Provided my boys don't kill him first."

Sven and Venn laughed.

"How many of our men are still in New Babylon." Rodge asked Felica.

She answered without hesitation. "All but four are searching for Tiller and his group."

"Good. Tell two of them my wagon and supplies are on the hill outside the eastern gate."

Felicia walked to me and pushed Venn aside. He raised his blade to her, but she paid him no mind. "You're lucky," she whispered in my ear. "I initially wagered two horses on you but decided a slave would be much more enjoyable." She bit my ear hard and kissed it. The pain sent waves of ecstasy down my body. "Be good, and I'll see you soon."

She disappeared around the corner with one last glance over her shoulder.

"What are you going to do?" I asked Rodge.

Rodge stared at me for a moment before his lips spread into a thin grin. "What I do depends on you. You cost me a good horse. I wanted to kill you, but Felica can be persuasive." He jabbed a finger into my chest. "You owe her your life. As for your troubled friends, I'm going to make them stars. Tonight, they fight for the crowd. One with blade, the other with a sling. It ends when one is dead."

"No! I ain't fighting nobody!" Tick railed against the bars. "You can kill me if you want, but I ain't fighting Little Man."

"My, my, you certainly have vigor," Rodge said. "The audience will love it. Unfortunately, I think you will fight. Sven, bring the girl out." Sven opened the cage and grabbed Susan's arm. She fought, but he outweighed her by two hundred pounds and drug her easily through the door.

"I'm not going to kill you, Tick. That is my young star's privilege. But, if either of you fail to give a convincing show, I will kill her." His demeanor grew hard. "I will make it painful."

What happened next happened fast. I only remember bits and pieces. Susan screamed, lunged at Sven and grabbed his wrist. The big man sunk my blade deep into her stomach as she wrapped her arms around him. Sven struggled to free himself, but her grip held firm. She draped herself over him, keeping the knife safely buried in her midsection.

Tick yelled her name, and I remember the confused look on Rodge's face. I remember the little one, Venn, running to Susan, waving his blade in short bursts of fury.

I don't remember dashing past Rodge and pulling Tick from the cage, but Willy told me later I did. He said Tick fought me, trying to pull Susan's lifeless body off Sven.

My memory clears with us running past rows of caged animals and stacks of boxes. Barking dogs and screeching birds added to the chaos.

I saw the door ahead and heard shouting from behind. Footsteps, light and quick gained on us as we ran. Ten seconds and we would be outside. Too afraid to glance over my shoulder, I focused on the doors and freedom five seconds in front of me.

Beside me, Willy screamed. I jerked to his cry and saw Venn clinging to his back, thrashing his knife with wild abandon. Bright light flooded the room as Tick banged the doors open. From a distance, more running steps. These heavier but slow. I grabbed Venn by his hair and yanked him off Willy. His blade made one final slash leaving a shallow slice across my arm. I flung him into a pile of crates, which toppled and buried him under a mound of vegetables and fruits.

Willy stumbled forward and collapsed. The heavy footsteps grew louder as I took him in my arms and ran to the light of freedom.

Tick mounted my horse and I handed him Willy. Blood streamed down the boy's face and onto my chest as Willy's eye oozed from its socket. I mounted behind him and held tight.

"Go!" I yelled to Tick.

# 24

**TICK KEPT** watch as Willy and I knelt by a stream. Big
Rodge's men found our campsite and pilfered through our
few remaining belongings. Tick wanted to fight, but we
couldn't take them, not without Willy. I almost said yes
anyway. One last act of vengeance before I left the world
for good. Vengeance against Big Rodge and his greed.
Vengeance against Grandview. Vengeance against
Outriders, their intent good or evil, I didn't care.
Vengeance against the girl, who might or might not exist.
The girl whose face would not leave my mind, and whose
voice now spoke day and night. One last act of bloody
insanity before I closed my eyes on this hateful world.
After weeks of crossing between madness and lucidity,
the final pain of death would be worth the freedom a few
moments of wrath might offer.

It was Willy's calm that persuaded us to let it rest.
As thick fluid congealed in the corner of his eye, he
suggested we circle west of New Babylon, opposite of our
hilltop camp, and head south along the border of the
Wastelands. Within a few days, we would find another
village. I argued we should ride north into Blanch.
Tiller's men would either be gone or dead, and Big
Rodge's men would have already searched the village and
left. Tick and I knew the land enough to find our way
around. We knew where to trade for cloth and ointment
for his eye. Willy convinced us otherwise, and again he

was right. If Rodge decided to send men after us, they would surely concentrate north and east, the direction we came from. So, we circled the city and rode south until the sun perched mid sky.

"Enough water, Sir Cole."

I splashed one more handful into the bloody mess that was Willy's eye. "I want to make sure we get it clean. You never know, it might heal."

Willy steadied himself and rose slowly. "I'm afraid my world is forever dark, sir."

I grabbed his hand and led him to the horse, where Tick took him in his arms and held him close. I moved to join them but hesitated. As much as I loved the boy, he and Tick shared a bond I couldn't grasp. I walked to the stream and drew a canister of water. A damp heat pounded my skin. The water looked clean, and we could follow the stream south to Newton.

"Thirsty?" I called to them.

A few moments later, they joined me on the bank. I handed fresh water to Tick who passed it on to Willy. He drank, refilled the canister, and gave it to Tick.

"Sir Cole, what will we do in Newton?"

"Find labor, rest, you can heal."

"And after that?"

I shifted away from them. "I don't know. I'll find my way to Lawsonville. Once you're better I suppose you can do what you want. Same for you, Tick. You don't have to be part of my misery." I started down the trail of self-loathing and couldn't stop. "Since we've met, I've been a curse to both of you. Look what happened to Susan. I don't expect either of you to go on with me. I'll do what I can for your eye Willy, but once I've gathered enough supplies, I'll-"

A crisp blow to my jaw sent me to the ground.

"You listen here. Don't you ever say that again." Tick's scrawny body trembled above me. "I ain't never had no friends, but I guess I do now. I ain't about to let you run us off because you're feeling sorry for yourself."

I reached up and took his hand as he helped me to my feet.

He didn't stop talking. "I don't understand all your talk about Outrider poisons, infections, and the girl, but that's alright. I don't need to. Little Man believes it, and I believe him," he paused, "and you. So, if we've got to wander for twenty years for y'all to figure it out, I'm with you." His voice calmed, and an awkward grin eased across his face. "Besides, ya'll done got my house burned flat. I ain't got nothing else to do."

For a moment, no one spoke. I wanted to apologize, tell him he was right, but my throbbing jaw wouldn't form the words.

Willy laughed, and Tick joined him. "Sir Tick...." Tick shot him a sideways glance. "I mean Tick. Our first attempt at social interaction certainly has been a roaring success."

The scowl Tick wore dissolved. "Little Man, I ain't sure what all that means, but I like it!"

This brought more laughter from the pair, now propped against one another and in danger of toppling. I imagine their laughter was, in a sense, a release. They had come close to leaving this world but for the moment were safe.

***

Against my better judgment, Tick and Willy decided to bathe in the stream before we continued south. I raised a brief protest but let it drop. After days in a cage, Willy stunk like a wild beast. The stench from Tick was worse. Rodge's men would smell them half a mile off, but it was a weak justification. We needed the refreshment momentary peace sometimes offers.

I leaned against the bank and opened The Holy Book. Drops of water splashed my arm as Willy and Tick laughed and played below. Ten minutes, no more, I thought as I scanned the page, searching for where I last read. Ten minutes, and we leave.

I found my place and followed the words with my finger. A civilization of people, bound as slaves, had been freed by their God after a series of miracles devastated their captors. Now, chased by the ruler and his army, they waited by a vast body of water, trapped with no visible means of escape. The story captivated my imagination.

Movement from behind startled me, and I dropped The Book.

"What have we there?" Alton stepped from behind a row of thick bushes. "Is that what I think it is?"

"How?" I stared at him, unable to speak.

"Son, is that how you welcome your savior? Especially after what I brought you."

I stumbled to my feet and saw our supply wagon. "How?" It was all I could think to say.

Alton chuckled and called for Willy and Tick. "A man like me has many friends. Saved it from the camp just in time. Which brings me to my next point. If you want to stay alive, we need to move. Rodge has two dozen men looking for you. North and east for now, but they'll circle south before long." He squinted against the sun. "Smart of you to come this way. Your idea?"

"No, Willy's." I said.

"Figures. For a ruined one, his brain works fine. Which way do you plan on running?"

"South to Newton."

"Won't work." Alton said.

Tick and Willy joined us. They couldn't hide confused looks as water puddled around their feet.

"Why not?" I asked, more out of defiance than curiosity.

"I've already told you. Rodge's men will head south, and eventually turn Newton inside out searching for you."

"What do you suggest, Elder Sir?"

"Willy!" I spun my head and shot him a look he couldn't see.

"Go easy on him son. He's the one who seems to know what he's doing." Alton's eyes bore through me. "First, answer my question. What is the book you're reading?"

"I don't see what that has to do with anything."

"It may or may not. Either way, we need to go soon, and thanks to me, we have plenty of food and," he pointed to Willy, "ointment for the kid's eye."

"You have ointment?" Tick asked.

"Told you I did, didn't I? He may never see again, but it'll keep him alive." Alton flicked his cane my direction. "The name of the book?"

"The cover says Holy Bible."

Alton glanced to the ground. "You sure?"

"Of course, I'm sure! You want to see for yourself?"

"No, I believe you. Now pack up, it's time we go."

"No. We're not going anywhere until you tell us what's going on." I said.

The old man mounted his horse. "You're searching for truth, correct?"

"You know I am."

"We'll, I told you Lawsonville is where you need to go. They teach the book you've found. It's also a place Rodge's men will never go."

"Where is this place?" Willy asked. "We'll go, if you're kind enough to lead us."

Alton's face went dark, and he pointed west. "On the other side of misery my boy."

Minutes later we set out into the barren nightmare of the Wastelands.

# THE WASTELANDS

## 25

**BORN FROM** the aftermath of war, life had abandoned the Wastelands centuries before. Brown, dusty, collapsed buildings, scorched stone, lifeless air...miles of ruin and devastation. I tried to imagine what the land was like before civilization collapsed during the great decay but failed miserably.

Our first night in the Wastelands, we treated Willy's eye, or what remained of it, and mourned Susan. Tick took it the worst, but we all wept for her. Even Alton shed a tear as we buried the few items she left at our hilltop camp: a wooden comb, two odd shaped rocks, and a small tin containing dried rose petals. Tick asked about her pendant, but I didn't tell, and the question died with a handful of dirt in the shallow hole. We slept under stars along an old hardtop road, our stomachs full and hearts burdened. I dreamed of home. When daylight came, we rode till midday, ate, and rode till dusk. The next morning, we started the cycle anew.

For a solid week, we rode hard and rested little. Little conversation, no laughter. We used the ointment, but Willy's eye grew worse by the day. He didn't complain. Finally, around the fire on our seventh night in the Wastelands, Tick told his story.

"When I was little, my mom and pop used to tell me stories about jeeters. Scared me real bad. Told me they took kids who didn't mind and made them work in caves...something like that anyways. I'd peek out my window at night and watch the forest across our field. We never lived in a village, always close though, so there was always a forest close. Lots of fun to play in during the day. Not so fun at night.

"Anyway, one time, I was about six I guess, I was playing in a tree. Climbed nearly to the top, when I felt a branch give. I grabbed hold of another limb as the one I was standing on broke. I couldn't call for help because pop told me if he ever caught me climbing trees, he'd give me to the jeeters himself. I hung there for about a minute till the limb broke. I don't remember anything until I woke up two days later in my bed.

"I was beat pretty good, broke foot, cuts and scrapes all over, nearly died. I yelled for momma when I first came to, but instead pop walked in. He didn't look mad. Just walked over, sat on my bed and started talking." Tick reclined and rested his head in his hands.

"What did he say?" Willy patted the dirt and found Tick's hand. "Did he punish you?"

"No, Little Man, he didn't. Said I'd been punished enough. Told me the jeeters saw me being bad and took me away for a while. He said they poked and prodded me to see why I couldn't mind."

I leaned toward the fire and warmed my hands. "You didn't believe him, did you?"

"Course I believed him. He was my pop. I ain't never told nobody that story. Ain't never had anybody to tell I guess, except for Cindy, and she would have laughed and told me I was an idiot."

Alton whirled his finger. "Lovely but get to the point."

"Leave him alone, Elder Sir! If you don't want to listen, go gather more wood!" Willy pointed across the fire to Alton.

I didn't fight the smile working its way along my lips.

Alton heaved out a characteristic grunt but didn't leave.

"I reckon the point is, I got this sense about those jeeters," Tick said.

"Shadows." Alton interrupted.

"Yeah, whatever you want to call them. I can almost smell them when they're around. Smells like eggs gone bad." He sat up and cocked his head to me. "Please don't take this wrong Cole, I said you were my friend, and you are, but I've been smelling them a lot since we met. I'm starting to wonder if they have something to do with that girl you and Willy go on about." He paused and scanned over his shoulder. "Maybe it's Outriders; I ain't sure. All I'm saying is we need to be careful."

*** 

**T**ick's scream woke me. I rushed to Willy and knelt beside his blanket. Tick held the boy's head to his chest. Sweat drenched Willy's clothes and heat radiated from his body. Alton joined us but didn't kneel.

"He ain't talking, Cole," Tick Said.

His chest rose and fell with each labored breath. "He's alive," I said.

"What do we do? What's wrong with him?"

"He has the fever." I knew the signs. Many neighbors had died from internal heat in Bethman.

"What gets rid of it?" Tick grabbed my wrist. "He can't die. You can't let him die."

Alton tossed a jar of ointment to us. "Use more of this and wait."

***

**T**wo weeks passed and we moved slowly. Willy improved, but not enough. We spoke little; each of us dealt with the loss of Susan and Willy's sickness as best we knew how. Overwhelmed by guilt and haunted by dreams of Alice, I watched our supplies dwindle but didn't care. I remember little about those days. Rosewood dulled the loneliness and boredom. I kept the seeds a secret, not because I was ashamed, but because I feared Tick or Alton might ask me to share.

Tick's paranoia grew worse each night. In the beginning, he was certain we were being watched. As days grew shorter and nights colder, he became convinced Shadows studied our moves from the dark. "I'm telling you, I felt eyes on us. I ain't seen one yet, but they're out there." Tick pulled a ragged blanket over his shoulders. "Last night before we ate, and again when I got up to pee. Scared me so bad I didn't finish. Had to sleep in wet underpants."

"Shadows, Shadows, Shadows. I'm tired of hearing about Shadows." Alton spat into the fire and wiped his mouth. "Someone's stalking us alright, but I assure you it's not a child's monster."

"Who then?" Tick glared at Alton. "You said Rodge's men wouldn't chase us through here. You think it's one of those fellows from Grandview?"

"It's not Rodge's men, or anyone from Grandview, though I'm fairly certain it's a single rider."

"Oh, you're 'fairly certain?'" I asked.

"I've traveled through more lands than you'll ever see. We don't have enough supplies for an assassin to bother with—especially three against one. My guess is either an Outrider, or gods have mercy, a Heathen scout."

"Heathen, you ain't ever told us about no Heathens." Tick said.

"I wasn't sure I needed to. I've encountered them before; four summers ago was the last time. Wretched people to deal with."

"Wretched? How?" I asked.

"Every way imaginable. Open sores, ripe with oozing fluids, hostile thieves who negotiate at spear point, stench that will turn your stomach…should I continue?"

"Well, I smell something, and if it ain't Shadows, which it is, whoever's after our wagon is going to be awfully disappointed." Tick said.

Alton wiped a dirty hand across his sweating brow. "Maybe so, but they'll want more than our supplies."

He wouldn't elaborate. We pressed, but he refused. Tick threatened to break his wrinkled neck, but Alton laughed and went to sleep. I laid awake, clutching my remaining seeds, thinking of a place to hide them from thieves. The Holy Book never crossed my mind.

# 26

**A WEEK** later, I carried Willy through rock formations and over cracked earth. He had regained partial strength, and we needed water. Alton insisted a stream ran through this part of the Wastelands; one he knew from years ago when traveling through. "Clean, cold water," he said with a nod. "Saved my life."

Ahead, a massive boulder towered above the jagged stone outcrops. Its top flat and wide, I searched for a clear way up, and found one.

"Someone's here." Willy whispered in my ear. "I hear them."

"Heathen?"

"I don't know, but they're close."

I crouched low without thinking. "Where?"

Pain erupted from inside my head and down my neck without warning, and faint laughter floated from behind. I swirled around and saw her. Willy fought my hold and dropped to the ground. "Vedia!" He stepped toward her and stopped. "It's really you."

"Yes, Willy, it's really me." She beamed and ran to him.

My legs gave as I watched them embrace. A whirlwind of contradictions swirled through my mind. Her body looked young, yet her countenance seemed ancient. Her laughter filled me with joy, but it hid terrible power. Her eyes sparkled with love, yet within them burned a mighty fire.

She kissed Willy on the cheek and came to me. "My beloved Cole." Flames danced in her eyes, drawing me, searching me, loving me. One word came to me as she took my hand. Something inside my body recoiled at her touch. Pain. Love. Despair. Hope.

From a place faraway, as the world dimmed, I heard myself mutter the word aloud.

"Holy."

*** 

Light flooded my brain when I opened my eyes. The sun sat mid sky and warmed my face. She sat to my right and Willy to my left. Neither spoke as I tried to sit up and collapsed to the dirt.

"What happened?"

"You fainted, good Sir. You mumbled and fainted."

I said the word aloud once more. "Holy."

She dipped her head in silence, and the sunlight shifted. But it wasn't the sun, it was her, just like Renenet's temple. The piercing light and the comforting warmth radiated from her. From the little girl.

"Who are you? What are you?" I asked.

Vedia closed her eyes and smiled. "You know who I am. The moment I first called to you; you knew. I am everything your mind perceived before you fainted. I am absolute joy and absolute power. I am unending love and consuming fire. I am an ageless teacher and comforter. I am a dove and the wind on which it rides. I am the oil and the fire it fuels." A bolt of pain stabbed me in the chest. "I am Holy."

"You left me The Holy Book and note."

"Yes, a gift from me, delivered by one who serves me. A man you'll soon meet again. Listen to his words and what he says about The Holy Book, and you will find truth."

Willy hung his head.

"What's wrong?" She asked.

He trembled as he spoke. "I was trying to remember your face...your smile, but the image escapes me."

"You're sad because you can no longer see me?"

He stifled a sob.

As I watched, the little girl, beautiful and full of life, faded from view. A gentle breeze filled the air, the first I'd felt since entering the Wastelands, and passed across my face. Willy stiffened and raised his chin to the sky. Strands of his hair flittered in the breeze as it swirled around him.

"I see you! I see you!"

Her voice came from all around. "Listen to me and love me. Hear the man I send. Guard your mind and heart against lies and follow truth." The breeze faded. "Follow my words. I am Truth. I am Holy. I Am."

# 27

**WILLY RELIVED** the encounter a dozen times to Tick and Alton. Tick listened like a child at bedtime, while Alton feigned interest. Around Willy's fourth time through the story, Alton found a soft spot of dirt behind the wagon and fell asleep. I let Willy tell our tale, offering a nod or smile as he spoke. For the first time in months, I desperately wanted to be alone. Not because I didn't care for my friends, but because I felt unworthy of their sincere, innocent love.

Tick's laughter caught me by surprise. "Tell it again! The part where she disappeared and blew across your face. That's my favorite."

Willy told the story again.

"Little Man, you think I can meet her?" He stretched out on his blanket. "I mean, you talk so much about her, I feel like she's part of the family. Like a little cousin. That's what I'll call her. She'll be my little cousin." He closed his eyes, and his voice faded. "I didn't have no cousins, and she sounds real nice." His breaths slowed and within seconds, he was snoring softly.

Willy wanted to talk more, but I patted his head and told him an early day awaited us. I helped him to his blanket and took his hand. I wanted to ask if he believed her, if he thought she could help me find truth, but I knew his answer. He would look at me with his hideous smile and remind me she said she was truth. I simply wished him goodnight.

Unable to sleep, I took The Holy Book and crept away from my friends. Ruins of dilapidated buildings spotted the sides of the road. Ancient machinery, long useless, made navigation tricky, but I managed.

I worked my way through a maze of scrap and into a structure twice the size of Marvels and Wonders, pulled a match I lifted from Alton, and struck a campfire. I needed to read. I needed to know. Ancient dust coated row after row of empty metal shelving, some standing, most lying in scattered, twisted heaps. Above, the night sky glared through gaping portions of the collapsed ceiling. I settled onto a sturdy crate and opened The Holy Book.

The people, children of Israel, had miraculously escaped the army of their captors and traveled to a land their God had promised. Along the way, they endured hardships. Many grew discontent and questioned the leaders, but their God took care of them. Eventually, that same God gave them laws which they accepted with enthusiasm, then broke.

Their God gave instructions on how to build a place where He would meet with them; a place where they could practice the rituals He demanded. Every detail, every material, size, and color were provided. Every act and restriction set forth for these people.

I didn't understand why anyone would choose to live a life bound by rituals after escaping generations of slavery. I didn't understand killing animals, lighting oil lamps, or burning incense. Many in New Babylon worshipped gods, but none like this. None who imposed rules impossible to keep.

I closed The Holy Book. Its stories captivated and frustrated me. My village believed in nothing but the long sleep yet maintained an alter to a forgotten goddess. Grandview had their own beliefs. New Babylon offered many gods and goddesses...if you decided one was necessary. Everyone I met had varying opinions about Shadows and Outriders, but what was the truth?

I couldn't stop thinking about the girl. For months, I skirted the edge of madness, struggling with the reality of her existence. Now, after seeing her in Renenet's temple and with Willy, after hearing her voice in my dreams and feeling her draw with each heartbeat, I knew she was real. If she was real, did that mean the stories from The Holy Book were real?

Shadows rose and fell along the floor, livened by the swaying flames of my fire. Twice I sprung to my feet, certain I was being watched, then laughed at myself for acting like a child on his first trip into the night woods. I remembered a time when I was nine. My father took me on an overnight adventure into the forest. Mom had packed meat and bread, and we sat and talked like men. I was afraid. Crackles and yelps from the depths of thick trees sent my heart racing. I tried to hide it, but I'm certain he knew. Seventeen harvests later, I felt the same fear.

"Cole." I fell back at the sound of my name. "Cole Creek?"

I reached for my blade and remembered I'd left it in New Babylon...in Susan. A man eased toward the fire, still a safe distance away, but drawing close. I spied a metal pipe leaned against one of the twisted shelves and grabbed it.

"Cole, my name is Charles, and I am an Outrider. I've been sent to talk to you. Answer a few questions I suppose."

"Stop!" I jabbed the pipe like a spear. If the man meant to poison me, he would have to do it from a distance.

The man froze and held out his hands. "No need for violence, young man. I'm not armed." He spread his long jacket wide. "I only want to talk. I can stay right here if you want."

"Who sent you?" A list of people with reasons to put me down scrolled through my mind.

"You know who sent me." His tone reflected neither good will or harm. "Now, are you going to calm down, or are we going to stand here like fools?"

"What is the name of the man?"

"What makes you think it was a man?"

"Was it?"

"You ask a question we could examine all night, but if it helps, you met a little girl."

I reminded myself this man was an Outrider. Many considered dangerous. Most considered mad.

He moved slowly, and his large hands, calloused and worn, grabbed my attention. One was different...odd. His finger. His pinky was missing. No, not missing. I knew exactly where he could find it. Chief Elder Gourd had tossed it into the grave with Elder Frank and Alice.

"You!"

"Vedia told me you were there." The Outrider sat and motioned for me to do the same.

I believed the girl when she told me to trust her servant, but my deep-rooted distrust of Outriders remained. I joined him at a safe distance, the pipe across my lap in case he made a move for his poison. "She said you saw it. I wept for days about that little girl, Alice. I see a lot with what I do, but watching her die, the look on her daddy's face." He drew a deep breath. "I still dream about it...about her I mean."

"We found your pinky." It was all I could think of to say. I didn't tell him where we buried it.

I flinched and gripped my pipe when Charles slapped his thigh and laughed. Not the laugh of a madman, but of one who understands joy. "Well, it healed. Still feel it though. Sometimes it itches." He rubbed the vacant end of his hand. "The Creator will work all of this for good."

"How? How can he do that? You lost a finger, Elder Frank lost a daughter, I'm losing my sanity. How is that anywhere near good?" I tried to keep my calm but the familiar anger toward him and his kind festered.

His smile faded, but the gleam in his eyes did not. "You're here aren't you?"

"Meaning?"

"It means you're searching for answers," he picked up The Holy Book and held it in his lap, "and I'm going to show you the truth."

***

"You are sick, Cole. We all are. But it's not from any poison we spread." He paused as if searching for the right words. "Do you know what a parasite is?"

"I know the word."

"A parasite lives in or on another species and survives by drawing nutrients from their host. Your sickness...our sickness," he pointed to himself then me, "works much the same way. Born into our world after our first ancestor rebelled against the Creator, it passes throughout generations, infecting our blood...our source of life." He stopped and patted The Holy Book. "Do you remember the story of the garden?"

I did. Not because of its profound wisdom or lasting spiritual impression, but because of the serpent. It talked. "The snake spoke to a woman."

"Yes, but what did the snake say?"

"It wanted her to eat from a tree. I can't remember what kind, but she wasn't supposed to."

"The snake intended to drive a wedge between mankind and the Creator."

I must have looked puzzled because he opened The Book, flipped through its pages, and handed it to me. "Read here."

I read and turned to him. "I still don't understand. The serpent played a trick. What does that have to do with sickness?"

Charles leaned forward and warmed his hands over the fire. "How many times have you met the girl?"

"Twice. I think I've dreamed of her before, but only twice in person. Why?"

"Tell me, what do you feel when she is near?"

"Meaning?"

He didn't answer but continued warming his hands. I couldn't help but notice how he rubbed the scar of his missing pinky. Slowly massaging the nub and letting his fingers slide along its imaginary path.

"Pain," I started. "Love and pain."

He raised his head. "Go on."

"I know she loves me, but I don't know why. I think I love her too. She draws me, but I...the pain comes when she is close. It's like she's trying to hurt me." I couldn't express in words the inexplicable force behind my need for her and my fear of her.

"Love, pain," Charles nodded slowly, "what else?"

I didn't struggle for an answer. "And a word. I don't understand its meaning, but both times it filled my head"

"The word?"

"Holy."

"Holy." He repeated. "Worthy of complete devotion. One perfect in goodness and righteousness. Perfect in every aspect. Perfect in thought, deed, and intent. Perfect in form, substance, and nature. Absolute purity."

Chills covered my body. The word painted a living picture of the girl in my mind.

"So now, Cole, do you see how the serpent's deceit was more than a simple trick? By convincing the first man and woman to defy the holy Creator, he drove a wedge of separation between Him and His creation. The cause of separation was once called sin, though this world no longer knows the word. It ravaged the blood of the first man and woman and passes from one generation to the next. Our hearts still beat, our lungs still draw air, but swimming through our veins, this parasite feeds on the core of who we are, children of the Creator. We don't feel it because it numbs us to its existence. It consumes our love, our empathy, our humbleness. It turns us into all He is not. It separates us from Him." His eyes narrowed. "Without the cure, it separates us forever, and separation from Him is death...forever."

Heat rushed to my cheeks. "I love! I love my parents and sister. I love Willy! Who are you to tell me what I can and can't feel? And if she loves me so much, why do I feel like I'm dying whenever she comes around? Doesn't she see what she's doing to me?"

He didn't flinch. "She knows. Without her, you would never know you were sick. The parasite would thrive undetected until your last breath."

I wanted to argue but movement from the corner stopped me. Charles saw it also.

"We don't have much time left tonight. Read The Book." More movement, this time from atop a pile of twisted shelving. "Read it and listen for the girl. There is a cure."

Dust and debris shot from ancient rubble, knocking me down. Bits of rock and rusted metal pelted my arms and face. I saw Charles, also on his back and reaching into his long leather coat. I struggled to breathe the dirty air, which now hung thick and heavy.

"What is it?" I coughed hard and wiped dust from my eyes.

Before Charles answered, I saw. Three dark forms emerged from the dust cloud and into the small circle of light cast by our fire.

"What are they?" But I knew...I felt. Shadows.

I scrambled to my feet, cutting my hand on a mangled piece of metal as I fumbled for the door.

"Run!" Charles called from behind.

I stopped and glanced back. He made it to his feet and faced the dark masses with The Holy Book in his hand.

Through the chaos, I found the door and fled.

I didn't tell anyone about meeting Charles or my brush with Shadows. I needed time. Time to think. Time to read. Willy knew something had changed, but when he asked about it, I snapped at him and spent the day alone with my Rosewood seeds. The barren landscape cast a dark spell over our group, me most of all.

\*\*\*

Days passed, then a week. We worked our way through the Wastelands, and the terrain mercifully changed in our favor. The sun still tormented us, and the air still hung lifeless, but we topped a hill littered with jagged rock and packed earth, and before us lay flat land for as far as the eye could see. We camped on the ridge that night, and as full dark descended and a multitude of stars gathered overhead, I saw something far to the west that filled me with hope. A pinprick of light emerged in the distance.

"Tick, come take a look. You too, Alton."

They left Willy by the blazing fire and came to my side. I pointed to the western horizon. "You see?"

"I don't see nothing." Tick squinted and leaned forward. "Nothing but stars and dark."

Alton peered into the void ahead. "I see it. It's still there alright."

"What? What is it? What are y'all seeing?" Tick squinted and leaned forward.

"Lawsonville, my friend." Alton turned to walk away. "That tiny speck of light is Lawsonville."

# 28

**ALTON PREPARED** our horses and wagon for the trip down the ridge, while Tick and I scouted the best route. Willy perched himself atop a boulder, his nose lifted to the impotent air like a hound searching a scent.

"Little Man, time to go. I'll come get you." Tick winked at me. "He thinks he don't need nobody. Don't need him walking off the edge though."

He made his way to the boulder and helped Willy down. They talked for a moment before heading back.

"Tell Cole what you told me." Tick's face looked the color of fresh snow. "Alton," he yelled over my shoulder, "get over here."

"What now?"

"Get over here. Willy smelled something."

"We don't have time to stand around cackling like a bunch of old women every time the kid smells something, hears something, or feels something. If I broke wind and he smelled it, you would gather us around for a discussion about my breakfast."

"Just do it," I said.

Alton slammed the latch into place and sulked over. Keeping the peace grew harder each day. Willy absorbed Alton's constant abuse with ease. Tick did not. I reminded him of the times Alton saved us. He was cantankerous, or mean as I put it to him, but he was keeping us alive.

"Go ahead Little Man," Tick said.

"Sirs, the air smells like..." He shook his head. "It smells like a latrine."

"You saying you smell dookie Little Man?" Tick asked.

Alton looked west and sighed. "What you're smelling, kid, is the Heathen."

***

**W**e worked our way down a narrow path along the ridge. Loose gravel and steep drops slowed our progress, but after Alton's revelation, it was the best option. Clear sightlines would warn us of an ambush, and the narrow width of the path would prevent us from being surrounded. If we encountered a tribe of Heathen, it could only happen from the front.

Halfway down, Tick's horse lost its footing and nearly toppled over the edge, but he managed to pull it to safety. I tried to concentrate as we went, but my conversation with Charles never wandered too far from my mind. I was more and more convinced the girl's words were true, which meant his words were true. That's what bothered me. If I was sick, and the sickness was universal, what hope did I have? What hope did anyone have?

Frustrated, I determined to finish The Holy Book. I left Bethman in search of truth, and if The Book led me to it, and Lawsonville understood its words, I would learn from them.

We reached flat land without incident (other than Tick's near catastrophic fall) and rode for another hour. Tick, Alton, and I scanned the barren landscape for trouble. Lack of trees and no hills let us see for miles in every direction, and though Willy insisted the stench lingered, none of us smelled it. Besides, we would see dust clouds of any approaching riders in plenty of time to react.

Dirt coated the flats on the western edge of the Wastelands. Structures taller than forest trees sprouted from the ground in rows. I recognized them from the Books of Knowledge. Ancient civilizations somehow used them to provide the mysterious force they called "electricity." Their dull gray metal struggled against the rust devouring their bones. Some lay in twisted heaps; others stood tall and erect, though the brown cancer foreshadowed their impending collapse. Patches of scraggly brush dotted the landscape. A cobweb of cracked earth stretched into the horizon.

Me and my band of travelers trudged forward through a part of the world that had abandoned all hope of life.

\*\*\*

We first heard them from a dry creek bed to our left. A moment later, a hoard of Heathen rushed us from behind. My first instinct was to race forward. Most were on foot, and our mounts would easily outrun them, but they covered the wagon within seconds.

They were exactly as Alton described. Dirty, savage, and covered in oozing sores. Some held spears, others rusted axes and blades. One old woman grabbed a metal box top and raked it across her arm. Yellow pus dripped to the ground in steady drops. Tick leaned over and vomited.

Alton pulled his horse to a stop and jumped off. "Keep your peace boys, let me handle this."

Mounted behind Tick, Willy spoke loud enough for all to hear. "I'm sorry. I knew they were close, but...I'm sorry."

Tick turned to Willy. I couldn't hear his words, but Willy quit apologizing.

As much as I hated it, we waited to follow Alton's lead.

"Heathen," Alton called out, "I'm the chief of this group. Which one of you monstrosities will I be dealing with?"

A wiry man, tall and distinguished despite the open sores spotted around his chest and stomach, hopped from our wagon. "Me." More yellow pus ran from his bald scalp, down his cheek and across his lips. His tongue flicked out and lapped it away.

Alton cocked his head and spit out the side of his mouth. "Alright, let's get to it."

The thin man gave a short yelp, and his people stopped and squatted in place. He and Alton began negotiations.

\*\*\*

Twice, I tried to join the conversation, and twice a fence of spears blocked my path. They talked, yelled, cursed, and laughed. Occasionally Tick leaned over and whispered to Willy. No one else spoke. The clan watched intently but didn't threaten us.

The sun had inched a hand width down the sky when Alton motioned me over. I couldn't read his face, but the Heathen leader's thin smile told the story.

"Cole, this is Ketman." The thin man raised his palm. "Ketman, Cole."

I shifted my feet, still unsure of the trouble ahead. "What's going on?"

Ketman started to speak, but Alton cut him off. "They want a fee for passage."

"Fee? They don't own the Wastelands. Call it what you want, but it's robbery." I cut my eyes to Ketman.

"They're robbing us, and you're negotiating with them like it's a business deal."

Ketman spoke. "You may call it what you wish, but we require barter for passage. Despite our obvious physical maladies, we are a civilized people. It is not our desire to slaughter you."

We were outnumbered four to one, and I counted five spears and four axes. The rest certainly carried blades. Eyes of all shapes and colors peered out from behind layers of grime. Brown, almond shaped eyes: round, crystal blue eyes: eyes green as spring grass.

Ketman laid his hand on mine. "Be wise young man; you do not have the numbers for resistance. Suppress your rage and you will survive our transaction. Allow its release only when we are far into the horizon."

He was right. I saw it in his clan's hardened faces. They spent their lives in this forsaken place. Brutality wasn't a choice; it was how they survived.

I jerked my hand away, and he smiled. "Good. As I was saying, the elder in your clan has agreed to the price. However, he felt it necessary you be made aware before we proceed. I'll let you two discuss the terms alone." He held up his palm and walked to the wagon.

I turned to Alton and shoved him. He stumbled but didn't fall. "What did you say? What promises did you make without talking to us?" I drew back my fist to swing.

He raised a boney finger and stuck it under my nose. "I'm keeping you alive! I'm keeping us all alive, that's what I'm doing. Look at them." I felt the wind as his finger flashed from my nose to the group of people scattered around our horses and meager supplies. "They don't have to leave us alive." He calmed and took my arm. "This is how they survive. They prefer negotiation over force and made us a good offer."

"What is it?" I asked.

"We're a day away from Lawsonville by horse, three days walk, maybe four."

"They're not taking our horses!" It wasn't a question.

"Yes, they are. And they're taking the wagon."

I jerked away. "No! We can't let them have whatever they want."

"We will. They wanted everything, but I convinced him we couldn't survive our trip without rations. He agreed we keep three days' worth. Enough, but barely."

"Is that it? Is that all the monsters want? We keep three days of water and food, then what? We hope for the best until we cross into Lawsonville?"

Alton turned away. "They want one more thing, and they'll take it whether we like it or not."

"What?"

He searched my eyes for a moment. I wasn't prepared for his answer.

"Tick's going with them."

I grabbed his collar and threw him to the ground. "No." I wanted to say more, but fury kept my speech simple. "No."

He stood and smacked dust from his shirt. "Yes. It's already done. They either take you or they take him. I chose not to put you two in the ugly position of deciding, so I settled it myself. He goes."

My fight dissolved to despair. Ideas of heroism seemed as far away as Bethman. "Why? Why do they want him? I understand water and food. I understand horses. But why me or Tick? Why not you? Did he include you in this absurd demand?"

He stifled a laugh. I lunged again, but he was ready, and I flew past and rolled onto the ground. He walked over and offered his hand. I swatted it away. He stepped back, his gaze focused on the Heathen clan. "Look at them Cole. Tell me what you see."

"Don't change the subject."

"Tell me what you see!"

I wiped dust from my mouth. "I see a bunch of savages unfit for civilization. I see ruined monsters who should spend their lives in cages."

"In cages? Like your friend Willy not too long ago?"

The words sunk into my belly like a blade. "No, that's not what I mean. Willy's not like them. He's good...decent. These people, if it's fair to call them people, are vile."

"Why do you think they are this way?"

I didn't get his point. "Why does it matter?"

"They live like savages because other villages cast them away. Civilized people don't want them near. Except, of course, for businessmen like Big Rodge, and you know his interest." He took a cautious step toward me. "Think about it, no way to trade for food, water, clothing. No chance to grow vegetables or raise meat in this barren land. No home."

"You're not answering my question. Why do they want one of us?"

"Heathen plan not days in advance, but years...generations. They want to be part of society. Trade with other villages, marry and interact with the rest of earth. Maybe not these men and women, but their children, or their children's children. It will never happen as long as they carry the effects of the great decay on their body." He paused and drew a breath. "They want

Tick to breed. They use unspoiled humans to eradicate the mutations from their bloodlines. And like it or not, Tick goes with them today."

He dismissed me with a cocky wink and joined Ketman beside our wagon.

They spoke briefly, and Alton waved Tick to them. Tick slid his arm around Willy's shoulder and whispered in his ear. Willy stifled a smile, but it broke through anyway. Like a coward, I turned away, ashamed and heartbroken.

I didn't see Ketman's men grab Tick, but I heard his surprised cry. Bound in rope, he struggled, but they held firm. Willy lashed out, his fist a windmill spinning through empty air. From the crowd of Heathen, a woman laughed. Another joined in and soon their laughter drowned out Willy's cries. Heathen dodged Little Man's fury with ease. His desperate attack found a victim when a younger man crept behind him, and Willy spun, catching a nose with his closed fist. Blood flew, sprinkling Willy's shirt and arms. Not one Heathen moved to assist, but the laughter stopped. Willy took another swing, but the man stepped sideways, drew back his fist, and hit Willy with the full force of his body behind the blow. Willy dropped and lay silent. His extraordinary courage mystified me.

Tick struggled against the ropes. "Leave Little Man alone! I'll go, just don't hurt him no more!"

Those words broke me. I no longer cared if I lived or died. Thoughts of sickness, Outriders, and the girl fled my mind. I snatched a blade from the young woman beside me and rushed the men guarding Tick. I made it three steps when pain ripped through the back of my head, and the world blinked away.

\*\*\*

Sunlight filtered through my closed eyes. From a distance I heard shouts, but they seemed miles away. I tried rolling my head for a better look but couldn't. Movement drove spikes of agony through my skull and out my eyes. The voices became clearer. Alton and Willy were arguing. I struggled to focus.

"Shut up, you little reject! I saved your life! I saved all of our lives. More times than this too! If it wasn't for me, you'd be strung up in Grandview or dancing in a cage for Big Rodge."

Despite the agony, I struggled to my feet. I tried to speak but doubled over and emptied my stomach in spastic heaves.

"Sir Cole!" Willy ran toward my guttural sounds, but I blocked him and stooped down to wipe up the mess. He eventually slipped past my outstretched hand and caught me in a hug. He wailed into my chest as I glared at Alton.

"We're through."

Alton walked to us, his eyes hard slits. "We're through when I say we're through, son."

Willy pulled away from me and spun to Alton's voice. His whole body trembled. Alton retreated but grinned. Maybe it was the heat, or maybe the blow to my head, but for a moment his yellow teeth looked like two rows of dirty knives.

I meant what I told Alton. I wanted nothing to do with him. I had tolerated him long enough. Too long. "We're done, old man. We split the water and food and go our separate ways."

He chuckled and shook his head. "Don't be a fool. You're going to Lawsonville and so am I." He stepped toward us and stopped. The awful grin crept across his face again. "Besides, if I know you, and I do, you'll want to find help and go after your friend."

I didn't answer, but he was right.

"Lawsonville's a different place, Cole. Much different than New Babylon. Not many people willing to risk their lives wandering the Wastelands looking for a stranger. Not many, but a few perhaps. For the right price, of course."

I hadn't considered the likelihood of not finding help, much less what I would do if they wanted to barter. "You know people who might help?"

"I know lots of people in lots of places. When you're a traveler like me, knowing people is more important than knowing the land."

Willy, calmer but still trembling, whispered to me. "He's lying, sir. I know he is."

I peeked at Alton. He rolled his finger telling us to hurry.

"Why would he lie? He doesn't need us, and he's the only reason we're still alive. I hate it, but that's the truth."

Willy sighed and dropped his head. He didn't trust Alton. I didn't trust him either, but what he said made sense. Every time trouble swallowed us, he pulled us out. He knew the land. He knew the villages. He knew people. The kind of people I needed.

"Okay, let's go."

"See son, that wasn't so difficult."

We gathered the few supplies left us and headed west on foot. Willy and I argued about Alton, and I said things I regret. I should have learned long before to trust Willy's instincts because Alton wasn't the man I assumed he was.

Alton wasn't a man at all.

# 29

**WE CAMPED** next to a field scattered with heaps of rusted, charred, and broken machines that resembled bulky wagons made of steel. Alton stayed to himself as Willy navigated his way around piles of twisted metal. Losing his sight had slowed him, but he learned to adapt. He said he loved the night; except he used the phrase "accustomed to darkness." I preferred solitude and read The Holy Book. Rosewood called to me from my satchel, but I resisted. I needed focus. I hadn't felt the parasite for some time, though the fear I was going insane had returned. Little girls don't bring walls to life or light darkened rooms. Snakes don't talk or play tricks. Only lunatics believed such stories.

The cycle of insanity rolled onward.

The Outrider's two words, love and holy, echoed in my thoughts. "Draw close to the Creator, and he will draw close to you." I had asked how someone can draw close if they didn't know where he is. He told me to listen for the girl. "She leads," he had said.

I closed The Book and pondered the stars. Thousands dotted the night sky. Beautiful and mysterious, they sparkled with clarity beyond description. I wondered if The Holy Book was true. If so, the Creator took time to set each star in its place and ordered their movements.

Footsteps from behind startled me a moment before pain ripped through my chest. The parasite made itself known again as the peculiar sensation of holiness permeated the air. The girl had come.

"It was an amazing time...creation." Vedia said.

"You were there?"

She laughed, and the beautiful sound filled the camp. Willy and Alton didn't stir. "Their sleep is deep tonight. It was a difficult day."

"They took Tick."

"I know." She walked to me and sat by my side. "You spoke with Charles; tell me about it."

"He said I'm sick." My whole body hurt now. From deep within my chest, the parasite thrashed.

I hoped she would laugh, even smile, but she returned a look of intense sadness. "Yes."

"I'm either dying or losing my mind"

She placed her small hand in mine. "Walk with me."

We walked in darkness, yet I saw. Soft light flowed from her and lit the path around our feet. "When do you feel it? The pain of the parasite."

If I lied, she would know. "When you're near. Are you doing this to me?"

"You've carried the parasite your entire life. I only help you see. I'm not the cause, but I will show you the cure."

Her words made my stomach churn. "How?"

Her smile lit the night sky. "What do people do when they are sick?"

"See a doctor?"

She reached up and ran a silky hand down my face. Under my skin, the parasite slithered from her touch. "You're dying. It swims in your blood, numbing your senses. You think you see, but you are blind. You hear music, but not the most beautiful notes. You smell flowers but detect precious few fragrances."

She withdrew her hand, and the writhing sickness inside my body stilled. Her face sparkled as tears trickled down her cheek like liquid diamonds. "You read My Book but doubt its truth and chase lies. You touch Holiness but long for the profane."

I couldn't look at her. "If there's only one truth and the rest are lies, how do I know the difference?"

"The Holy Book is truth. The Physician is truth." She took my hand, and my knees unhinged at her touch. "I am truth."

My eyes watered. I wanted to believe her. "But how? How do I know?"

"You never will until you realize the nature of your sickness."

"It doesn't make sense. I read the books in New Babylon. If I'm sick...what is the cure? What plant will heal me?"

"There is no plant. Only pure, uninfected blood can overcome the parasite. The blood of The Physician."

"Blood?" The idea disgusted me. "Blood isn't medicine."

"The Book teaches the life of all flesh is in the blood."

The morbid phrase sounded familiar. Charles spoke similar words before the Shadows attacked. "You can't take a man's blood and put it in another. He'd die. Both would die. Besides, if everyone is born with the parasite, how can a physician help?"

She bent, retrieved a lifeless stick, and held it in her palm. Green shoots sprung from its side and grew into thick leaves. Its grey color melted into a healthy brown. Light cut through the night as she smiled. "He gives you life because He loves you."

She wasn't getting it. "But how? Even if what you say is true, how is his blood better than mine?"

"He wasn't born with the parasite." She answered with patience.

"But you said all born of man carry it from birth. How am I supposed to believe if all I hear are contradictions?"

"The Physician wasn't born of man, Cole. He was born of a woman who did not know the touch of a husband."

"A virgin?"

"Yes."

"Impossible."

"Nothing is impossible with the Creator, for it was He who moved upon the woman's womb and formed the child."

"What about the mother? Wasn't she infected?" Frustrated, I tried to form a cohesive argument. "A bucket of clean water poured into a bucket of dirty water doesn't purify, it contaminates. Correct?"

Her soft smile remained. "Yes."

"Then, if uncontaminated blood existed, mixing it with parasite infected blood would contaminate, not cure."

"Yes, but a human baby doesn't inherit its mother's blood. A mother provides nourishment and shelter in the womb, but blood forms within the baby itself. The tainted blood of The Physician's mother never mixed with the blood of her child. He was born of The Holy and with the blood of the Holy. Since life is in the blood, The Physician's blood provides the only cure."

"How does it work?" My mind reeled. "I still don't understand."

"Read my book Cole, and you will." She stood on her tiptoes and kissed my cheek. "And remember what I've told you."

She laid the healthy stick at her feet, and it sprouted into a small tree. Beautiful pink and white flowers blossomed from its branches, while green leaves swayed in the dead air. Its beauty enthralled me.

I felt the parasite stronger than ever. Its cold touch defiled my blood and dulled every sense but pain. Memories of men I had put down, women I had betrayed, and neighbors I hated, overwhelmed me. I understood why the parasite survived by concealment. No one could stand the pain it wrought as it ravaged a body and consumed a soul. I turned to the girl, but she answered my question before I asked.

"It can't hide from the Holy. You feel the parasite when I'm near because it rages against my presence."

I didn't meet The Physician that night, but I found a sliver of truth. Not only because I had heard or read, but I had felt. I knew the parasite infected me, not Outrider poison, and I wept for the first time since I was a child.

# Lawsonville

# 30

**AFTER TWO** days of hard travel, signs of life appeared. Sprigs of green grass poked through the ground in lonely patches. Above, a hawk drifted lazily, ultimately circling out of sight. Ahead, the horizon changed. No longer a hazy, hopeless void of flat earth, undefined colors and shapes rose from the land. I described what I saw to Willy. He listened with no reaction. Ahead, Alton walked in his normal, miserable silence.

Islands of sparse vegetation merged, and skeletal growths of wood gave way to robust trees adorned with the color of life. We walked a worn path between rows of wildflowers and tall grass until we saw a wall towering above the tree line. Still a half day's journey on foot, the sight poured energy into our drained bodies.

Near dusk, we reached the gate. It stood higher than any structure I had ever seen, I looked to Alton. "What do we do now?"

"Wait. They know we're here. Someone will let us in."

He no more than spoke when the door creaked open. Two men stepped through. Both middle aged and dressed in long white robes that extended to the ground. I glanced to Alton, and he gave me a reassuring nod.

A redheaded man extended his hand and spoke first. "Welcome travelers. My name is Greg; this is Eric." He gestured to his friend. "Our lookouts saw you coming two days ago."

I shook Greg's hand and turned to Eric. He averted his eyes and stuffed his hands in his pockets.

"We debated whether you would make it," Eric said. "And from the stench, it seems you almost didn't." He inched away from us.

"Forgive Eric. Hospitality isn't a gift in which he excels."

I wanted to tell him not to worry; we tolerated one of those in our group, but I didn't. Alton would open his mouth soon enough. "My name's Cole. This is Alton and Willy."

We exchanged polite greetings with both, though Eric's hands remained out of sight. Greg ushered us through the gate as Eric lingered behind to close us in.

"Our wall is more for show than protection. Trouble doesn't find us too often this side of the Wastelands." Greg led us forward.

Rows of white houses with well-maintained lawns met us. The streets, void of the usual trash and waste found in most villages, lay silent; a stark contrast to a city center bustling with people scurrying in and out of buildings. Firelit lampposts lined the streets and guarded each house. Most people wore the same white robes as Greg and Eric. I noticed a few in shirts, pants, or dresses, but even those looked new, without rips or grime, as if they had never been exposed to hard labor. Most scurried along without a glance our way.

Eric caught up to Greg. "We need to get them cleaned right away."

"Calm down."

"But Greg, we can't let them wander around town like this. What will people think?"

"They've seen it before. Everyone who crosses through the Wastelands comes to us like them." Greg glanced over his shoulder to us. "We maintain a certain image in Lawsonville. It helps remind us of how blessed we are to live here. Don't worry though; we have showers and clean clothes."

"Do you have any color other than white?"

My attempt at humor fell flat as Eric spun to me. "The robes are not for you."

Surprised by his cold tone, I stopped, and Willy ran into me from behind. Greg took Eric's arm and eased him back. "What my friend means, is only citizens wear robes. The others are visitors. We allow them access to our community, but they must live outside the walls."

Eric wrestled his arm free from Greg's grip. "After they are clean of course."

"Yes," Greg's voice sounded weary, "after they are clean and given proper attire, we allow them to visit our community."

"And water please, good sirs?" Willy's voice cracked as he spoke.

Greg and Eric's eyes met for a brief moment. "He speaks?"

"Who? Willy? Of course, he speaks. Why wouldn't he?"

The two men passed another glance.

"Yes," Greg finally said. "We have water. I'll send for a jug as Eric shows you to the bath houses."

"Follow me," Eric said. Greg disappeared into a small building off the main street.

We followed Eric through a narrow alley, overgrown with flowers and herbs. The scents of lemon, mint, and rosemary filled the small space. The alley ended in a stone wall, and we turned right, taking us directly behind the building we had passed. Lawsonville's showers stood beside a set of steps leading to the building's backdoor. The five wooden enclosures each had three walls and a large tub overhead.

"Little things, aren't they?" Alton mumbled more to himself than anyone else.

"They serve their purpose," Eric said, handing us each a worn rag. "You can put your soiled clothing in this," he produced a large sack, "and your weapons in this." Another sack, this one much smaller but thicker.

Alton pulled his blade and held to his side. "I'll hang on to this. The handle is worth more than three of your houses." The handle didn't look special. Faded white with spots of brown, it looked primitive, yet its simple elegance suggested the hands of an ancient craftsman had carved it into creation.

Eric opened his mouth to speak but closed it and studied us for a moment. "I'll have your change of clothes waiting when you're finished." He folded the sack intended for our weapons, stuffed it under his arm, and marched up the steps.

"Odd man, isn't he?" Alton's gaze followed Eric through the door.

"Yeah. Let me ask something. Did you lie about your blade's handle? How much it's worth, I mean."

"Worth is relative, son. An acquaintance gave me this blade ages ago. It's older than the Books of Knowledge in New Babylon. Much older." He ran his finger along its smooth surface. "To me, it's worth more than you could ever know."

I undressed and picked a stall. I remained cordial with Alton, but I meant what I told him earlier. We would part ways once we found Tick. I would find the answers I desperately needed, and he could do as he pleased. I knew the way home and hoped Willy, Tick, and I would travel it together.

***

Clean and dressed in new clothes, we sat in Greg's well-furnished office. I marveled at the oak plank walls and imagined the effort invested in smoothing them to their beautiful finish. On them hung maps, letters, and sketches of Lawsonville. His desk, also oak and also polished to a fine sheen, covered a third of the room. An orderly stack of books sat in the center. The Holy Book sat on top.

"Much better," Greg said and looked to Eric. "What do you think?"

"Better."

"Yes, better," Greg said. "Now gentlemen, we prefer to know visitors to our community, so tell us your story. From the beginning"

I rose to my feet. "Later. I'm going after Tick."

"Ah yes, the unfortunate gentleman taken by Heathen. Nasty lot of animals. No regard for law." Eric said.

Greg held up a hand. "Eric, speaking of the law, would you check the preparations for our unpleasant ceremony later today?"

Eric paused but eased from his chair. "We were on schedule, but I suppose it wouldn't hurt." His eyes darted between Willy, Alton, and me. "I'll return in a moment."

Greg grabbed a slip of paper as Eric's footsteps faded. He wrote something and handed it to me. "Go see this man. He may be able to help but tuck the note away and don't let anyone see it—especially Eric."

It held a single name, "Luke," and the words "north gate."

"What's this?" I don't know what I expected, but it certainly wasn't on that slip of paper.

"Luke will help get your friend back. He'll be away from his tent for another hour or more, but when we finish here, you should be able to find him. Now please, put it away." More footsteps, this time louder, sounded outside the door. I crumpled the note into my pocket as Eric walked in.

"Everything is ready." He slid into his seat. "Your story please. Then we will explain the rules of our special community if we decide you belong." No emotion came with Eric's words, and he looked at Willy. "We have high standards for citizenship, and I don't like what I see."

"Harsh words." Greg said like an amused father scolding a mischievous son. "Kindness, remember Eric? We show kindness to visitors." Willy slumped in his chair but didn't argue, and while I'm not certain, I thought I heard Alton chuckle.

I jumped to my feet. "All I want is to find my friend. I didn't say anything about joining a village. I have a home."

Greg shot me a nervous glance and cleared his throat. "I'm sure your friend is fine for now." He dipped his head to Eric. "And my colleague and I understand you have a home, but most who travel to Lawsonville are searching for something," he paused, "something other than a missing friend. Maybe answers."

"Or truth," Eric added.

Truth, the hidden treasure of my journey.

I outlined my travels, beginning in Bethman and ending at Lawsonville. I told them of Frank's daughter Alice, Grandview and the testing, meeting Tick, New

Babylon, and finally of the Heathen. Both Eric and Greg looked grim in all the proper places but neither interrupted. For an hour I spoke, and for an hour all I wanted was to leave and find the man who would help find Tick. I omitted any mention of my growing madness, my conversations with the girl, or talk of Shadows.

When I finished, Greg folded his arms across his considerable gut. "Fairly typical, wouldn't you say, Eric?"

"Yes, though you seemed to enjoy telling of your friend, Felica." Eric's eyes searched mine, but I didn't look away.

"Gentlemen," Greg said, "we've fellowshipped nicely for an hour. Let's not spoil it now." He pulled several odd shaped coins from his drawer and handed them to Eric. "Go to the market and get us cucumbers and tomatoes. I'll speak to our new friends about the laws of our community."

Eric glared at him but left without protest.

"Please forgive him." Greg watched Eric leave "He has a mind for numbers and organization but lacks much in social skills."

I peeked at Alton. "Sure, and thanks for the clothes and shower."

This brought a smile to the big redhead. "You're welcome young man. Now, let me tell you a little about Lawsonville, then tonight, after our gathering, we can talk more if you wish."

"No disrespect sir, but I don't plan on being here tonight." I said.

His bushy eyebrows rose slightly and rested back in place. "Very well, when you return." He took The Holy Book from his desk, blew its dusty cover, and opened it near the beginning. "Our laws are simple. We take them directly from this book."

His words brought hope. Alton hadn't lied about Lawsonville teaching The Holy Book. If they based their laws from it, surely, they could interpret its meaning and show me truth. I recalled only a few rules. Do not steal. Treat your parents with respect. Also, killing others was forbidden by this particular God. A jealous God according to other rules. Rules, laws, commands, I must have read hundreds.

Greg leaned forward. "You see Cole, our ancestors believed in the truth this Book contains. They built this," he motioned out the window to the picturesque village, "based on the principle of one Creator, and He shows the way through The Holy Book. Our laws, our customs, our traditions, all started from its words."

"Are you saying the laws of your village are the same laws carved into the stones?" I asked.

Greg shifted in his chair. "No, I wish it were that simple. Our laws expanded from those. Not to worry though; we understand it takes time to learn a new way of life. Our role is to welcome you, teach you, and then determine if Lawsonville is the right home for you. Of course, until then, you are exempt from our mandatory gatherings."

"Mandatory gatherings?"

He waved me off. "Nothing for you to worry about now."

"But you will teach me The Holy Book?"

"Yes."

Alton walked to the window. "Tell us about Luke. If I know my friends, they'll want to take care of business in the Wastelands before any theological or social instructions." He peered at me. "Am I right son?"

I hated it when he called me son. I also hated it when he was right. "Yes."

Greg rose and walked to the door. "It's not complicated. Go to the north gate, ask someone to point you to Luke's tent, and tell him your story. He'll help."

"How do you know? Is he one of your citizens?" I asked.

Greg face grew solemn. "Luke? No, he's a rebel who refuses to conform to our rules."

"But he lives here?"

"We allow him to camp outside our walls, but we furnish food and water when we can. We are kind to visitors, but until he chooses our ways, he'll never be cleansed of the sickness and can have no fellowship in our community."

"Why does he stay good sir?" Willy asked.

Greg cast me a questioning look before answering. "You'll have to ask him." He shrugged. "Find me when you're ready, and we'll talk."

Half an hour later we stood in front of the north gate. A young woman, proper in speech and appearance, reluctantly pointed us in the general direction of Luke. Willy asked if she might escort us, but she recoiled, face twisted in disgust, and walked away without answering. Five minutes later, standing with Luke outside his tent, I understood why.

# 31

**OPEN SCABS**, highlighted by his pale skin, covered Luke's arms, neck, and portions of his face. He leaned on his cane as we introduced ourselves.

Without speaking, he walked to his tent and waved us inside. I expected disarray, but his small, sparsely furnished tent was spotless. He patted dust off a chair and tossed a pair of pillows to the dirt, while I maneuvered Willy into the seat. Alton and I took the pillows, and Luke sat cross-legged facing us. We stared at each other until Willy broke the silence.

"Our friend is in trouble, kind sir, and we were told you might help."

Luke held up his hand and quickly dropped it. He pulled a stick of chalk from his pocket and grabbed a slate board. I glanced at Alton as the man wrote. "How can I help?" He pointed to me, and I gave a quick nod.

"Not a talker?" Alton asked.

He shook his head no and pointed to the words already on his board. I told a condensed version, leaving out most details except for our journey through the Wastelands and Tick's abduction. All the man needed to know was that the Heathen had Tick. Anything before the Wastelands would have been breath better spent searching for our friend.

When I finished, he erased the board with his sleeve and wrote more. "Did Greg tell you who I am?"

"Only your name," I said.

Willy patted my arm. "What did he write, sir Cole?"

I read Luke's part of our conversation aloud.

"They don't enjoy speaking of me. Or those like me," Luke wrote.

"Who? Greg and Eric?" I asked.

He nodded and scribbled on his board. "Most."

"Is it because of your..." I fumbled for the right word.

"Appearance, yes. And more."

"More?" I asked.

"Not important yet." Luke's hand worked furiously. "But you need to understand my motivation."

Alton sighed and rolled his finger. "Get on with it."

He wrote his story piece by piece. "I was born into a Heathen clan, as was my mother. My father was not. He was taken from a group wandering through the Wastelands. I lived with them twenty winters. I grew up a Heathen." He closed his eyes, cleared the board and continued. "Late one afternoon we ambushed a small group of travelers and seized their wagons. Much like what happened to you. Ketman negotiated for a woman, and we allowed her companions to continue. Her name was Maria, and she was flawless. No malformations, no sores, no stench of disease.

"Maria and I grew close." He paused and bit his lip. "You must understand, those they take, are treated well. I told her of my childhood, and she told me of hers. We fell in love and had a little girl. I dreamed of more than the desolate existence we endured. My family's life of violence and deceit troubled me. How we escaped isn't important, only that we did and fled into the Wastelands. We hoped to reach Maria's home, a village called Newton, and followed an eastern course for weeks. We ran out of water, and Maria died four days outside her village. My little girl survived."

"How did you find your way to Lawsonville kind sir?" Willy asked.

Luke paused, erased the board, and wrote. "After we buried and mourned Marian, I turned south. Her family wanted me to stay, but the pain proved unbearable. I took our baby and rode into the night. Eventually, we stumbled across a community called Hopewell. They clothed and fed us. The women helped with my little girl, and the men taught me from The Holy Book."

"Another village knows of The Holy Book?" I asked. He glanced up from his board, and I continued. "Like Lawsonville?"

His hand worked furiously. "No!"

"But Greg said-"

He stopped me with a grunt and more frantic writing. "I will explain but let me finish." Satisfied he had our attention; the chalk went to work. "My life changed. I changed. I lived in Hopewell eight years with my daughter, Susan. We left when I was called to serve The Physician as an Outrider."

I jumped to my feet. "You're an Outrider?" The revelation brought both anxiety and relief.

Luke dipped his head and calmly waited until I sat. "Yes," he wrote, "I serve The Physician."

"Your daughter is named Susan?" Willy asked.

His countenance melted into anguish. "Yes. She died the year after we left. We rode into a village hostile to my kind. I was tried or tested as they call it. After removing my tongue, they took her away and hauled me into the forest. I escaped, but not before their leader told me of her death."

"Grandview." Willy and I spoke the word together.

Dust flew when Luke fell back and knocked over a chair. Trembling, he tried to speak, but only managed sporadic, unintelligible grunts. Willy reached for him, but Luke flinched away.

Willy pleaded with me. "It can't be true. It can't be our Susan."

But it was. We told him how we met Susan, and how she died. We told him of her bravery and kindness. I held the Outrider as he mourned her loss. Whether tears of joy because she had lived past childhood, or tears of regret for believing Tiller's lie, I don't know.

All afternoon we talked, and he wrote. Willy told of his childhood and how he and Susan became friends after they fled Grandview. Luke wrote of exotic villages, scattered over the earth. Some rejoiced at his message, but most shunned him. A few tried to kill him. I never spoke of the pendant now hanging around another woman's neck.

When our conversation returned to Tick and how to save him, Alton, silent all afternoon, spoke. "I don't like it, Cole. I don't like it at all."

"What? What don't you like?" Luke flinched at my outburst.

Alton stopped behind Luke. "This!" He poked Luke in the back of his head. "His story, his disease, his face-" He paused and took a deep breath. "Isn't it convenient we meet a man halfway across the earth who claims to be the father of your dead friend?"

"What are you saying?"

"I'm saying he's a liar."

"But his tongue, he knows of the testing in Grandview-"

"Means nothing. He's an Outrider alright, but I've told you they're poison."

"Elder Sir, I believe you said they carry poison. I don't understand how they can *be* poison." Willy said.

"Shut up!" Spit flew from his mouth as he yelled at Willy. "I suppose if the mute fool agrees to help, it's his business, not mine."

I threw my hands into the air. "What do you suggest? I'm going after Tick."

"We're going after Tick." Willy navigated his way around the chair.

Alton sighed and lowered his voice. "Luke said they treat captives with respect...with kindness. I say you rest. Let Greg and Eric teach you the truth that sent you on this journey. If Luke wants to go, let him. But you stay and learn. He claims to know the Heathen. Let him prove it." He moved from behind Luke and leaned over me. "Think, son. Start trusting your mind."

"Forget it. I'm not asking a stranger to risk his life alone."

We turned to Luke, who was already writing. "I can get him."

He wrote his plan, but I didn't like it. He argued I shouldn't go. Heathen would meet him without harm but might demand an exchange for me. Without the temptation of another healthy male looming over negotiations, he would offer donated supplies...assuming he could acquire them. It had worked twice before.

I fought the logic as best I could, but I knew he was right and agreed to stay behind. Willy begged to help Luke search, but we both forbade it. I'm certain Luke's reasoning stemmed from Willy's lack of sight or severe deformities. Not mine. Willy could handle himself, sight or not. My reasons were much more selfish. I wanted him with me.

"It's settled." Alton grinned as he spoke, and I clinched my fists. "I hope you find him, I doubt it, but I hope you do. He and our ruined companion became quite close." He cocked his head to Willy. "Makes sense they're friends though. The little guy's own parents betrayed him for a sack of meat. You should have seen how fast they hauled him into the testing." His grin sprouted into a chuckle. "And Tick's wife left years ago for coffee. Poor souls like them always find one another."

"Sit down, Elder Sir! Sit down, and don't speak again unless Cole allows it!"

Alton jerked his head to Willy. His lips stretched chin to ear. Not a man but a picture of a wild beast sketched by a talented child. "And if I refuse?" His voice dripped with hate.

Willy worked his way from behind the chair and to Alton. He stopped a hand's length from the old man's chest. His voice didn't waiver. "Then I will kill you, Elder Sir." It is my fondest memory of Willy.

Alton's face flushed pink, then pale, and he disappeared through the tent's flap.

"I'm sorry." Willy backed into his chair and sat. "I don't know what possessed me, sir Cole."

"Don't worry about it, Little Man. You did fine."

***

**A** gruff voice from beyond the tent called. "Luke, brought your food." A thud and heavy footsteps walking away.

Luke rose and clapped his hands. He scurried outside and reappeared a few moments later carrying a small crate.

I gazed at the half-eaten vegetables and moldy bread at my feet. "What is this?" The smell worked its way to my nose.

He picked up his board and wrote. "Gifts from Lawsonville. They make sure I'm fed and have water." He knelt by the crate and dug through its treasures.

Luke handed me a lump of hard bread. I declined, but he insisted. Even after I dipped it in water, the dismal morsel caught in my throat.

We stayed the night with Luke, all but Alton. He hadn't returned and no one suggested looking for him. Luke offered Willy his cot, but he refused. He curled up along the wall and fell asleep shortly after Luke's first snore. I tossed on hard earth, not able to find a position comfortable enough to still my racing mind. The truth was close. I felt it. I believed the Outriders, both Charles and Luke. But more important, I believed the girl.

# 32

**LOUD AND** obnoxious bells ringing from within the gates woke us. Before I asked the obvious question, Luke's chalk scribed. "Gathering."

"The mandatory gathering?"

He blinked. "Yes, you know of them?"

"Greg mentioned them."

He erased and wrote. "I'll take you if you want. You're not required, but we can find supplies to trade with the Heathen while inside the walls."

Not required. The words brought both unease and comfort. "Then you go for Tick?"

"Yes." He wrote and slipped into a clean jacket.

***

Eric met us on the steps, hands behind his back, foot tapping. "Luke." He frowned as he spoke. "I see our new friends decided to join us."

Luke extended his hand, but Eric didn't return the gesture.

"You know where to sit." He stepped aside and ushered us through the doors. "And please, no disruptions."

"Where to sit?" I whispered to Luke. "Disruptions?"

Luke pulled us into a small room littered with trash. Crumpled paper, discarded clothing, and torn books covered tattered rugs. The air smelled curdled, as if the room itself needed to vomit. Dozens of white robes lined the walls. Though hidden behind tall trees, the eastern sun provided enough light to see Luke's board. "We sit near the back with other visitors. Watch and listen."

"Are they worried we'll disrupt the...whatever this is?"

He wrote. "The warning was for me. They don't appreciate my view of their teaching."

From behind came loud rustling and a crash. Willy lay sprawled out against the wall, buried under a mound of robes. An overturned woven basket and relics from the world before, rested at his feet. "I'm okay, good sirs."

I helped him up and took a robe. "You're sure I can't wear it? Might not hurt to fit in."

Luke scribbled on his board. "Not how it works. Watch and understand."

We followed Luke into the nearly full gathering hall and claimed our three seats. Luke, sitting between Willy and I, leaned back and propped his board on his lap. People of all ages, shapes, and colors, mingled the room. Most wore broad smiles; all wore white robes.

"Hello, visitor." An older lady with a plump face as smooth as an apple, hovered beside my seat for a moment, then scuttled off leaving the scent of pine behind. I glanced at Luke, but his gaze remained forward.

Luke started to write but stopped when a young man approached our seats.

"Welcome. My name is Marcus."

"Name's Cole. Nice to meet you." I faked a smile which he matched with practiced ease.

"Glad you're here. Did you check in with Eric?"

Willy leaned to our voices'. "We did friendly sir, we-"

Marcus didn't afford Willy the slightest glance. "I'm new. Became a full citizen three weeks ago." He pointed to a slip of black paper pinned to his robe. "Have to wear this for a season. A trial period they call it. Anyway, wanted to welcome you. You picked a good one for your first visit."

"Why?"

"Bringing in a sweet couple this morning. Good kids. It took the boy time to accept our truth, but he's ready."

A short, balding man bounced up behind Marcus and grabbed his arm. Marcus turned, and the two embraced and walked off laughing in hushed tones.

I tapped Luke's thigh. "What's he talking about?"

Luke wrote. "I want to show you why I stay."

Noise from the front drew my attention before Luke responded. "People! People! Take your seats please. It's time we begin." Eric waited for conversations to die. "Take your seats. Thank you.

"I know we are all eager to welcome our newest citizens, but we follow order, and first we must hear from The Holy Book."

I leaned to Luke. "Should I have brought mine?"

He pressed a finger to his lips and pointed to the sea of white before me. Only Eric held The Holy Book.

He recited the laws, both the Books' and Lawsonvilles'. He cursed the parasite and spoke eloquently about the Creator. The words of his prayer sang in my ears. Despite Eric's brash personality, he understood how to command an audience.

After a final prayer, Greg joined him, a white robe in each hand. A man and woman passed me as they walked hand in hand down the aisle. She wore tattered cloth pants with roses painted down the legs, and he wore farmers' clothing. Two ladies sitting in front of me sneered and whispered in a voice loud enough for me to hear. "Inappropriate."

Greg put his arms around the couple. "Citizens, today Jerome and Jade join us. They have chosen the robe and are ready to fully accept our ways...to follow truth." He handed each a garment. "They understand the Creator requires purity, an unblemished servant, and nothing less."

He looked at Jerome and Jade in turn. "Do you understand the importance of the robe, and why you must wear it?"

Both said yes.

"Do you understand that without the robe, the parasite prevails, rendering you unclean before the Creator?"

They agreed.

"Do you promise to obey the rules of Lawsonville, and understand the consequences if you falter?"

They did.

"Excellent. You may clothe yourself with purity."

Jerome and Jade slipped robes over their heads, and the sea of white rolled into thunderous applause. Luke tapped my leg and pointed to his board. "Remember his words." He flicked his hand toward the exit. No one noticed as we followed him into the street.

"Why did you want us to see that?" I asked.

Luke quickly wrote. "Those lies are why I stay."

Luke flipped a hand over his shoulder and waved us forward without slowing. Trees canopied the path outside the building. Whitewashed homes with perfectly ordered exteriors peered down at us as we walked. No children laughing. No farmer sowing his seeds. No one fishing the creeks or plowing the fields.

I described it to Willy as best I could. "The houses are white...all white. Not many windows: one on the door and another on the west side, identical. I'm not sure about the back. Nice flowers, all yellow."

About halfway, Luke stopped and pulled out his chalk. "Wait here." He shoved the board into my hands and disappeared behind a house.

"What did he write?" Willy asked.

"He said wait here."

"There is no one around?"

"Not that I can see. They're all at the gathering." On impulse I added, "I'll be right back."

"Sir Cole!"

"Hush! I want to take a peek."

I crept to the house on my right and eased onto my toes. Its dirty window didn't allow clear vision, but I saw enough to understand. The room was filthy. Flies swarmed over bowls of congealed food. Piles of dirty robes dotted the corners. In the center, ragged chairs surrounded a torn rug, barely visible under mounds of trash.

I spun at footsteps from behind. Luke walked past me carrying a large crate and stopped beside Willy. The crate was loaded with food. Good food.

"To trade with Heathen?" I asked.

He nodded and started back down the street.

"Where did you get it?"

Luke sat the crate at his feet and took his board. "From one who seeks truth but has lost his way. He left it for us."

"Who?"

He hesitated, scribbled, and handed me the board. He was already walking away with our gift when I told Willy the name. "Greg. It came from Greg."

# 33

GREG CAME for me later, though I almost didn't go. Per Luke's request, I didn't mention the food. He explained Greg and Eric didn't always agree on how Lawsonville should handle visitors. Greg had helped before, but he insisted on anonymity in order to keep peace in the community.

Greg extended his invitation to me alone. Willy didn't argue, but I did. In the end, Willy forced me to go. He claimed he wanted to explore outside the gates. My arguments about his blindness fell on deaf ears.

Greg and I left Luke's tent and walked into Lawsonville. The streets bustled with activity. A round man passed and gave a polite smile. He moved along without a word, his countenance a stoic glare. A common look along the street.

"Where are we going?" I asked.

"I have something you need to see," Greg said. "The best way for you to learn truth is a practical example. We'll talk along the way, but our conversation will flow much smoother if you see truth in action."

"When are we going to talk about The Holy Book? And the girl? Do you know of The Physician?"

He stopped short. "Yes, I know of them." He spoke softly, the way a mother explains hard concepts to a child. "And I'll teach you all about them—after we attend to this business."

"Don't you understand? I am sick."

"Yes, I do understand. I was sick." He swept over the crowd. "We were all sick. But we're better now. Our symptoms are gone. We defeated the parasite and work daily to keep it at bay." We walked. "That's what this is all for. This city, built in blood and sweat, keeps us safe. It's our sanctuary. Our refuge from the death outside these walls."

"But the girl and The Physician? You know of them?"

"I do, and we'll discuss them later. First, we have unpleasant business to attend."

A roar sounded from down the street. Ahead, a group of men and women gathered by the main gate. Bursts of laughter joined the shouts. People parted as we approached. A man, woman, and child huddled close and held hands. Similar to the others, white robes, clean skin without blemish or deformity, only the pain in their eyes separated them from the gathered hoard.

A familiar figure stepped to them.

"Clyde Harmon," Eric's voice hushed the crowd, "you are accused of blatant disregard for purity. How do you answer?"

Clyde fell to his knees. "Please, you can't see the stain," he turned down his collar. "Look! It's on the inside!"

A dark red tomato arched toward him and splattered his chest with stinking juice.

"What is this?" I asked Greg.

"Watch, and we'll talk."

Clyde's wife knelt beside the little boy and wrapped him in her arms. More putrid food smacked her cheek, and the crowd shouted its approval.

The scene fell silent when Eric raised his arms. "How do you answer?"

Clyde lifted his head. "I worked hard in the fields, I labored for you and this village. I didn't mean to let it get dirty. Please don't do this!"

A young man approached and handed Eric a cloth sack. He reached in and pulled a wad of rags, torn and caked with dirt. He tossed it to Clyde. "You broke the law. You are no longer well and must leave. You and your family. We can't allow the infection to spread in our community. You refused to exert the effort needed to keep your robe clean and control this sickness." Eric walked to Clyde and lifted him to his feet. "It's time. You and your family may change in privacy." Eric pointed to the stalls we had showered in when we first came to Lawsonville. "Now." He kicked the crumpled mound of clothes.

Clyde's wife gave one last cry which dissolved into sobs. He gathered her and his son and herded them into the stalls.

Greg leaned close and whispered. "Do you think it's harsh?"

"Do I think it's harsh to exile a family because of a stain on his robe? Yeah, it doesn't seem right."

"Are you familiar with a disease the ancients called Smallpox?"

"No."

"Exceedingly nasty according to the records. Whole families and villages suffered and died of the illness. It spread like fire across withered grass. How do you think they defeated it?"

"I assume they found a cure."

"Not a cure, but a vaccine. Until then, they separated the sick from the well. A measure to prevent the disease from spreading. We follow their example. Strict separation from the infected and adherence to law."

"Why did you let us in? By your standards, aren't Alton, Willy, and I all infected?"

"You are, but you're not part of our community. He was." Greg motioned to the stalls Clyde and his family had disappeared into. "This casting away is how we stay holy."

Holy. The word again. I started to ask him to tell me more, but a cheer from the gate interrupted us. Clyde and his family emerged from the stalls wearing the filthy clothes from the sack. They held hands and walked to the gate. The child wiped a runny nose on his mother's dress.

Two men, thick with muscle and hair, slid the latch aside and pulled open the massive doors. Beyond them, sparse patches of green and the barren desolation of the Wastelands.

I whispered to Greg. "They'll die out there."

"No, we're not savages." He pointed to a pile of sacks. "Enough provisions for a week. Maybe ten days."

"And when it's gone? There's nothing out there."

"No longer our concern. They are in the hands of the Creator. Once Clyde has paid the price, we may allow them to return. Assuming the Creator doesn't judge them with death." He clasped his hands behind his back. "But that is not our decision."

Eric's voice rose over scattered conversations. "May the Creator show justice as you cleanse yourself. When the seasons have come full circle, you may request restoration into our community. Until then, you are hereby exiled to the land of the profane."

Two men shoved Clyde and his wife through the gate. Their child teetered after, falling once, and crying out before his mother scooped him into her arms. The doors slammed shut, and everyone dispersed without emotion.

Greg paced in front of his desk. He held The Holy Book in one hand, a piece of paper in the other. "Adherence to our laws and tradition is vital for survival. You must grasp that truth before we go any further with your instruction."

"So, a little dirt on your robe is cause for casting a whole family into the Wastelands. I don't remember reading that in The Holy Book."

Greg stopped by the window and gazed out. A group of children walked by single file and waved. Each carried a small book under their arm and moved without talking. Greg dipped his chin in acknowledgement. "The sickness we fight is powerful. Do you agree?"

"Of course."

"Of course," he repeated. "Do you know the result if not treated?"

My last conversation with Charles came to mind. "Separation from the Creator?"

"Yes, and do you know why?"

"Holy." The word rolled off my tongue.

He smiled and eased into a spacious chair by the window. "Holy, you know the word. The infection profanes our bodies, soiling our holiness. We no longer are connected to the Creator. Our fellowship is severed."

Scattered pieces of knowledge clicked into place. "You overcome the infection's power by not allowing the infected to be part of your community and observing rules."

"Not just observing, enforcing." His fingers formed a steeple under his nose. "Our rules serve as a buffer. They ensure no one comes close to breaking a law from The Holy Book. Think of them as a fence that protects the integrity of the law. You are correct, there is no law in The Holy Book concerning a bit of dirt on a piece of clothing, but it does speak of robes and garments. It promises one day a great king will return wearing a robe of pure white, and all who are with him will wear robes of pure white." His eyes searched mine. "Do you understand what I'm saying?"

"Yes." I lied. "But surely you can give him a new robe, or try harder to wash the stained one."

"And dilute the importance of our rules? If no one worked to cleanse their robes because they could simply find a new one, our society would collapse. Lawsonville would be no better than New Babylon. Our rules prevent us from coming close to breaking The Holy Book's laws." A smile spread across his face. "And the infection cannot survive in the presence of the law." He handed me the slip of paper. "Take this. Learn them. No one expects immediate change, but if you wish to become one of us, you will need to act like us."

I skimmed the paper, flipped it over, and skimmed the back. "I have to learn this?"

"Eventually, but it will take time. Think of these next few weeks as a period of grace." He ushered me to the door. "A subject we shall discuss another time. I'm afraid I have a prior commitment and must take my leave."

I followed him into the hall and shook his hand. "When can we speak again?"

"Study our ways, and we'll meet here tomorrow afternoon."

"And Willy?"

He stroked his chin for moment. "Just you tomorrow."

***

Luke left for the Wastelands like he promised. We spoke briefly, though I avoided my conversation with Greg. My mind was on Tick. I wanted to go instead of Luke. I was his friend. I was the reason he wasn't sitting in his yard wasting metal balls with his sling. But I needed to stay. I wanted to learn.

I tied the crate to his horse and wished him luck. He dipped his head and took me by the shoulders, before kissing my forehead. The simple gesture touched me. With a final smile, he turned and went to Willy. The two embraced, and after another forehead kiss, was gone. We watched him ride until darkness overtook him.

*** 

I tried not to think of Tick as I read Greg's list to Willy. He asked me to read it again, and I did. When I finished, he wiggled his arm and asked me to go through it once more.

"Tell me what you think. I'm not reading the whole list again."

"Okay, but I do not like it." Willy said.

"Of course not, but does it sound like truth? It makes sense. The girl gave me The Holy Book. The Holy Book tells of the parasite. Lawsonville teaches the Book and has a cure." I wanted him to believe with me.

He tilted his chin to the air. "They spoke of a physician. Have you met him?"

"No, not yet, but I meet with Greg again tomorrow."

"And the girl? What does he say about her?"

I slammed my palm on the table. "I'm just saying it sounds logical."

Willy felt his way along the table and took a chair beside me. "Let's talk about the list."

We spent hours debating the sixty-seven rules of Lawsonville. They observed laws concerning leisure time, music, dress, speech, attendance to town functions...every aspect of daily life. Bread, corn, beans and water on Mondays. No intimate actions during sunlight. No more than five unexcused absences from mandatory gatherings in one year. Close fellowship with visitors was forbidden unless approved by Greg or Eric. No chance I would remember them all.

The night grew long, and I folded the list and stuffed it into my front pocket. Willy drifted to sleep, while I waited for Alton, who had disappeared again. I had almost given up when he slipped quietly into the tent.

"Didn't think you'd be awake." He sounded tired, and though I was curious, I wasn't in the mood for more conversation...especially with him.

"Not going to be for much longer." I said.

"Don't let me keep you up."

"Goodnight Alton." I spread a blanket and grabbed another for cover.

Alton grabbed several potatoes from the table and stuffed them in his sack. "I talked with Greg today. He said your visit went well."

I rolled away from him.

"He thinks you'll fit in well here. I think he's right."

"I said goodnight."

"Have it your way."

Footsteps shuffled out the tent, and within minutes I downed two Rosewood seeds to calm my frustration and drifted into fitful sleep. I didn't see Alton again until the day he tried to put me down.

# 34

I **SPENT** the morning with Willy walking around the perimeter of the city and reconnecting. We talked mostly about Tick and convinced ourselves Luke had already found him. We imagined the two making their way back to Lawsonville with enough extra water for a week. Willy tried to hide the loneliness in his voice as we spoke.

When the sun reached mid-sky, I left Willy alone in the tent and strolled to Greg's office. Before I reached the gate, it opened. Two guards dipped their head as I passed. As before, people marched along the pathways and streets, speaking when spoken to and smiling where appropriate.

A woman approached from the opposite direction. Tufts of curly brown hair bounced against her brow as she walked. We passed, and though she offered the standard Lawsonville smile, her stunning beauty brought it to life.

"Wait!" I fumbled for an intelligent introduction. "My name is Cole."

She stopped, and her eyes darted across the street and back to me. "Heather." I offered my hand, but she pulled away. "You're new here, aren't you?"

"Yeah, a few days. I'm not sure if I'll stay, but..." I stuffed my hands into my pockets.

"Nice to meet you." She pivoted and continued down the street without another word.

I watched until she disappeared around a corner.

"What's on your mind Cole?" Greg's voice caught me by surprise as he walked up behind.

"I...I met a woman."

His eyes probed mine. "Pretty, don't you think?"

"Yes."

"Good. Honesty is among the most valued laws." He furrowed his brow. "Though you certainly violated several rules as you watched her walk away." His expression softened, and he clapped my shoulder. "You'll learn. Just don't let Eric catch you."

"Catch me what? Admiring a pretty woman?"

"Not admiring. Lusting."

"I'm not sure that's what I was doing."

"Maybe. Maybe not. But, even if an action appears inappropriate, we consider it in violation of our rules. Again, a safety measure, put in place to keep our citizens from crossing the line."

"Who decides what is appropriate?" I asked.

A brisk gust of wind whipped through trees sending a handful of leaves tumbling across our path. Greg stopped and watched them before answering. "Our ancestors handed many of their rules down to us—rules they received from their ancestors. Eric and I have modified some to keep current with our time. Occasionally we find the need to expand the list."

"I'm having a hard time understanding how that fights the sickness."

His lips formed a thin smile. "Have you met anyone here who looks sick? We are careful about who we accept into our community. Prospective citizens must be able to maintain a certain appearance. Maintaining a spotless robe or well-groomed hair may seem minor to outsiders, but to us it's everything. We fight the parasite from the outside in."

"And it works?" I asked

"Look around." He spread his arms. "The only way to win the victory is to ensure our community follows the laws we set forth. I would say it works quite well."

"What about Willy? When can he join us?"

Greg didn't move when a misshapen fly landed on his head. The insect stretched its absurdly long front legs as Greg gnawed his bottom lip.

"He can't join us. Some of our leaders believe allowing the ruined into our community will soil our holiness. I feel different, as do others, but we are the minority."

The news should have angered me. A better man would defend his friend, but I wasn't a better man. No guilt. No remorse. No empathy for the ruined boy banned from the community. I simply nodded and asked if he had news of Tick.

"No news, and we're not likely to get any for another week, maybe more. Once or twice a month a traveler stumbles in from the Wastelands and lets us know what is happening out there. If any arrive, I'll let you know if they have information on your friends."

***

I met Greg for lunch every day and learned The Holy Book along with the laws and traditions of Lawsonville. Mornings with Willy, afternoons with Greg. Evenings alone, missing home, my family, New Babylon, and Felica.

Alton had been missing four glorious days when I chose Lawsonville over Willy. The boy sat cross-legged on the dirt floor, twirling his sling. He didn't offer his polite greeting. "Have you received any news about Tick?"

I dropped my hat on the table and pulled out a chair. "No."

He didn't turn to my voice. "When may I speak with Greg or Eric?"

"You can't. They won't see you." I struggled to explain...to ease my guilty conscious. "I tried, so did Greg, but the leaders..." The words wouldn't come, so I lied. "They decided you are too young to be involved in decisions. You can visit but not have close fellowship."

The news didn't seem to bother him, and he lifted himself from the floor. "I saw Vedia last night."

My heart picked up a beat. "Here?"

"By the gate." He felt his way to a chair and sat. "She said you're afraid, sir Cole. Afraid of the truth."

I smacked the table. "What truth?'

He didn't hesitate. "The Physician."

I snatched my hat and shoved it in his face. He was right, but pride fights dirty. "Leave it alone Willy. I found what I was looking for. Everything I've learned fits." I jerked my finger to toward Lawsonville. "Look at it! It works! What they do works! Can't you see? Can't you see anything?"

His expression didn't change. "Sir Cole, please listen to her. This can't be the way."

"What makes you so sure The Physician is?"

He inched toward me; his good arm stretched forward. I waited till he was close and stepped aside. He tilted his head, and though without sight, I know he saw through me. "Listen to yourself, sir Cole. The way taught here can't be truth."

"I suppose you'll tell me why." The words flew sharper than intended.

"I will, if you will listen."

Ashamed, but not to the point of apology, I told him I would.

"You say a parasite infects our blood." He wiggled his crippled arm against his chest. "All of us. Yet, Lawsonville's cure only dresses your flesh. It's like bathing in a cold stream to cure stomach rot."

"So now you know medicine?"

"No, but I know this is wrong. Sir, it's true, I have never met The Physician Vedia speaks of, but her words feel true." He paused and shook his head. "She feels true."

I didn't admit it, not to him, but she did. I wanted to trust her. I wanted to fling myself at her feet and beg she introduce me to The Physician. But I didn't. It sounds absurd, considering the wonders she had shown me, but the parasite's power of deceit is strong.

I changed the subject before I lost my temper. "No one has heard from Alton. I asked Greg, and he asked around town."

"We need to go after Tick." Willy reached for me again.

"Tick is safe! We're talking about Alton!"

Willy spun to walk away and stumbled over a crate of fuzzy bread. Dust flew as he hit the ground. "Sir Cole," he struggled to his feet, "I am leaving tonight with or without you."

"Leaving for where?"

"To find Tick." Willy said.

I laughed. "No, you're not. You can't walk around this tent without falling. How do you expect to survive the Wastelands, much less track him? Even if we went together, it would be impossible. Let Luke handle it. He knows the Heathen. He knows where they camp. Give it time. Luke will find him, and until he does, give this place a chance. These are good people. Their customs might seem strange, but they mean well."

"Are they good people?"

"Give it time, Willy!"

"I'm worried we don't have time, sir Cole."

I stormed away. "I'm through arguing about this. If you don't want to stay in Lawsonville, you and Tick can leave when he gets back." Angry at myself for snapping at Willy and angry at him for making sense, I wanted solitude. "I need air. I'll be back before dark." I hoped Willy wouldn't ask to join me, and he didn't.

I left him alone in the tent, sure he wouldn't leave, but I was wrong. When I returned later, I found his note. Scribbled with care by a boy who could not see, its words tore me apart.

HE IS OUR FRIEND. Willy

I cursed the day I left home and drifted through the night in a constant stupor of Rosewood. I cursed Willy and the Wastelands.

# 35

**I SPENT** the day alone tending to a pounding head and angry guts. Guilt, anger, confusion...the emotions blended as one. More than once I gathered supplies intent on going after Willy. I never made it far.

I tried reading The Holy Book, but its words stirred more rage, so I threw it aside. Food tasted bland. My mind and heart warred to a stalemate. Night came, but sleep wouldn't.

Bored and alone, I grabbed half a dozen Rosewood seeds from my bag, tossed them in my mouth, and waited. First came the nausea, but it passed quickly. I needed to forget, if only for a few hours, and I succeeded. I woke at dawn, naked and lying in the doorway to Luke's tent. Steady blows of pain battered my head to the pulsing rhythm of my heart.

I pulled myself together enough to venture into Lawsonville. People crowded the main street as usual. Men, women, and children strolled into and out of shops. No laughter, few smiles.

An older gentleman, clean shaven and in a hurry, crossed in front of me. I dipped my head in respect. His reaction should have been a warning. No smile, no return nod, no acknowledgment.

A plump woman corralling two rambunctious children approached from the opposite direction. Our eyes met and she spun, grabbed the children's arms, and drug them across the street, away from me. She glanced once over her shoulder and hustled the boy and girl away.

A young woman with fiery red hair, an elderly couple sitting on a bench, a group of young men standing outside the food dispensary; none acknowledged my existence except for an occasional look of contempt. What had changed? I focused on the night before. A handful of seeds, nausea, overwhelming sadness...not like the euphoria I experienced in New Babylon. My recollection of the night ended there. Me standing outside Luke's tent, looking toward the desolate Wastelands, then to the secure gates of Lawsonville. One offered the hope of finding my friends and probable death, the other, the hope of truth and security. I don't remember how long I stood there. The seeds had gained control, and time dissolved into a meaningless theory. I knew nothing else until I opened my eyes to blinding rays of sun the next morning.

I neared the center square and heard my name from behind.

"Cole!"

Greg and Eric walked briskly in my direction.

"We need to talk." Greg reached me first. His face ashen and drawn. "We need to talk now."

Eric didn't speak.

"I was on my way to see you," I said.

"There's been a report."

"About Tick? Has Luke found him? Or Willy? He left yesterday."

Greg's brow wrinkled in a look of surprise, but he didn't respond. Eric prompted him with a hard scowl.

"No. No news about your friend...either of them. Now please, if we can speak privately in my office." He motioned in the direction of his building.

We walked in silence, Greg to my left and Eric to my right. Flashes from the previous night rolled through my mind. Silent streets...standing in front of the gathering hall...crying as I snatched a robe from the messy room inside...drying my eyes with that same white robe and using it as a blanket from the cold.

Eric mounted the steps first and unlocked the door. I followed Greg into his office.

"Do you want to tell us about your incident last night?" Greg asked.

"I don't remember last night. I took medicine for my shoulder and..." And what? I threw up my hands.

Eric started to speak, but Greg stopped him.

"Cole, last night you came into the city and created a situation."

Eric sprang to his feet. "You profaned the purity of Lawsonville!" He slammed the chair with his fist. "That is what he did, Greg! He defiled the law!"

"Calm down. Let me handle this."

Eric huffed but sat.

"Cole, last night several men witnessed you wandering the streets in a robe. They claim..." He paused and glanced to Eric.

"Go ahead. Tell me what they claim."

"They claim you accosted them and blasphemed our laws."

Eric jumped from his seat and shot me a look saturated with hate. "I'll make it very clear! You wore a robe of righteousness without our consent! We have laws for a reason." He took a breath and lowered his voice.

"Otherwise, we risk the parasite returning to our community."

I waited for him to continue, and when he didn't, I burst into laughter. "You're yelling at me because I tried on one of your robes?"

"You still don't understand, do you? It wasn't just about the robe." Eric sat. "Cole, you came here for a cure. You came because you know you are sick. Yet, we show you how to make yourself well, and you refuse to listen." He raised a finger. "Which violates another law, might I add."

Greg cast a pleading glance. "Eric, please."

"Very well. You know how I feel."

"Thank you." The relief was evident on Greg's face. "You are new here. It takes time, as we've discussed before, but eventually you need to give in to the truth. Our laws serve a purpose, and not just for a single person. They ensure the purity of our community as a whole. They protect the testimony of our city. They guard the reputation of our people.

"But, the single most important reason you should conform, is because of the truth you seek. The only way to drive out the parasite is to obey the rules set forth by the Creator."

Eric interrupted. "And the only way to accomplish that is to follow the rules of Lawsonville."

Greg obliged a nod and continued. "Yes, our rules also."

Absurd rules. Impossible laws. Beauty and order on the outside, sickness and rot from within. I thought of the way they treated Luke...the way they had treated Willy. I thought of the girl and her words. "You feel the parasite when I'm near because it rages against my presence," she had said. I believed her. I also wondered how many in Lawsonville had ever experienced the rage she spoke of. My guess was few.

I stood and dipped my chin. "Thank you for the kindness, but it's time I leave."

"Leave? Why would you want to leave?" Greg sounded genuinely hurt. "We're not casting you away. We're trying to save you, so the Creator doesn't cast you away forever."

"If he hasn't already." Eric said it under his breath, but I heard.

"I'm sorry. I really am, but I'm going after my friends."

"Is that the only reason you're abandoning our community?" Eric asked.

"No. I've tried to follow the rules, attend every gathering, think only pure thoughts, and you know what? I can't. No one can. Underneath the perfect image you've created here, we're all the same. I'm sorry, but if this is truth, I don't want it."

Eric smirked. "Don't apologize to us. Apologize to the Creator."

"Shut up." Greg spun. "This is why we lose so many. You and your mouth."

Eric raised his hands in mock surrender. "It's the truth."

"If it's truth, so be it. I can't do it. I'm done. I'm going to find my friends," I said.

Greg ran a hand through tousled hair and walked to the window. "We'll see you off with rations for a week."

"No," Eric interjected.

Greg growled. "Yes. He gets supplies, same as any we turn out."

Eric flinched, but held Greg's stare. "We turn him out then. We can use his indiscretion last night as a learning opportunity for the others. We can send a strong message that flagrant disregard for our laws will not be tolerated."

Greg looked to me.

"I don't care." I said. And I didn't. I wanted to believe that following their laws would lead to a cure, but belief meant I would spend my life scrubbing a white robe and pretending nothing unclean existed inside those walls. I couldn't do that. Not after the words of Vedia, The Holy Book, and Charles the Outrider.

"Splendid." Eric dipped his head. "I'll spread the news and return for you shortly." He left without another word.

Greg shook his head and sighed. "You don't have to go along with this charade. I'll give you the food."

"Like you did Luke?" I asked.

He smiled but didn't look at me. "You know about our arrangement?"

"Why? Why show kindness in secret?"

He studied his hands before he answered. "We trust in law. It exposes the parasite and heals our bodies from its effects. Kindness, however, is deceptive. Its motives are often misconstrued...or worse, interpreted correctly. Rarely does a person act without expecting something in return."

"Did you?"

Eric stuck his head in the room before Greg answered. "It's time we conclude our chat and get to the gate. People are anxious to get on with their chores."

Greg and Eric marched me through the streets. It hurt, losing hope, and I debated if I was doing the right thing...leaving. What was on the other side of the gate? Nothing but death and the friends I had abandoned.

\*\*\*

Citizens jeered as we walked toward the gate. We pushed through a group of young men, all primly outfitted with clean robes. Three of them held assorted decayed fruits and snickered as we passed. Greg stopped, and the guard handed him a box: two canisters of water, several ears of corn, and two worm ridden apples. I took it as he leaned in and whispered. "It's enough for four days. I added corn and extra water."

He addressed the gathering. "Citizens of Lawsonville, today we turn our back on Cole Creek." A cheer rose when a hail of the rotten fruit smacked me in the chest and head. Greg waited until the uproar died before continuing. "As a visitor, his contempt for our ways jeopardize our safety. According to our laws, he must be separated from us." With a loud click the gate opened, and I was thrust out. Utter desolation lay before me—miles of cracked earth and loneliness.

I didn't find Willy and Tick in the Wastelands. I wish I could claim I truly searched but that would be a lie. My intentions were honorable. My willpower was weak. I did what I always had—thought only of myself, chased pleasure, and succumbed to enticing lies.

The parasite's influence is strong...stronger than any of us.

# 36

**OUTSIDE THE** gate, I salvaged a day's worth of supplies from Luke's tent, giving me five, and traveled south for a day before turning east into the Wastelands. According to Greg, several towns and villages dotted the border in that area, some welcoming like Lawsonville; some hostile; but all offered food and water for a price.

I walked for hours with nothing but my own imagination for company. My seeds called to me...reminded me of the escape they offered, but I forced myself to ignore them. I feared they would take me on a journey from which my splintered mind would never return.

On the third day into the Wastelands, I stumbled over a piece of ancient metal, hidden beneath centuries of dust. The last of my water spilled, and the earth greedily drank it down. I considered making my way back to Lawsonville, but opted to press forward, and let the Wastelands take me if it was their will. Blisters rose in angry swells on my feet, screaming curses with every step. My legs moved by sheer will. One step, then another. One step. Another. I didn't stop. I didn't rest. I plunged deeper and deeper into the Wastelands.

The fourth day my blisters broke open. I know because dampness seeped through my sock. An hour-long conversation with the scorching sun ended when my tongue stuck to the roof of my mouth. I had begged it to relent, to ease behind a cloud and leave me in peace. It laughed and grew hotter.

The fifth day, I fell to my knees and cried dry sobs. I was going to die in the Wastelands and didn't care. I pulled the Rosewood from my pocket, laid on my back, and brought them to my lips. Dying might not hurt if you didn't know you were dying. I popped them in my mouth and tried to swallow. They stuck to my tongue, refusing to slide down my throat. I considered chewing, then fished them out with my fingers. I couldn't work up enough saliva to spit.

I struggled to my feet and walked.

***

**B**irds circled the distant sky as I stumbled along a steep path down the ridge. Loose rock and dried earth threatened to carry me over the edge. I made the mistake of glancing down, and jagged stones greeted me from below, begging for company. Drowning in despair, I almost accepted their invitation.

I descended and briefly lost sight of the scavengers circling above. Near the bottom and around a sharp bend, they reappeared along with their meal.

The corpse was too small to be Willy. A host of buzzards crowded around the lifeless form, pecking it and each other. Dust obscured details, but it was a man.

The scavengers scattered as I approached. Missing most of his face, a dirty white handle jutted from the man's neck. I knelt beside the form and studied a dark patch of earth beneath the body. It wasn't Tick, but I knew the man that blood once belonged to. A clean slice extended from Luke's ear, across his throat, and out of sight.

I ran my fingers along the handle of Alton's knife and jerked away. It felt like bone, not smooth ivory. Indecipherable markings and symbols rose from its sides. Luke's writing board lay beside his lifeless body. The message, addressed to me, was signed by Alton.

"The only way is death."

\*\*\*

**I** dry chewed three Rosewood seeds, sat under the stars, and waited to die. The twinkling lights patiently listened to me rail against the injustice of Lawsonville and curse the misery of my infected body and mind. They watched me threaten the Creator with Alton's blade. They comforted me as I cried over Willy and Tick and counseled me about the truth I no longer wanted to believe.

Sharp steel pricked my skin and opened a cut on my palm. Small drops of blood trickled down my wrist, and I moved the blade to my other hand. Rosewood numbed the sting of another shallow slice. Did each drop carry the parasite? Would deeper cuts rid it from my body? Was that the message Alton left? No option but death? I flicked my palm over the fire and imagined the parasite screaming in agony as the flames consumed drops of infected blood. It deserved to writhe in agony. It deserved the fire.

Felicia's familiar voice drifted through dead air. "Cole, my love. Maybe it's all truth. Or, maybe there is no truth."

I focused on clearing my head. She wasn't there. My only companionship was the lifeless tree thirty paces from my campfire. I had never encountered one, but the tree told me it was a Rosewood. Birds covered its barren limbs like black leaves rustling in a fall wind. Beyond, cracked earth of the Wastelands stretched as far as the moon's dim light allowed.

"Felicia?"

"Yes?" From a different direction…above, between the stars. "Up here."

The seeds. I closed my eyes tight and concentrated on fighting the hallucination, but it didn't help. "The girl, The Holy Book, the Outrider," I mumbled.

A cool breeze passed close beside me. "Shh. You think too much." The air grew warm and crossed my lips. "What does your body say? You want so much to believe, you ignore your flesh."

"What do you mean?"

"Does your body tell you you're sick? Are you weak or burning with fever?"

"No," I told Felica's voice.

"Does your skin show signs of disease?"

"No."

"You don't sound sick. You don't look sick. You don't act sick." Her invisible touch traced a line down my face. "Follow your instinct, and you'll find happiness."

The words danced in my ears, and I wanted to believe. Dying men grasp at lies of hope if given the opportunity. "There's nothing more?" I looked to the stars when I spoke the words aloud.

"What else is there but mind and body?" Soft kisses skipped along my neck. "Cole, my darling, your body is well, but your mind is sick. Which should you trust?"

"I think I trust the girl." I hadn't intended on saying it aloud, but Felicia's voice didn't anger.

"Don't you trust me?" Sweet, warm breath caressed my ear.

"No." I fought the urge to taste lips that didn't exist. "But if you met her, I think you would see. She could explain truth. We could learn together. We could heal together."

Her voice moved away, and I opened my eyes. She and the desolate Rosewood tree were one. Dozens of birds dipped their heads in unison as she spoke. "Healed from what? Love? Passion? Pleasure?" Condemning yellow eyes opened along twisted branches as her bare shoulders swayed in cadence with the constant rumble of distant thunder from the direction of Lawsonville.

The horrific vision enthralled me. If I ran to the tree, it would devour me. If I fled, I would destroy myself for rejecting its embrace. Lightning sparked the black sky with her last words. "Do you trust me, Cole?"

# 37

**THOUGH I'D** rationed, I ran out of food the next day. Worse, only two Rosewood seeds remained. Twice I held Alton's blade to my throat. Twice I threw it aside and cried.

Sometime after dusk, I surrendered to the Wastelands. Determined to numb the sting of death, I savored the bitter aftertaste of my last two seeds. I hoped Felicia would return to see me one last time. In death, a hallucination would be better than loneliness and self-loathing. I let the seeds work and called her name.

"Felicia."

Silence. Not even a soft wind called back. The only sound was a dull thud as my heart spread the sickness with every beat. I pressed Alton's blade to my throat and cried out one last time.

"Felicia!"

From behind, a voice called my name. "Cole, my boy." Alton emerged from the darkness; his arms spread wide. "Why couldn't you have listened? Why did it have to come to this?" Susan's pendant dangled from his neck. He stroked the chain with his finger and sneered. "I chatted with Luke about it before I drained his blood. Emotional fellow. I don't think he liked me wearing it. I wish he could have told me what was on his mind. It always amuses me what Outriders say right before the end."

In my heart, I knew. Alton played the savior, but as a master of games, he hid his true motives until necessary to reveal them. I thought back to Grandview and the Dead Trees. How he marveled at the hanging Outrider—his look of wondrous joy. I remembered arguments about the girl and his contempt of Willy and Tick. He led me to New Babylon. He led me to the Wastelands. He led me to Lawsonville. He led, and I followed.

I tried to stand, but my head swam under the influence of Rosewood. He patted my shoulder and eased to the ground across the fire. "What to do? What to do?" Alton leaned forward and rested his chin in his hands.

"You're not real." My thoughts came faster than my lips moved.

"But I am. I'm as real as Felicia, the one you chose over your friends. I'm as real as the merchant who sold you Rosewood. Time and time again, I saved you...gave you countless opportunities to embrace my generosity. I hoped you would listen because I like you. I really do, but how do you believe this will end? I'm running out of patience. If you refuse to accept my counsel, I can't save you."

"Save me from what?"

He looked surprised. "From yourself. What else? You're dying Cole. Either your body, your mind, or both. Here you are, days from food or water, exhausted from heat and losing your sanity." No dust stirred when he moved to sit beside me. He picked up his blade and slid it into my hand. "Your parasite is fatal. Now that you've discovered its existence, your only options are to let it eat you alive from the inside or allow it to destroy your mind." His cracked lips curled into a thin smile. "Unless you've thought of another way."

I clinched my fingers tight around the sharp blade and didn't feel pain. Warmth trickled down my wrist. I considered flicking my blood into the fire, listening for the parasite's scream, but wiped it on my leg instead.

Alton sighed and lifted his head to the moon. "Did you know it hasn't rained in the Wastelands for a decade? And before that, eight summers." A puff of breath flowed from his lips, and when it did, thunder growled from the horizon. Angry clouds rolled from the sound and swallowed stars one by one. "And before that, I waited seventeen years before I allowed a drop to fall. Lawsonville and villages north and south? Yes. But not the Wastelands."

Clouds drifted across the moon, leaving only our small fire for light. Alton still gazed into the heavens. "Never too much rain here though. Do you know why?" He flipped me a glance then turned away. "Of course you don't. I give enough rain so the Heathen experience the joy and refreshment unearned water brings. They didn't negotiate it from travelers or trade for it from a village. My joy comes when the final raindrop falls. It's always an exhilarating moment when the Wastelands swallow that last drop of water; to see their hope rise then crash. The power to give and withhold life is true power. Besides, if I offered blessing without restraint, they would never appreciate my grace." A deep laugh rumbled from his chest.

Silent rain pecked my naked arms. Drops fell without a sound except for an occasional sizzle as some disappeared into the flames and died an imperceptible vapor. I envied them. No pain. No confusion. No despair, birthed by countless moments of shattered hope. The drops endured a simple fall from the heavens, into the oblivion of a slowly dying fire.

Alton stood and stretched his back. "It didn't have to end this way for you."

I held the blade to my wrist. I wanted it gone. If its death meant mine, then so be it.

"Can't think of anything to say?" Alton pointed south and lightning crashed. The dead Rosewood tree emerged in its flash. Felicia turned her naked shoulders and faced me. The branches' yellow eyes opened wide and stared unblinking. Her...its...hideous beauty intoxicated me. I gazed at the figure; no longer certain I was hallucinating.

"I know you don't understand, and that's okay. This entire drama is beyond your comprehension," Alton said.

Water or tears splashed the blade as I touched it to my skin. This time the cut would sink deep when I opened an escape for the parasite.

"It's not so hard to believe, is it? You trusting me, I mean." A rattled laugh escaped him. "You've trusted many of my kind in our time together. Tick sensed me, and the ruined one, he might have known the whole time. I spent many nights arguing with my counsel on how best to remove him from the battle." He wiped a line of drool from the corner of his mouth. "You were easy, my boy."

"I'm waiting for you, Cole." Felicia's voice called from the darkness.

Alton took my chin and lifted it to meet his eyes. "Free it from your body. Death is the only cure. Go to her."

Pain tore through me as I pierced my wrist. Familiar pain, not like a blade, but of the parasite. The peculiar sensation of holiness washed over me before I saw her. Vedia had come for me.

Time stopped. Rain froze mid-air. A glowing ember, which had escaped from the ashes, hung inches from the ground. Perfect peace in the midst of anguish. Locks of hair shielded her eyes, but I felt them on me. Raindrops parted in worship as she walked. Pure, beautiful, Holy. I fell forward, face first at her feet. "Why do you keep leaving?"

Her smile devastated the night. "Cole, my love. I have never left since you first heard my call." She pulled me to my knees. "Do you want to see the truth?"

Unable to speak, I nodded. Whirlwinds of fire stormed in her eyes, and she faded into a blue mist. Alton was no longer the aged man I despised. I knew instantly what I was looking at. Surrounding my camp, a hundred more creatures cowered like stone statues; captured in a timeless state of frozen terror.

"Shadows," Vedia said. "They fought hard for you." Her presence, Her majesty, paralyzed every muscle. I wanted to embrace her. I wanted to run from her.

She lifted my chin and wonderful bursts of power radiated through my body. "They serve darkness and its master."

Her words trampled my mind.

"It is part of the truth you seek...a war you are not ready to comprehend."

"War?"

"The Serpent rules in darkness, and Shadows war against the light under his banner. They thrive on the infected and fight to nurture the parasite. Few villages understand this truth, and those that do are in danger. Much like the parasite, Shadows succeed best when dismissed as myth and allowed to fight in obscurity."

Flashes of heat sparked in her eyes. "Shadows are born in darkness.

"My servants, spoken of as Outriders in this age, travel the earth warning people of the parasite, proclaiming the cure, and teaching of the war. The Serpent's Shadows fight to keep the truth hidden because when light encounters darkness, darkness must flee. Pure light vanquishes shadows. Shadows fight out of rage, and hate. They fight to maintain their kingdom."

"Are you The Physician?"

Her voice remained constant as the blue mist changed forms in front of me. "I am fire...I am wind... I am the dove and the One who comforts." The misty form of a little girl reappeared. "I am the One who draws, and the One who teaches."

The Holy Book's words pierced my heart and thundered through my bones. Every conversation with Charles, every encounter with the girl, flooded my memory. Draw nigh unto God, and He'll draw nigh unto you.

Pain shot through my legs and up my chest as the parasite wreaked havoc with my blood. I felt its darkness as it writhed in my veins. I needed healing, not just my mind, but my blood—the source of life.

I cried out for The Physician.

Without warning, her form exploded into fingers of lightning. I fell to my face, certain I had spoken my last words. Above, the air crackled with heat and energy. The sensation sent chills along my arms and neck. Even through closed eyes, brilliant bursts of light threatened to blind me. Then it was over. No screams or pleas. Total silence.

A soft hand touched my face. Afraid to look, I spoke into darkness. "Take me to him. Take me to The Physician."

"Open your eyes." Her tender voice carried more power than I imagined existed in all the earth. "Open and see."

Alton lay dead, smoke drifting from his charred body in lazy wisps. Susan's gold pendant with the symbol of an Outrider lay in a circle of blackened earth.

Instead of Shadows, brilliant beings filled the valley. Some circled overhead carried by wings as broad as a man. Sunlight sparkled from each, creating a glistening sea of diamonds in the sky above the Wastelands. I'll never forget the sight. Hundreds of magnificent creatures sang in unison, and though I didn't understand the language, their words spoke truth to my heart.

"Cole, my beloved." I spun to a man's voice. It was Him. The Physician had come to me.

# 38

**THAT WAS** three weeks ago, and I'm a new man. The small village I've called home for the past twenty-one days is Hopewell: Luke and Susan's old village. Hopewell lies somewhere on the southwestern edge of the Wastelands. The people, all followers of The Physician and friends of Outriders, have cared for me, taught me, and loved me. Charles, the Outrider who prompted my journey, has not left my side. I fought to leave—to search for my friends, but my nurse assured me I would die if I ventured into the Wastelands without rest.

Yesterday, an Outrider came into Hopewell for rest. He had passed a Heathen camp two days outside Lawsonville and saw a young boy with a severely deformed arm. He was alone and dared not venture close, but the vague description he gave was enough for me to know he was talking about Willy. I questioned him about every detail. He described a man that fit Tick's description. He assured me they seemed well. My tears flowed when he told me he saw the boy laugh. I pray I find them soon. They need truth, and I need them.

I still crave Rosewood. It's a secret I've kept from Charles and the others. I know the deceit is wrong, but the shame of addiction is powerful. Here, in the safe confines of a village dedicated to The Physician, the temptation calls from far away. Eventually, access to the seeds will be easier. I'm not certain how I will respond when the temptation finds me.

Also, Felica haunts my dreams. Two nights ago, a sound startled me from sleep, and I smelled her perfume beside my bed. For a moment, the thought that she was near exhilarated me. I lit my torch to an empty room and whispered her name. She didn't reply, and I spent the rest of the night reading The Holy Book, trying to erase her from my memory. My addiction to her has not faded.

I don't understand much that happened to me in my time with The Physician, but I know the nature of the parasite I carry. I know its deceit and destructive personality. I know its origin and objective. Most importantly though, I know the cure. I haven't comprehended how the process of my healing worked, but I hope to learn more. Charles told me the Who is more important than the how. I believe him. I trust The Physician is the truth I sought for so long.

I don't know when I'll see Bethman again, but when I find Willy and Tick, I'm going home. I miss my family. They need to know my story...Who I met.

The Physician is still a mystery in many ways. So is The Girl. Their nature is beyond my comprehension. However, I'm learning. Charles has taught me much—The Holy Book has taught me more. I know the way to life and will spend the rest of my days proclaiming the truth. I go to my family and friends. I go to them as a neighbor, a brother, and a son. I go to them as an Outrider.

My testimony for His Glory,
Cole Creek

# Author's Note

Dear Reader,

I hope you enjoyed Parasite. It was a difficult book to write, but I thoroughly enjoyed the process. Tick was by far the easiest character to put on paper. Not sure what that says about me, but I think he's an alright guy. He reminds me of someone I'd spend a Saturday afternoon grilling burgers with and drinking sweet tea. I can't wait to see Cole reunited with him and Little Man. The Heathen are certainly not the friendliest of people, but I was encouraged by the report of Willy smiling and laughing. I think they'll be okay.

I worry about Cole. He met the Physician, but I have a feeling his battles are just beginning. That's the way it is though isn't it? That's when those "fiery darts" really start to rain down. Paul understood it when he wrote to the church at Ephesus and told them to take the shield of faith. It's a powerful thing.

For His Glory,
Jason Parrish

# WORDSLINGER

From A Piper's Song Short Story Collection

With bonus, Last Confessions and Introduction to A Piper's Song

## Jason Parrish

Copyright © 2019 Jason Parrish

East Star Publishing, 2019

# WORDSLINGER

**M**arvin Blick never knew about the tumor that didn't kill him. Only two more months until the nasty little trespasser fingered its way to the base of his skull and flicked the right cell, shutting Mr. Blick's lights off permanently. No need for the drama though, Marv handled the final chapter himself. For eleven months he chalked the nightly headaches up to stress and blamed the hallucinations on sleep deprivation. Even in his last moments, when he had a change of heart, he doubted what he saw and heard. He dreamed of writing a best-selling western novel and poured himself into The Slinger's Revenge, his one shot at infamy. Yes, Marv the middle-age middle-child. Filled with anger and mild with rage but can't fight or write a readable page. Middle Marv this, middle Marv that, Middle Marv the Wordslinger. Marvin Blick got the middle finger. His attention span also shortened as the cancer that would have killed him slunk towards the switch at the base of his brain…

"Marvin? Marvin! Do you understand? You got three months to prove you're worth what we pay you. I'm done trying to get through to you." Stanley Newton leaned across his solid oak desk and beckoned Marv close. "Off the record, here's where I am. I want you gone. HR says I have to follow protocol; verbal warnings, written warnings, reviews, meetings like this." The plush leather chair took it without complaint as all three-hundred pounds of Newton Steel's VP of Manufacturing plopped back. "It's not that you're bad at what you do, but you bring absolutely no value. None." Stanley cracked the top on a diet soda and sipped. "Do you know what an Oxpecker is?"

Marvin Blick did not like Stanley Bear Newton, and he'd never heard of an Oxpecker. Marv grew up poor and knew it. Kids like Stanley Newton reminded him every day. For three years at Longview High, Bear reminded. Sophomore year... "Marvin, do you know what a wedgie is?" Junior year... "Hey Marvin, why do you smell like cat piss?" Senior year...

"Marvin! Look at me! Oxpecker?"

"No, I've never heard of it."

"I'll tell you. It's a bird that lives in a beautiful symbiotic relationship with some animals, like the Black Rhinoceros. Do you know what that means?" Stanley slowed and hit all four syllables, "Sym-bi-o-tic?"

Marvin knew. Not because of the science, but the language. The interaction between two different organisms living in close proximity. Symbiotic. A bird and Rhino, fungi and roots, writer and reader.

"Do you know, Marvin?" Marvin nodded, but Stanley regurgitated the definition anyway.

"Which are you Marv? The bird or the Rhino?"

"I assume I'm the bird."

"You assume wrong. You are neither to me. I am the Rhino, but you provide no value to this company, my bank account, my business life, or my personal life. So, you can't be the bird. You're the irritating litle tick gorging yourself on the rhino's blood. Symbiotically attached but not mutually beneficial." A sneaky diet soda burp slipped into Bear's monologue, but he recovered without apology. "The little parasites drink Rhino blood which irritates the Rhino, but Oxpeckers like to eat little parasites. The only loser is the tick, and that's you Marvin, a tick." He took another sip, "and a loser." Stanley finished his drink and trashed it.

He stood and four strides later reached the far wall. A large oak-framed aerial view of the factory grounds hid Bear's safe. The forty-two-year-old accounts payable clerk wanted to vomit all over the family fortune and the treasure it protected.

Three medals hung from Bear's paws, all with the same style ribbon, same shade of gold. Not Olympic but still impressive. Three medals he'd won twenty years ago in Track and Field. State? Regionals? Marvin couldn't remember and didn't care. Bear didn't always use them as props, but the speech stayed consistent over the years.

Problems at home? Suck it up. Be a man. Bear threw a discus over two-hundred and two feet with a broken finger. Having trouble keeping up with those young bucks Marv? That bald spot got you feeling impotent? Bear chucked a shot put sixty feet after a dozen bad egg rolls. Spent three hours hunched over a toilet before the meet and still won this baby. Overcome Marvin.

"At least pretend to be a man." Stanley dangled the medals inches from Marvin's nose, "or you will never have anything." He motioned to the door before dropping the gold onto his desk. "Get out of my office."

And that was it, freedom...almost.

"One more thing Blick. The Christmas party this year is plus one. Good profit last quarter so we're renting the back room at Ruby's Smokehouse out on twenty-seven. Bring Jill. Can't wait to finally meet her." Stanley shooed him away and buried his face in a file.

Marvin fled to the hall without looking back. He would never let Jill meet an animal like Stanley.

Al the janitor met Marvin outside his office. Of the sixty-seven current full-time employees of Newton Steel, Al was Marv's favorite. If he was honest with himself, no one else in his life made much sense.

"Get another pep talk?" Al blocked Marv's path. "If I was thirty years younger," the old man's eyes disappeared into a wrinkle line, "you know what I'd do with those medals?"

"He's in a bad mood today."

Al nodded. "How's the book coming?"

The Slinger's Revenge, Marvin Blick's first serious attempt at a novel. "Have a couple of changes to work through but no sweat. It's a winner."

Al smacked Marvin in the jaw. Smacked. Open palm. Stiff finger. The younger man froze, and Al the janitor came across for another whack. "You're an idiot."

The fight instinct existed only in Marvin Blick's alter ego from The Slinger's Revenge, Roland Slick, a rugged cowboy, con-man, gambler (the emphasis of each changed through various rewrites) in 1870's Kansas. The Marv Blick in 21st century Georgia always opted for flight and without a word slipped past Al into the safety of his office.

The janitor followed and plopped into the padded chair across the desk. "You'll thank me later."

Marvin jiggled his mouse, chasing Jill's picture from the screen. His face stung. Not bad, but enough for a single tear to slip, hopefully unseen, out of the corner of his eye.

"Aren't you going to call me a summabitch or something as equally charming?" Al's playful tone masked a dark side Marv knew well, "at least give me the finger. You know, flick me the bird." Al shoved his middle finger at Marv's face.

Marvin pushed it away. "I'm not in the mood today." The headache that pecked at his crown in Stan's office now snaked its way down his neck.

Al nodded and relaxed back into his chair. "You angry with me?"

"What?"

"Are you mad? Are you filled with rage? Do you wish violence on me or someone else? Answer the question Marv!"

Marvin flung the mouse. "Why did you hit me?" His outburst fizzled when its cord caught the tower and smacked the baseboard.

Al smiled. "Mother smacked me three or four times a week when I really needed to listen." The smile disappeared. "Strike a match to the hate and watch it burn. Fuel your anger. Go home and write. Use it to bring cardboard to life." Al cackled and moved towards the door. "Your book is not going well. Seven, yes count them young Marvin, seven complete rewrites, no character arcs, multiple continuity chaos from the rewrites, but here's the best part Marv, all by hand. Computers can't be that expensive."

"How? I mean, you?" But Al was gone.

Marv rubbed his jaw. The old man's wisdom always came with a price.

***

Marv flicked the light of his one-bedroom apartment, passed the window that looked out over Phil's Primetime Pizza and his mouth watered. In a couple of weeks, he'd take the twenty dollars he put aside every other paycheck and head across the street for an evening out. A treat he allowed during even the leanest of times.

A quick pass through the fridge, another through the pantry, and Marvin had his night's writing fuel. Two slices of thick cut bologna (the kind with fancy red paper around the edge), eight fresh saltines, and a bottle of yellow mustard.

Background bar fights from Channel 7's twenty-four-hour Eastwood marathon would help quiet any lingering echoes of the day's meeting with Bear. The scripted chaos calmed him. Clint's voice guided him through a tough scene edit just last week. Four hours of reading, scratching out, scribbling, re-reading, more scratching. Exhausting work but he didn't mind.

Jill strolled into the kitchen and made a beeline to her bowl by the closet door.

"Hungry, girl?" Marv unloaded his supper onto the table and grabbed a fresh can of tuna from Jill's cabinet. He butt-bumped the fridge door, popped the can, and sat the tuna on the floor.

The three-year-old Tortie sashayed to the smell and chirped her disdain. Marv used a fork to cut the lunchmeat into cracker sized squares, lining each with three yellow squirts. He grabbed a bottle of warm water from the pantry and set up camp in front of the TV.

Twenty-minutes. No more. Enough time to eat and take in some good lines. Maybe something he could use, not copy, an idea. That's all he needed. An idea.

Jill swatted the half-empty can, watched it clink across the checkered linoleum floor, then vanished after it into the living room. Not to eat. She hadn't finished a full can of tuna in months. Months of worry, vet visits, and tests.

Dr. Murray still hadn't called with the latest round of lab results. Blood work this time. X-Rays last month. Pills, shots, special food...the kind you can't find on aisle 11.

He refocused on Clint's voice. He watched and learned.

Thirty minutes later Marvin moved to the kitchen and deposited his empty plate into the sink. Time to write. He massaged the finger shaped bruise under his left eye. Al was right. Maybe what he felt wasn't rage, but something deep within him stirred in Bear's office that morning.

At 8 PM Marvin Blick's little apartment went dark, and he remembered the power bill. In shadows cast by small town streetlights, Marv didn't stop writing. The something that once stirred opened its eyes, and Marv wrote well in the darkness.

***

"I told you." Al kicked back in the little padded chair across from Marvin. "Best writing you've ever slung, right?"

Right. Words flew into beautiful lines of prose. Sentences lined up into solid paragraphs which, in turn, formed fertile plots of story. If Roland Slick didn't need electricity, neither did Marvin Blick.

"Marv! Pay attention." The chair's front two legs slammed onto the concrete floor. "Tell me about it."

Marvin's email dinged. Bear's secretary. He fought the urge to open it. "I don't know. It just felt good. I finished the scene."

Al scooted a few inches closer to Marvin's desk. Metal on concrete. Not a pleasant sound for someone with headaches like Marv. "No, no, no." The old man's eyes twinkled. "What did you write? Details my friend."

Another email, this one from Emily, Human Resources Manager. The momentary thought of her sparked a dim memory from childhood. Pleasant. Safe. Secure. Real? He didn't know but also found it didn't matter.

"Marvin!" Al smacked the top of the desk. "Tell me about the scene."

"The scene. It was great. Buck," he paused. "You remember him?"

Buck Anderson, Roland's latest antagonist, one of many depending on the draft, living their fifteen minutes of fame through Marvin's head, all rolling through the same plot.

Al twirled his finger. "Get going."

"Anyway, Roland figured it out. He could never beat him, right?" Marv's tempo picked up steam. "In poker I mean. Roland could never take Buck over enough hands. Once I figured that out, it was easy. Roland used a prostitute to distract Buck and take his gold. Left him a sweet gift in its place. You see, Roland was never meant to play cards for a living. He was a con, and cons don't come in just one shape and size, do they?" Marvin didn't wait for a response. "Anyway, Ro-"

The phone interrupted. He reached, pulled back, then jerked the receiver to his ear. "Blick."

"My office." No roar. No growl.

***

"What the hell is this?" Gooey brown chunks oozed through Bear's considerable clinched fists. "Just what the hell is this?"

"Stanley." Emily's voice floated from the corner. "Have a seat please."

Her posture relaxed once Bear settled into his chair. "Marvin, Stanley has accused you of stealing his medals and replacing them with chocolate replicas."

"What!?"

"She said-"

"Marvin," a controlled, formal kindness in her voice, "someone broke into Stanley's safe and replaced his gold medals with chocolates wrapped in gold colored foil. Halloween candy."

"Not someone!" Bear rose out of his chair.

"Stanley, do I need to remind you that I report to the Board, not you?" Emily's question dropped him back into his seat.

She pivoted to Marvin. "Stanley believes it's you, so I have to ask. If it was, tell us now, give the medals back, and it's forgiven." She shifted her attention to Bear. "Forgiven. Isn't that right Stan?"

Bear grunted his agreement.

"Did you take them?"

"Of course not. I went home yesterday, watched T.V., and wrote. That's it. Wrote until I passed out."

"Wrote?" Emily's voice perked. "What do you write? You know we're looking for an assistant in marketing."

"Westerns. I write western novels." He padded the truth.

Chocolates. Candy. The moisture in Marv's mouth thickened. His scene was not a perfect copy, more of an old sepia tone photo of the digital original. The details look a tad different, but you get the picture.

Deep inside Marvin's dying brain he wanted to laugh, and for the first time in months, he almost did. Instead, when his mouth opened, a partially digested, though hefty portion of the previous night's fancy bologna feast escaped onto Bear's desk...mostly. Emily, an innocent bystander, took a few small chunks to the arm and cheek.

His last memory of the workday was her telling him he should go home. Maybe for a few days. She worried about him driving, but he convinced her he was fine. How? He had no idea, but Al joined the conversation at some point.

***

"Do you think it was him?" Jill rubbed Marv's calf as she slithered through his legs.

He'd napped several hours, an unfruitful exercise considering the dull ache at the back of his neck and throb behind his eyes.

Al had access to every office, closet, and bathroom in the building. How he cracked the safe's code was a mystery, but who knew what Newton family secrets the old janitor uncovered in the company trash?

Jill slid another round through Marv's calves and purred. "Yep, it had to be Al." She chirped in agreement, hopped onto the counter, and sat. "But I didn't tell him about the scene, did I?" Jill licked her paw without answering.

After four rewrites Marvin had not crafted a plausible scene in which Roland beat Buck at the card table. Nothing worked...until he realized the goal was simply to take the gold. His hero, Roland Slick, could do it any way he pleased. A con was a con whether at the card table, the boardroom, or in the bedroom. Roland opted for the bedroom and hired a friendly lady escort to help pull it off. Miss Samantha kept Buck occupied while Roland made the switch. A pile of yellow penny candy for Buck's gold. Not chocolates but still goosebump irony. Marvin loved it.

Jill broke his daze with a short cry for attention. Marv grabbed her bowl and held it under the faucet. Nothing. He'd pay Longview Sewer and Water after the power company got theirs.

"We'll figure it out girl. There's water in the toilet for now."

Jill hopped from the counter and exited down the hall. Seconds later, a high-pitched meow wormed its way through his ear canal and married itself to the now never-ending throb living in the base of his skull. Jill called out again, this time a deep long plea. The toilet lid. Marvin grabbed a handful of candles and a box of matches. Tonight's scene should come easy, but first, water the cat.

\*\*\*

Stanley pounced as Marv walked into an unusually quiet lobby. Arms crossed, feet squared, Bear blocked the door to the factory floor and Marvin's coffice eighty-one steps and three turns away. "Follow-me."

Marvin lagged several paces behind as they walked in silence down the hall. The deep thud of Stanley's boot-heals echoed off each closed door they passed.

"They're on the plant floor for a surprise safety meeting," Stanley spoke without breaking stride.

Marvin wanted to run. Drop the brown bag with left-over tuna and run to freedom. He knew Bear was not going to kill him, but the urge to flee only grew as they passed the copy room down the hall from Stanley's den. Something stunk. Bad.

The smell reminded Marvin of a dead dog. Not the whole odor palate, only the spectrum that deals with shit. Marv had no other word. The kind that ER doctor's or coroner's can best tell you about. A nice bit of trivia he learned at sixteen when he found a neighbor, Mrs. Carlock, properly deceased for at least twelve hours sprawled out on her kitchen floor. Nightgown cocked up her veiny thigh, the stale smell of Sunday morning's left-over eggs had no chance against Betty Carlock's eighty-year-old guts when they let go and showed the world their true colors.

Bear opened the door to the source of the smell. "After you."

Three larger-than-life, hand patted, fecal replicas of Stanley's medals rested on the center of his desk. Each sparkled from a heavy peppering of gold glitter.

Marvin stepped through the door, stumbled to the chair, and sank down. Closer to ground zero but it was either the chair or floor. The door closed behind him then clicked locked. Bear's heavy steps crept from behind and passed.

Stanley leaned with his butt on the desk, arms crossed, face flat. "Marvin, Marvin, Marvin. I had no idea what a nut job you are."

The putrid smell of patted intestinal leftovers four feet away intensified when Bear pulled a latex glove from his jacket pocket and slid it over his right hand.

"I-"

"Shut your mouth," and Marv did. "Keep it closed until I say open." Bear paused, "I want them back." Stanley resumed his resting position against the desk. "I always knew you were a nobody Marvin. No more than that little tick gorging yourself on everyone around you." Bear slid his gloved middle finger through the middle medal and held it up to Marvin. "What I didn't know was that you're insane." He eased the glittery nugget under Marv's nose for a moment before taking a better look himself. "I mean Marvin, come on. You have some serious mental health deficiencies. That's why I'm not calling Baxter to come lock you up. You'd probably get off clean and end up living off Uncle Sam's tits. No, no, no, Marvin. We've known each other for a long time, so we're going to handle this ourselves."

Marvin wanted to scream but his lungs wouldn't pull the air.

Bear, middle-finger standing in salute, wagged it. "Not until I say." Stanley eased the finger down, careful to keep the clump intact. "You see Marv, you've had me all wrong. I'm not a bad guy, but I could care less about you." He eased off the desk toward Marv. "I do however, care about my medals."

Bear moved directly behind. The big man's hot breath warmed Marv's bald spot despite the distance. "Look at me Marvin."

Marvin leaned back his head to reveal an upside-down Bear towering over him. Stanley's soiled middle finger hovered a foot above his nose. "Open."

Bear's clean hand clamped down on Marv's cheeks. His jaw muscles, no match against Stanley's huge fingers, lost a quick fight and Marvin's mouth opened.

Stanley slid his shitty finger inside and brushed.

***

Marv came to, slumped against a toilet, in one of the seldom used bathrooms closer to his own office. Al leaned on a mop outside the open stall door. "You look like shit," he cocked his nose to the ceiling, "smell like it too."

Marv tried to flip him off but couldn't muster the strength and flashed him an awkward peace sign.

Al squatted close. "Are you ready to write like a real Wordslinger?"

Marv nodded, leaned over the toilet, retched, nodded again.

"Good, I think you are. Get yourself cleaned up and ready to go. I'm going to take care of your mess then take you home."

Outside, a train warned any would be crossers not to try. Inside, Marvin spit a bit of nastiness into the toilet. "What time is it?"

"Like you my good friend, I don't carry a watch, but by the sound of that train, I'd say 6:30 is about right." Al side-stepped a puddle of puke as he eased out of the stall. "Time to go. You've got a busy night. Lots of ideas the world needs to see, and you get to show them Marvin. Show them who you really are."

***

Jill didn't greet him in the kitchen as usual. He called but his heart wasn't in it. He had Roland all wrong. He wasn't a con or a man of cards. Roland Slick was a gunslinger, and real gunslingers don't chase gold. They deal justice.

By seven-thirty, Marvin's steno brandished four hundred new words. Jill passed through around eight, sniffed under the table and left. At nine, Dr. Murray called with a message. Three-hundred sixty dollars for Jill's next round of tests. Lab costs bill separate. No more special nights dining on the town.

Marv wrote harder. At ten o'clock he filled his last steno book and panicked. Last week he'd bought Jill a toy instead of restocking writing supplies. She played with it five minutes before a stupid bottle-cap grabbed her attention. Selfish, self-absorbed Jill. Always about her. He flung the pantry door open and scanned the shelf. There, on the floor, spare toilet paper. He grabbed a roll, yanked a fistful off, and scribbled a note. No idea what he wrote, but he knew it was good because it came from rage. Rage at her. Rage at him. An ancient hatred once locked away...all it needed was a prick to release the venom festering within.

Marvin slammed his pencil onto the table and screamed.

By midnight he filled two more rolls. Roland's mission became simple. Track down Buck and shove the gold down his throat. He was tired of his antagonist out-smarting him, out-playing him, and out-matching him. Marv's lead flew with power. Every word hit its target. The slinger knew it and laughed while he wrote.

Around two, toilet paper supply exhausted, Marv's concept of time clocked out. His panic over the paper outage might have lasted a paragraph or an entire library of works. Waves of anxiety pounded his heart and poured from his skin as the words piled up in his mind.

A frantic search for something new to write on yielded something new to write with. His thumb slammed into a black marker stashed in the back of his kitchen junk drawer. He started the next sentence right there, high on the patch of empty wall beside the fridge. He paused a moment to wonder why he'd never thought of it before. Then his hand came alive and danced with the permanent marker in every room. He'd never felt closer to his writing, to his characters, to Roland.

***

Hundreds of words peered from above when Marvin Blick opened his eyes. His final draft of The Slinger's Revenge. More scenes greeted him from the hall's once barren walls. No page numbers or chapter breaks, Marvin needed neither. He knew his story by heart and now so would the world. Instead of a shower Marv opted for a hand-towel and strategic scrubbing. He pocketed his keys and headed to the office with a smile.

His morning commute didn't change, same sharp curve on Forrest Street, same pothole on 3rd., but Marvin knew everything else had. Finally, a Wordslinger whose lead mattered.

He remembered the note when he turned onto Industrial Blvd. The one he wrote on toilet paper. It seemed important then, a matter of life, even death. Not so much now. Marvin understood his part was over. The Slinger's Revenge was complete. He could move from writer to reader and enjoy. Buck got what he deserved.

Flashing lights, emergency vehicles, and caution tape didn't take him by surprise as he pulled into the employee parking lot. The chaotic scene needed no introduction. He parked in his normal spot and headed toward the lobby doors. A group of guys, none of which looked familiar, lingered outside next to the dumpster.

"He's dead, isn't he?" The group of three looked up in tandem but only for a moment. Their hushed conversation continued without him.

"Anybody else hurt? Emily from HR?" He remembered her kindness. "She okay?"

A big guy, whose shirt called him Jim, offered a smoke. "I'm sure she's with the family. Baby sister's gotta step it up now. Or with Sheriff Baxter."

Marvin waved the cigarette away. "Baby sister?"

"You alright Marvin?" This from another big guy whose blue denim shirt didn't have a name. "Stanley's little sister. Emily Newton, class of 95'. Couple years behind us." The big unnamed man shot a look at Big Jim. "Married Scott Williams. You sure you're okay man?"

Marvin had no idea what No Name and Big Jim were talking about. "Yeah, just..."

A younger man, also nameless but a lover of bluegrass according to his t-shirt, spoke up. "I know, crazy. Those medals shoved down his throat. I heard there was nothing left of his mouth but a freakin' hole...like a cave with those jagged things coming down from the ceiling except with blood and pieces of bone and teeth. Said it looked like an animal had been slaughtered in there." The pitch of his voice dropped with his chin. "Anyway, that's what I heard."

No Name fished a can of snuff from his back pocket and plopped a couple of pouches into his cheek. "Emily found him at his desk this morning. I heard Vickie from sales found her passed out."

Big Jim aimed his unlit cig at Marvin. "Hey man, we're all supposed to stick around and talk to the police. Give a statement or whatever."

Marvin turned to leave before Big Jim finished his sentence. He didn't need to hear more. He had read the gruesome details on his way out the door less than an hour ago. It's what he came to see, the climax of the final draft of his best novel. Writer turned reader. A trick he enjoyed but didn't understand.

Marvin sidestepped an overturned mop-bucket and paused. "Any of you guys seen Al?"

"Alvin Oliver? Pack Line Supervisor?" Bluegrass lifted his head.

Marvin knew the name but not the man. "No. Al the janitor. Old guy, cleans our crap, worked here...well forever."

Marvin turned to three concerned faces. Big Jim leaned on his janitor cart. No Name and Bluegrass squatted beside theirs.

Bluegrass eased into the obvious. "You sure you're okay, Marvin? You're looking at the only cleaning crew we've had the past two years. That right Bo, two years?"

No Name nodded, "Yeah, that's about right." He stood and reached out to Marvin. "Dude, you don't look good. You want a water? Couple of us are riding down to that church on the corner, the white one with the big cross by the road. They're cooking and everything, you know, because..." a stream of tobacco-spit shot from his pinched lips. "Well, I heard Emily goes there."

"No thanks." Marvin did not want the Jesus talk today. "I need to get home."

Big Jim called after him. "What do you want us to tell the police?"

"Shut-up Jim, ain't none of our business." One of the others, maybe No Name, but it didn't matter. Last night's work, however? Now that mattered, and the spectacular red and blue lightshow proved it. He wished Jill could see it. Her image triggered an echo in his mind.

Toilet paper words written in anger. Words he wished he could take back. A flicker of moist heat swept up behind his eyes, over his forehead, and down his face. Why did he write her name?

He needed to go home. He needed her and she needed him. He knew he shouldn't have written it. He was a Wordslinger now, and a Wordslinger's prose has power. The power to give life and take life. Too much power for a little man like him.

Marvin found a spot in front of his building and opened a car door for the last time in his life. He walked into his quaint, quiet apartment certain Jill was no more. In his rage, he'd killed her off. Wrote her sentence on a fistful of toilet paper. Actions consistent with a person unfit to sling lead.

He called her name in every room, but she never answered. She didn't come running when he opened a fresh can of tuna. He emptied it onto a paper-plate and called again. No Jill. Outside a train sounded, the morning tourist train from Chattanooga, and Marvin thought of Al. He couldn't get him out of his head, but he didn't know where to find him. Ten lonely minutes later, Marv's infected brain convinced him to open his nightstand drawer and slam the bottle of pills.

The Wordslinger's last lucid scene came moments before his last breath. Marvin Blick's smile vanished, replaced by a long scream heard only in his head.

Jill the cat, healthy and happy, strolled out of the closet and toward him on the bed. He tried to pet her, but his arms wouldn't obey. Too late. No more energy. Too many little sleepy pills. Way too many pills. She was alive, but all he could do was watch the final scene...one he didn't write. Images produced by the drug, the cancer, the demon, mental illness? The drama played out all around.

Very few people receive life changing enlightenment in the precious moments prior to death, and those that do have little time to enjoy the new perspective. Marvin's enlightenment came too late. A sentence written in permanent marker. No rewrites.

Marvin Blick watched his cat and listened until his heart quit beating. He died in his own vomit, terrified, confused, and surrounded by the only friends he knew. He was forty-two and left no wife or children.

For some, the final moments of dying come with waves of peace and joy...anticipation of the reunion that awaits. For others, like Marv, the experience might foretell hell. A few later mentioned the whole thing was rather mundane. Just like Marvin Blick's short life, right up 'till...

## The End

# LAST
# CONFESSIONS

Last Confession of Catherine Michelle Lewis, October 21st, 2039
Prisoner No: 16.18.1.25.14.15.23

Transcribed: October 22nd Andrew L. Lewis. Western Hemisphere
Operations. Headquarters: Appalachian Valley Execution Group,
Indigo Valley Execution Network- Andrew L. Lewis.

Filed: October 25th Ronald T. Hanover. East Georgia Office,
Southern Province, Execution Lab, Outrider Files. Captain Hanover-
Records, Information, Surveillance, Technology.

*All words transcribed as found in original form*

"My name is Catherine Michelle Lewis, Cathy to everybody but
daddy, and this is my written confession. Fancy words for saying I did
it, and I don't care what people think of me. I'd do it again.

I'm waiting on The Authority to get here, spread a blue tarp
over the floor, put a gun to my head, and pow. Nothing like laying it
right out there is there? Nervous habit, I guess.

The Authority doesn't make a spectacle of executions now like
they did when mamaw and papaw was alive. I heard they packed
people into a little room and let them watch a doctor give the criminal
a shot of poison. Or something like that. Now, the whole thing is
private...if you don't count the person in the cell across the hall. They
see it all...But still not as much as the eye in the corner. Every cell has
one. I know somebody is watching me through that thing, and I'm

pretty sure it's the guards. I never see them (unless they're carrying a tarp ha, ha), but they always seem to know what we're doing. Also, it follows me around sometimes. It creeps me out.

Enough chatter. I tend to ramble when I'm nervous. Already said that didn't I? (ha ha ha) Best to focus. Can't waste my last chance to say what I have to say.

I did it. I had to, and I ain't sorry. They call me a monster and spit in my face, but like I said, I'd do it again. They know it too...The Authorities that is. That's why they have to kill me. 'Remove me from society' was what the papers said. Saying it out loud scares ILLEGIBLE. My hands are shaking and my hair ILLEGIBLE matted with sweat. And it's cold. Why is it always so cold in here? I'm ILLEGIBLE ILLEGIBLE take a break. Be back ILLEGIBLE.

I'm back. I'm not shaking anymore, but the announcement just came over the speakers that C Wing is on lock-down. That's us. They keep the worst of the worst on this end. Misty (she's the chatty redhead two cells down), helped her boyfriend kill his parents, and the girl down from her stole a pack of smokes. All of us just watching the eye watch us wait for the end.

I've never seen exactly what happens once they go into a cell. It don't take long though. Misty told me how they lay the tarp out. She saw them remove Amber from society two days ago. I couldn't see her from my cell, but I heard. I heard her scream, and I heard a boom. I cried when they carried her (rolled up in the tarp) past my cell and out the door.

I'm rambling again, so here I go. They want me to write down my confession. If I do, The Authority said they won't go after Bill. He's my brother. He didn't do anything but that don't matter. The family is as guilty as the criminal. Some law passed after the War of Liberty. My uncle Evan called it something different, but daddy said he was a little touched in the head. Anyway, I never understood all the laws and rules passed after the war.

I knew The Authority was coming for me. I'd hid out in Bill and Gina's shed for 3 days. They didn't know I was there. Nobody did. I got hungry and wanted a can of beans from the top shelf. I reached up, tripped, fell on my wrist, and broke it. Sometimes it hurts so bad I forget what's coming. Thankfully it was my left wrist, or you wouldn't be reading this (ha ha ha).

Bill called The Authority when I screamed. He didn't know it was me. He thought somebody was stealing his new tractor. The one he bought when he got his insurance money from the county. I don't hold it against him that he called. I'd like to think he wouldn't have squealed if he knew it was me, but it's done now. If The Authority gives my babies to Bill and Gina, I hope they raise them right. They know what to do. They're good kids. Tell them this ain't their fault. Oh, ILLEGIBLE. I want to see my babies. ILLEGIBLE, please let me see them one more time. ILLEGIBLE SENTENCE.

Okay, I'm back. The door at the end of the hall just clicked open. Got to hurry.

They pulled me from the shed five days ago. I ain't talked to anybody since, except for the girls in here. Couple times The Authority came got me. Told them same thing I'm telling here. I begged them to let me see Danny and Beth one more time. Danny had a snotty ILLEGIBLE the last time I saw him. I hope it's not the flu. Please check. Please.

Close now. They're laughing. I guess I missed the punchline (ha ha ha). I gotta ILLEGIBLE.

I love my kids. They ain't old enough to understand why I did it. Maybe one day they will. I don't blame them for telling Principle Morgan it was me. Like I said, they're too young to understand.

Danny. Beth. If they let you read this, I love y'all. Momma ain't mad at you. Mamma ain't mad you told them what I said. I did it so you could be free.

There they are, punching the code outside my door. I'm not sure if they'll ILLEGIBLE me finish ILLEGIBLE.

Okay, Captain is motioning me to hurry, and two men are spreading the tarp on the floor. I thought it was blue, but it's green.

This is it. I hope it don't hurt. God, please don't let it hurt. I did it and I ain't sorry. I'd do it again. I did it for them...my babies. Danny, Beth, mama loves you. They're killing me for it, but that's ok. I told you about Jesus, and I would do it again. He loves you. Mama loves you. Mama loves you. Ma" end of confession

Headquarter Execution Group: Appalachian Valley Executions. Andrew L. Lewis.

---

Last Confession of William Albert Jackson, October 21ˢᵗ, 2039 Prisoner No: 13.15.12.5.19.16.25

Transcribed: October 22ⁿᵈ Andrew L. Lewis. Western Hemisphere Operations. Headquarters: Appalachian Valley Execution Group, Indigo Valley Execution Network- Andrew L. Lewis.

Filed: October 25ᵗʰ Ronald T. Hanover. East Georgia Office, Southern Province, Execution Lab, Outrider Files. Captain Hanover-Records, Information, Surveillance, Technology.

*All words transcribed as found in original form*

"They said if I confessed, they'd let Gina go. Nothing I could do about Cathy, she'd already made it clear which side she was on. I don't know who you think you are tearing up my house looking for contraband! This ain't right! I thought they was stealing my tractor. I called you!! You hear me? I CALLED YOU!!!

Anyway, I guess there ain't no use in crying about it now, so here we go. If I said the Bible was mine, I could pay the debt to society and Gina gets to go free, right? She'd get to raise Danny and Beth? Baby, if they let you read this, I love you and I'm sorry. I don't know what else to do. Yes, the Bible is mine and mine alone. I love you baby. Tell the kids about Uncle Bill and their mama. I love you."

end of confession

Headquarter Execution Group: Appalachian Valley Executions. Andrew L. Lewis.

---

Last Confession of Gina Margret Jackson, October 23st, 2039 Prisoner No: 20.8.5.25.11.14.15.23

Transcribed: October 24nd, Andrew L. Lewis. Western Hemisphere Operations. Headquarters: Appalachian Valley Execution Group, Indigo Valley Execution Network- Andrew L. Lewis.

Filed: October 26th, Ronald T. Hanover. East Georgia Office, Southern Province, Execution Lab, Outrider Files. Captain Hanover-Records, Information, Surveillance, Technology.

*All words transcribed as found in original form*

"They lied. Danny, Beth, if you ever get to read this remember they lied...and remember why."

end of confession

Headquarter Execution Group: Appalachian Valley Executions. Andrew L. Lewis.

---

Last Confession of Andrew L. Lewis, October 31st, 2039 Prisoner No: 021.52.395.6844.7

Transcribed: October 31st, 2039 Susan K Marshal. Western Hemisphere Operations. Appalachian Valley Execution Group, Indigo Valley Execution Network-

Filed: October 31st, 2039 James David Roberts. East Georgia Office, Southern Province, Execution Team, Outrider Files. Colonel Roberts-Surveillance Technology, Records, Information.

*All words transcribed as found in original form*

"Treason? Because we cling to the cross of Christ? Because we kneel at Jesus' feet? You murdered my friend, Ben Johnson, after breakfast this morning because he spoke the name of Christ. You'll murder me tonight for the same. You lie and call it a war instead of an extermination. When did the madness begin? Last century when public prayer to our God became offensive? Sixty-six years ago, when the killing of unborn babies became legal or twenty when we cheered their outright murder? Maybe three years ago when possession of a Christian Bible meant death?

My hands shed the blood of innocents until His shed blood set this guilty man free.

You say a confession is required of me. I freely give it for Him. Jesus Christ is Lord.

To all who have given all for The Gospel of Christ, I join you with a smile and a song.
Andy Lewis"

end of confession

Headquarter Execution Group: Appalachian Valley Executions. James David Roberts.

---

The End

# INTRODUCTION TO A PIPER'S SONG

**AUTHOR'S NOTE:** *Of the three stories commanding my attention when I experienced my very own "Remember when I almost died?" moment, this one changed the most. Wordslinger and Last Confessions remained basically intact.*

*More lyrical poetry than short story, this version wasn't initially written for publication. Most lines began their journey to this page out of pure frustration. Each writer deals with creative struggles in their own unique way. I let myself write with the intention that no one will ever see. My go-to medium is poetry because I'm a storyteller not a poet. Freedom from the fear of scrutiny loosens our minds.*

*As the bleed in my stomach progressed and infection worsened, several characters in my little collection of shorts decided to switch plots. Their mischievous escapades multiplied through the Christmas 2018 holiday season. Most nights word production ceased with plenty of lines but very little forward progress. So, during those crazy weeks when my blood wasn't staying where it should and neither were my characters, I scribbled and typed a lot of 'frustration freestyle'. Somewhere along the way, I decided to clean it up, slick back it's hair, and toss it the keys to the family car.*

*If you're a pure "story" reader, this model probably isn't your style. If, however, the prospect of navigating a dimly lit, sometimes disturbing, psychological house of mirrors excites you, then hop in for a quick trip. I'm with you the whole way.*

*Jason*

Follow along and see, how often lines deceive. Subtle lies open eyes, so learn the story of me.

He was a young lad who almost died.
*Almost but not*, a foe Piper cried.
*I'll summon dark.*
*Kill this spark.*
*Unless he agrees to hide.*

But to The Throne many saints did go.
To save his life, a plea from below.
*Feed him bread.*
*Revive his lead.*
*Craft him for war, so he may show.*

The same young lad could not hide.
Words poured onto the page as he cried.
Arrows from the spark.
Light over dark.
Evil shall wish this Piper had died.

See how fun learning can be? Even when the writing is lazy?

My tales stand for right, though some feel born in the dead of night. See, some Piper's sing. Here, others write. Lyrics, lines, notes, and prose. All used by Pipers, all gifts He chose.

Next glimpse into a war of words often waged in-between. Down below...dig deep. Meanings can mean much more than they seem.

Lock me in a box with no keys. Bars slam down, click click click I'm free.
Some see prison but at the end hope.
I hear notes and grasp language by the throat.
Like Alice in a hole, the deeper you dig the further we'll go.

Last lesson my child then some fun. Follow along with me and speak.
My song is smooth, my voice was weak.

Marv's note read, "i'm a c-type, oh my head, never in bed, slingin' lead,
Jill's not fed, no more dough for her meds, wish she was dead"
It's all said.
If you can't hear it, you're not dead just lazy.
I break rules, some sea red...and the doctors say I'm crazy.

Dear child, come along and uncover hidden treasures only some will
discover.

Poor Marvin regretted popping the pills.
Now that he knew he didn't kill Jill.
When the closet door opened, Marv saw his cat.
Al stepped out with her, chuckled and sat.
He said "young man, young man, this is what I do,
I travel in search of fools like you.
I drew you to Bear and watched you run.
I even bet my friends the slinger wouldn't use a gun.
I gave him the gift and left presents on his desk.
I fed you lies, said you were the best.
I know, I know, I didn't cut you any slack,
but at least I'm no thief. I gave his medals back.
Alton stretched, smiled, and stroked Jill's chin.
"She wants a last kiss. You'll never see her again.
Oh, and don't worry, she'll be fine.
Dr. Murray called, he's an old friend of mine.
Now close your eyes, let Alton tuck you in.
I'm ready to move on. This is your end.
It's time to go, your rhyme is done.
You're not a Wordslinger, can't even draw a pun."
Jill the cat watched as the young man cried.
The old man cackled as the first one died.

Speaking of the dead, Andy Lewis hid what he said.

That's how they caught him, one extra in the math.
Follow along...the not a Haiku will start you down the path.
His messages involved letters and numbers,
The first of one, the partner of the other.
It's a puzzle I know.
An easy one though.
Not like the puzzle of life,
Scattered about, full of strife.
Put it together we shout,
Or people will think our light Blicked out.
God's plan...the puzzle of life. Man's pride...I've got this! Won't work...I've tried.

We can walk together, you and I, but please remember, often there's more than meets the eye. So, follow along and find the real me. It's not far. See...I am a Kat dead in the car, same two Ben slammed at that bar. I'm the Earworm chanting your name at night. When we meet please don't fight. Just relax my host, you'll feel better soon...before we say night night to the moon.
I'm a wife's soft voice whispered into a phone. The voice of a loved one too soon gone.
Yes, I'm Araphel, telling my story. Little children and those of weak stomach beware, that one's gory.
I am Cathy Lewis mother of two. Shot in the head. Ended up dead but stood for what was true.
I'm the Wordslinger who wrote while he bled and the Daniel who peed his bed.
Dear child draw near and follow along.
I am a Piper. This is our song.

# ABOUT JASON

I'm Jason Parrish...husband of an amazing woman, introvert living as an extrovert (exhausting), and author. My books, written from a Christian perspective, combine a love of scripture, fascination with the human psyche, and desire to better understand the supernatural as it relates to both. Years of small town southern living bleed into my characters and settings. Add a decade of teaching theology, biblical history, and leadership. Sprinkle an interest in the macabre, and you have a recipe too bitter for some, too sweet for others.

To learn more about Jason or his books you can visit his website:
jasonparrishbooks.com